BLOOD
AND
WHISKEY

August Lee

Dear Eve,

When I dreamed of love, you came to me.
When I dreamed of writing, you gave me the key.
I walked the path to finish a book,
and stopped at times so you could have a look.
Without you there, walking beside me
I would have ended up alone, stuck in a tree.
But you were my light when it was too dark,
my sun, my guide, my northern star.
So, it is with great pleasure, love and glee
That I dedicate my work, my love to thee.

ACKNOWLEDGMENT

As the famous saying goes, "It's not what you know, it's who you know?" and that couldn't be truer in my case.

My darling Evelyn, if I had never met you, I would never have gone to that secret "detective" bar in London. You wouldn't have suggested I solve people's fictional cases online, and so starting my adventure of writing this book. But you didn't stop there. You read my drafts, my ideas, listened to my plans, read my stories (again and again…). You helped me soar like an eagle through the sky, believing this dream of mine, would come true. At the beginning of 2019, you gave me a gift I will never forget. You gave me the gift of freedom to write, not worry about work, money or other stresses of life. You told me how much you believed in me and wanted me to finish my book. A year has passed since then, it took a little longer than planned, but you never complained, always encouraged me, and that's why you are my angel and my queen. Thank you.

To my friend Emma Roche, a great writer, with whom I've had many a thousand cups of tea and coffee with, I thank you. A writers' journey can be a very lonely one, locked in our own world's. So, having you there to share this journey with and share yours too, has been an immense pleasure. All of our writing meetings in coffee shops (and a few cheeky cocktails in Wetherspoons) added up to fun, laughter and my finished book. You have helped and inspired me throughout my journey, something which I will never forget. After spying on our favourite booth to sit at, (for hours sometimes), waiting to have the luxury of a wall socket, we have sat and often dreamed about our lives after our books have sold worldwide. I look forward to spending time in our dream homes together, discussing our latest writing adventure.

Copyright © 2020 by August Lee

First edition

Cover design by August Lee

ISBN 978-1-5272-8151-6 (e-book)

CONTENTS

MEMORIES REBORN

Case #221

T he last pieces of ash fell off my cigar, and so I reached for a new case file from my desk. Before my hand could reach it, the phone rang. An international number.

What have you got for me today, God?

I picked up the phone. "Detective Banks."

"Surprise!"

I knew that voice and held it close to my heart.

"Nancy, it's been a while," I said with a slight grin.

My niece Nancy, the closest thing to a daughter I've ever had. She'd grown up so fast. Last time we spoke, I'd wished her luck as she left the country for university. Three years had passed, and I realised how much I'd missed her.

"Yeah...sorry about that. Life kinda passes you by, I guess."

I could tell she was eager to tell me something. "What's running through your mind, Nancy?"

"Well, umm... You're not gonna believe this, but I've got a mystery for you to solve," she said with a hint of a nervous giggle.

Nancy started to tell me everything about the case. As she did, I closed my eyes and took a deep breath. I imagined she was sitting in front of me, just like old times.

In 1981 four friends headed on a couples' trip to/of a ghost tour in Savannah, USA. They never made their destination. Now, Nancy and three others have claimed to be those exact four people reincarnated. Vivid flashbacks came to her about

2

how they were killed. She saw their organs had been removed and nearly threw up when the smell of the sweaty killer flashed back and ran up her nose. The trouble was that the general public didn't believe Nancy or her friends. She thought to herself, who was the best person to solve this mystery? Who would believe her and fight 'til all the facts were found and shown to those who mattered? I was that man.

It was hard to believe what I heard at first. If it had been anybody else talking, the phone would've been hung up right away. There was something so sincere in her voice, however, and as crazy as it sounded, my intuitive brain was now alive and kicking. Nancy had also never lied to me in the past. She hated liars, and I think that even if she wanted to lie, she wouldn't know how.

I had heard enough, for the time being. "I'll be on the next flight over."

The plane landed just before the witching hour; the sky was black, and the moon sneaked behind a cloud. My mind and body didn't feel ready to sleep. I walked down the road, with a strong wind rustling through my clothes, until I found a bar. I ordered a large whiskey and asked where the best place to get cigars in Beaufort, SC was.

After a brief walk to the store the following morning, I sniffed my fresh new cigar and lit it up. I let the smoke linger in my mouth before exhaling. *Not bad.* I headed over to Nancy's place to meet her three new friends.

I soon arrived at Nancy's tall apartment building. She hadn't changed one bit. Her wavy blonde hair flowed like a river down her back, and she still wore those dorky t-shirts with jeans.

"Unc!" she shouted and threw her arms around me. "It's so good to see you!!" she said squeezing me tighter.

"You too, Piglet," I said, pulling myself back and capturing this moment. "Love the shirt," I said, looking at the cat hanging from a tree.

"I once saw it on your office wall, and so when I saw the t-shirt, I had to have it," she replied and smiled.

I smiled wider and longer than I had in a long time.

"Well what are you waiting for?" she asked, twisting her hair. "Come in."

I stepped inside and took off my jacket. The floorboards creaked as I walked over to the kitchen table, narrowly avoiding a hidden black cat, and took a seat. Nancy introduced me to Tom, a tall skinny skeleton of a man, Jane, a brunette no taller than five foot, and Mike, who had Cheetos stuck in his long black beard. After greetings were over, I placed the lie detector on the table. *It was interesting taking that through security at the airport.* Everybody went silent.

"Can I get you a drink, unc? Too early for whiskey I reckon." She looked to the ceiling trying to think. "I have… green tea with lemon, urm…"

"I'm fine, Piglet, but thanks for asking. I'd like to get down to business if that's okay with everybody?" Heads nodded around the room. "Thank you. Mike if you'd join me, please."

Mike was a little hesitant as he rose from the sunken brown sofa and walked towards the table.

"This will only take a minute. Take a deep breath and relax." I reassured him as a drop of sweat cascaded down his face. "Let's start with something simple. Is your name Mike?"

"Y-yes."

"Very good. Are we in America?"

A deep breath was released. "Yes."

"Have you been to the moon?"

"No."

"Are you Mickey Mouse?"

He let out a small giggle, "No."

"Are you a reincarnation of a man killed near Savannah in 1981?"

"Yes."

There were no jumps on the lie detector. So far, he was telling the truth, or at least he was according to the machine.

The questions didn't last too long, and Mike was relieved when it was all over. He left the chair and headed outside for some fresh air.

Jane was next, and confidence vibrated from her.

Before any words left my mouth, she smiled and said, "I'm ready for you."

As I placed the pads on her, she gave me a subtle wink.

Keeping professional, I carried out the test, and the results came out the same. According to the machine, she was telling the truth about the reincarnation as well.

Last to the chair was Tom. His left eye twitched, and as he placed a hand on the chair, it nearly fell over. Embarrassed, he sat down and forced a smile. I turned the lie detector on and turned to Tom. He'd turned pale, beads of sweat travelled down his forehead. He clutched his stomach and threw up all over the desk. He'd had chunky carrots at some point, along with sweetcorn. I was about to hand him my handkerchief when, as if from nowhere, he let out another moan and covered the floor and his feet in vomit. This guy wasn't passing the test, I thought. After a series of questions, Tom knocking over the lie detector and nearly choking on air alone, we were done. Surprisingly though…he passed. Tom passed the test.

People often say that lie detector tests can't always be right. This was something I disagreed with, but as this was such an unusual case, I felt other methods were needed just to be sure.

Having witnessed people being questioned under hypnosis before and getting positive results, it felt like a good thing to try next. Question was, where could I find a great hypnotherapist here?

To my surprise, when I asked the group if they knew of a hypnotherapist, Nancy stood up and said, "Actually I know of an excellent one. I've never met him, but he comes highly recommended."

"Great. So, who recommended him? A former patient?"

"You know what?" Nancy said while scratching her head. "I can't remember…"

"Okay…well, can I use your laptop?"

You can find anything online these days, including a therapist's credentials. He checked out, and it turned out his office wasn't too far away.

"Right ladies and gentlemen, we're going to head over to a hypnotherapist's office now. You all okay with that?"

Everyone nodded, even *Vomit boy*.

We arrived at a small red brick building and were greeted in the foyer by the therapist, who wore an overly false smile. It was like he was trying too hard. A lot of people in businesses can be like that I know, but still, I took a mental note of it. Force of habit. We walked into his office and he shut the door. The room was small and had shelves full of academic books, a peace lily, and even a… teddy bear? *Strange.* Having taken our seats, we ran through my case.

With a Cheshire Cat smile, he said, "This all sounds very intriguing! I'll clear up my schedule and start immediately!" Clearly, this guy had never come across something like this before, and I was glad I didn't have to wait.

The therapist pointed Tom towards a leather chaise lounge. "Have a seat. Relax. As for everyone else, could you please wait outside? This will work much more efficiently if I do it one on one." I nodded and gave him some instructions before I left. While under hypnosis I wanted him to ask the four people about the murders, any details they could give me of the time. I also wanted to see if they could talk as the people from the past life. I wanted to know if they could give me intimate details about themselves.

After everyone had been seen, the therapist gave me a file with the information he had gathered. From the session, he told me, it pointed towards them telling the truth.

"I must say, Detective, this has been amazing. Reincarnated murder victims, here, in my office," he said with a smile and then handed me a book. "Just in case you're still not as convinced as I am." It was a book by Dr. Stevenson called "Reincarnation Exists" I turned the book over and read that this man had spent his whole adult life proving that reincarnation was real.

After saying goodbye to everyone, I headed for a liquid lunch. I pushed a heavy wooden door open and entered my kinda bar. Dark, quiet, and it turned out, as I approached the bar, a good selection of whiskey.

"Whiskey—"

"No ice?"

"Only way it should be drank."

"My man. I couldn't agree with you more. Try this one, stiff but pleasant."

He placed the drink in front of me, and after a sip, I gave him a nod of approval. I took my head back to the case. The main details I got off the four during that session were:

1) The killers all had the same tattoo, skull and crossbones surrounded by a flying dragon. Could be a gang tattoo.

2) One of the men had a scar across his lip.

3) The other female said her past life self had a scar across her left butt cheek from an accident.

Later that day, once I was alone, I paid a visit to the hospitals where the four victims had gone over the years. I wanted to check for anything significant, like an accident leaving a big scar.

After receiving a dirty look from a nurse sitting on a bench near the entrance, I extinguished my cigar and headed for the reception desk.

"Can I help you?" someone said from a low desk, eyes still on her screen.

"I was hoping you could do me a favour. I have some past records I need digging up."

"And why would I do that?" The face of a short haired blonde now stared at me.

I put the twenty-dollar bill away. "I'm working on a case, trying to help some unfortunate people, and you would be helping me a great deal."

Without even a blink, she replied, "It is against the law to give out confidential information, sir."

"I'm sorry. What I meant was…" the twenty-dollar bill now shown in my palm, "…I would love it if we could help each other."

The woman nodded and began typing on her computer. Minutes later, the printer started to speak. As the woman approached it, she took a long look in both directions of the corridor. As if feeling it was safe to do so, she collected the papers, put them into a folder, and slid it to me. The bribe worked, but I missed having contacts in the hospital like in London.

Outside, with no nurse in sight, I lit a cigar and pulled out the sheets of paper. It turned out one of the past life victims had indeed had a large scar on her ass, caused by a motorcycle accident. It was a big tick off my list. Now I wanted to find out information about that tattoo.

I don't have a lot of contacts in America, but the several I do have come in extremely useful, for work and as friends. There was one man in particular whose life I had saved several years back. His task force is dedicated to bringing down organised crime and the black market.

The clouds rolled over the light blue sky and a swift breeze ruffled through my hair. I watched a gardener pruning the trees outside the entrance of the skyscraper building and waited for my contact. After fifteen minutes, a man in a sharp black suit, with gelled back hair, came out of the entrance and straight towards me. With a stern look, he approached me. "What can I do for you, John?"

"What? No hello?"

"I never saw you as one for chit chat, and some assholes from a gang just slipped through my fingers, again, thanks to a sleazeball lawyer."

"They wouldn't happen to have a skull and crossbones tattoo—"

His fists clenched. "With a flying dragon?"

"How did you—"

He had fire in his eyes. "Hijos de puta! Those fuckers are every-where." His teeth clenched. "Anything you need on these assholes, I'll give you. Do me a favour though, cause these guys some pain."

"Sore spot I see."

"I've been trying to nail these guys for years. You know the drill. Witnesses never make it to court, or they end up richer be-forehand. Look, I'm real busy, but I'll put some time aside today and send over all the information I can find for you."

"Appreciate it."

With a final nod, he turned and walked back towards the building.

I sat in a diner with a strong black coffee and skipped through the book the therapist had given me on Dr. Ian Stevenson. His research began in 1960 (before this original incident). He'd au-thored 300 papers and 14 books on the subject of reincarnation, and this one was an interesting read. This book and the case so far had me starting to believe.

Later, I went to Nancy's home unannounced, but she didn't mind, of course. Sitting down in a worn leather chair, I smiled wider than I had in a long time.

"What?" she asked. "Is my hair a mess or something?"

"Not at all. It's just so good to see you."

"Aww, you too, unc," she gave a smile that could melt gold.

"Listen, through what I've found out and book I've been reading, I wanted to tell you," I stared into her eyes. "I believe you, and I'm gonna do all I can to help you."

She placed a hand over her heart and gave a little smile as a single tear rolled down her cheek.

"It's okay, Piglet," I said, holding her hand.

"I know, Unc. It's just been so hard, you know?" She wiped the tear away. "Having so many people call me a liar, and the looks they give me…With the help you've given me, well, I feel I can hold my head up again. Oh!" she said and walked quickly over to a cupboard.

"What is it?"

"I got your favourite whiskey," she said with a sweet smile.

"Why thank you, Piglet." I said, pretending to take a hat off my head.

After finishing a second glass, Nancy went to stand up to get me another.

"Allow me," I said and walked to her kitchen.

As the whiskey hit the glass, I noticed something out of the corner of my eye. There was some something sticking out, down the side of her microwave. I slid it out and saw it was a letter with the office address of the hypnotherapist on it. *She said a friend told her about him*, I thought to myself. I read the rest of the letter, it was an invitation to go to his office and cure her smoking. This letter was handwritten to Nancy; it wasn't just some junk mail and the therapist was asking for no fee. For a practice that had been around for five years, I found that quite odd. Just then Nancy came into the kitchen.

"Everything okay?" she asked. "I thought you might've got lost."

"Nancy, I thought you said you hadn't seen this therapist guy before."

"I hadn't."

"Then what's this letter? Why did you tell me it was a friend who knew him?"

"I've never seen that before, and it was a friend, I just can't remember who. Where did that come from?"

I looked her in the eyes for a moment. "Leave it with me. Thanks for the drink." I kissed her on the cheek and left, the letter still in my hand.

My head was filled with questions. *Why would she have this letter and not tell me? Why would she have it and not know about it? Why did he want to give her a free session? Could she have opened the letter but not read it? Had someone else been in her apartment and opened it by mistake?*

A quicker way, I thought, was to go straight to the source. With questions on my lips, I headed back to the hypnotherapist's office.

The tyres of my car skidded to a halt as I slammed the breaks in front of the shrink's office. I slammed the door and spotted him about to leave the building. Greeted with that same false smile as before, I handed him the book he had lent me.

"That was fast," he said and invited me up to his office.

"I haven't got much time to read when on a case. But I have always been good at skimming through a book and collecting the main points. Thanks for an interesting read."

I looked around his office, my detective senses running. "So, tell me, have you ever met Nancy before?"

"Nancy? No, why?"

"Just curious. She was the one who recommended you but couldn't recall who had told her about yourself."

"The mind can be a wonder at times. It will remember and reveal the deepest emotions and secrets, but just as easily forget a simple name."

Something flashed into my eyes. *What was that?* I squinted my eyes to focus clearer and looked around. I looked at the shelves opposite his desk. I saw a peculiar looking book. *What is that?* I saw another reflection of light. *Is it a...a...yes, a secret camera! Son of a bitch.* I decided to look into it, but when it was…a little quieter.

Later that night, as the roads came to a halt, and the sky hid the moon, I let myself into the therapist's office and headed straight for the camera. Taking it from the shelf, I plugged it into my laptop and started going over all the footage.

I was searching for Nancy, one fist clenched as the other caressed it. *There!* I hit pause, went back a few seconds, and there she was. Thing is, my findings didn't end there. On this footage were the three other "reincarnated" friends of hers!

It had all been a lie! It had all been a fucking lie! They weren't reincarnated people; he had planted the memories inside their heads! I almost smashed my laptop as I watched him brainwashing Nancy but managed to stop myself. Instead I hurled one of his expensive looking decanters at the wall, sending shards of glass spraying across his office.

I waited in that damn office for what was left of the night. Luckily, the bastard had good taste in brandy. This was not my drink of choice, but right now I just needed something stiff.

With the bottle almost empty and the sun up, a video message popped up on my phone, with the words "You won't believe this!" My contact had sent me a video. I pressed play. It was footage from a phone in some sort of ghetto. An old man walked past the camera. *Wait. What was that?* I played the video from the beginning, checking my 'brandy eyes' hadn't been playing tricks on me. *There!* The old man walking past. He had the tattoo I'd been looking for! But with too much booze in me and anger still coursing through my veins, I merely shoved the phone back into my pocket.

✲ ✲ ✲

"Detective Banks? What are you doing he-?"

"Thereee you areee you sackless piece of shit!" I slurred as I grabbed the therapist by his coat, anger coursing through my veins.

I threw him across his desk like a rag doll. He bounced off it and his head crashed into the wall. Droplets of blood fell onto my hand as I picked him up and shoved him against the wall.

"M-Mr. Banks. What's going on?" he dared to ask.

"You know damn well wha-ss going on youuu son of a bbitch!" I yelled shoving him into the wall again. "You brainwashed my kid! Niece, my niece!" I crashed my knee into his ribs.

Bent over and wincing he said, "I don't know what you're talking about."

I backhanded him with my right hand, for such insolence. He then tasted plastic as I shoved his camera right into his little mouth.

"I-I- can explain," he said in a muffled voice, as he stumbled nervously across the wall, trying to get away from me.

"Start talking before my fists do!"

"J-just give me a second, please!" He sat down and with his hands shaking, reached for his liquor cabinet. He opened it and looked confused.

"Looking for this?" I waved the brandy bottle in front of him.

He nodded, took a deep breath, and rearranged his clothes that were...out of shape. Then he told me everything.

"I was eighteen when it happened. My sister...my sister was one of the victims. She was the one with the scar across her ass." He took a deep breath. "Not a day goes by that I don't think about her. I torment myself thinking of how I could've saved her, should've saved her." A teardrop fell onto his clasped hands.

"But what about the tattoo?"

"Wh...what?" Tears stained his face.

14

I launched the brandy bottle into the wall behind him, "The tattoo. Did you just make that up?! Cos your sister sureee as hell didn't come back from the dead and tell you."

His eyes were glazed over as he looked out the window. I backhanded his face, "Snap out of it! The tattoo, ex- explain."

"Well. For weeks after my sister's death, I went back and forth down the same route she had, looking for anything that might help. On my final trip down there I pulled over, got out of the car, and screamed in frustration. That was when they got me."

"Who?" I said, through clenched teeth.

"The same men that took my sister," he said looking at the floor. "I didn't see them coming. One minute I'm screaming at God and the next I'm waking up in the back of a truck with a bag over my head. I could just about make out shadows if I focused hard enough."

I shook my head and tried to focus. "Go on..."

"Right. Well. When we finally stopped, I was dragged out of the truck and brought to my feet. I heard several men talking as they pushed me inside a building, something about selling things on a market. I couldn't see much once inside, but I counted my steps, trying to remember the way out in case I needed it. They threw me in a room that smelled of damp and had dirty water dripping from the ceiling. They tied my hands behind my back and then broke my nose as if to show me what would happen if I didn't do what they said."

"Tell m-me more about the men. I need details. Details!" I said, my hands on his shoulders and my face inches from his.

"Okay!" his chest puffed in and out rapidly. "Well umm, they all had skull and cross bone tattoos. One guy had a scar across his lip. They were young. Perhaps no older than twenty-five, twenty-six."

15

"And?"

"I don't know okay?! I was just trying not to die and get the hell out of there!"

"Okay, okay," I said as I wobbled from side to side. "One thing I don't understand. How the heeeell did someone like youuu escape?" I asked, my pointed finger an inch from his eye.

"Well, due to a skiing accident I had as a child, I've always been able to easily dislocate my shoulders. When I was left alone, I was able to get my arms around and free myself. Um…detective?"

"I'm awake!" I said, opening my eyes wide.

"Okay. Well, a while later, an ugly man approached me. I fought with him, struggling to match his strength. After a while of wrestling, he took a swing at me, but slipped on something on the floor, bashed his head on a door handle, and fell unconscious. Nothing too heroic, not for 'someone like me', as you put it. But it allowed me to get out my cell. I poked my head out the door but to my surprise, the other guys were nowhere to be seen. Probably out to get another victim… I told the police everything. About the incident, about my sister. I gave them as many details as I could, including the scar I told you about. But when they went to investigate, there was nothing there. They thought I'd made the whole thing up because of my sister and closed the case! Personally, I think the bastards ran cos I'd escaped and didn't want the police wrecking their rotten operation."

"And so what? The case is never taken seriously, and so thirty-four years later you decide to fuck with my girl, my niece's head?!" I slammed my hand down on his desk.

"Okay, okay, I know you're mad. Please don't hit me again!" he squealed.

"Give me what I need and I'll consider it," I said, grabbing his shirt collar. His crumpled white shirt had gained some pools of red. But it wasn't his blood. I let go of his collar and stared at my fist, drip, drip, drip.

"Urm...detective?" he asked with a shaken voice.

"What are you waiting for? Talk!" I said, snapping out of my daze.

He proceeded to tell me how ten years ago he came across a case. Through memory planting, a therapist convinced a child that her father had raped her. It ripped the family apart, but later the truth came out. Of course, he said, he didn't want to do anything horrific like that. But after reading Dr. Stevenson's book, he came up with the idea of reincarnation. Everyone had given up on his sister and the case, and he was convinced nobody would listen to him again.

Scientists had started building up cases and convincing people that reincarnation was possible. Imagine if people claimed to be reincarnated from his sister's case, he'd thought. Then everyone would stand up and listen. He would have media coverage, the best people in the country on the job. They would solve this case once and for all. Well, that is what he thought would happen. He had spent four years at university studying and another six years getting experienced enough to do this. After all this work and effort, the public didn't believe in reincarnation.

I still couldn't bring myself to entirely give a shit for his sob story but wanted to know more.

"So why Nancy?"

"I didn't target her specifically. I hacked into patient files at the local doctors. I then found people who were born when my sister was killed and people with addictions. One of the guys was a gambler, Nancy wanted to quit smoking. That's how I picked. I offered them a free way to get cured, and they came."

The desk creaked as I leaned onto it and gave him a stern look in the eyes. Grabbing him by his tie, I pulled him in close. I pulled back my clenched fist, he winced. My fist hurled towards his face but stopped an inch from his nose. Breathing heavily, I released my grip, stood up, and headed for the door.

"Wait!" he shouted. "What about my case?"

"Fuck you, AND your case!" I yelled, hurling a nearby vase towards his head. He ducked and with a final thunderous look at him, I turned and left.

I was awoken the next day in my car by a drill trying to pierce my skull...and my *leg*? I was confused. I opened my eyes and realised it was my phone from inside my pocket.

"Banks?!" yelled a man's voice at the top of his lungs! Well, that's how my brain heard it.

"Ahem!" I cleared my throat. "Yes, Banks here."

"Did you get the video?" It was my contact.

It took me a few seconds to shake my head clear and remember the video I had seen.

"Yeah, I got it."

"You won't believe this. A rookie had heard me talking about you and the case you were on. When he heard about the tattoo, he came to me with this video."

"Listen, I gotta get my head straight."

"You don't wanna talk more about it?"

"I don't know what my head wants right now. I'll get back to you alright?"

"Err...sure."

I hung up the phone and headed for a pancake house.

The bell rang as I opened the door and the coffee aroma danced around me. A sweet kick ran up my nose and I could practically taste the pancakes. After I sat down and ordered some, the waitress took one look at my face and kindly left the full pot of coffee on my table and gave a wink. She headed back to order my pancakes with extra sausages and bacon, humming all the way.

I ate breakfast and slowly sparks flew around my brain as it started to reboot. While tapping my fingers on the table, I played a staring contest with my phone, and it was winning. The therapist had pissed me off. He had messed with my niece and got what he had coming off me. I'd thrown him around, scaring him half to death. Nancy and I wouldn't be bothered again. But still…sitting there sober I could start to see things from his point of view. Sure, he went about things entirely the wrong way, but it was all for his sister. *Is there anything that I wouldn't do if it were Nancy that had died in his sister's case?* With that thought, on top of never liking to leave a case unsolved, I decided I would indeed solve the case.

After breakfast, I called my contact, and he told me that the rookie gave him an address for the old man with the tattoo. Turned out it was only a half-hour drive away. I struck a match, lit my cigar, and headed over there.

After I arrived at a rundown bungalow, a man in his late fifties approached the front door, keys in hand. I took out the binoculars from a bag on the passenger seat and took a closer look. As he lifted his hand to put the keys in the door, there it was, the tattoo.

With these types of guys, you can't just knock on the door and ask them a few simple questions. No, it took something more than that. I let him enter the house and then headed around the back.

After walking through knee-high weeds, stepping over an old car tyre, and scaring the hell out of a squirrel, I reached the back door. I've picked my fair share of locks over the years, and this one was no different. One by one the components of the lock clicked as the tools did their magic. With one final turn…the lock clicked open and I was in. The man was bending over to grab a beer from the fridge as I approached him from behind. A stench of sweat and cigarettes oozed from his body. I grabbed a nearby glass and smashed it over his head. As he fell to the ground, the man didn't know what hit him and when he woke up, couldn't see who. I shone a bright light in his eyes the whole time, he wouldn't have been able to make out a thing.

"This is how it's gonna go. I'm gonna ask you some questions and depending on how co-operative you are with me, will depend on what I do to you."

I questioned him for hours. I plugged him into my car battery and lit him up like a Christmas tree, then nearly drowned the guy, but nothing. They don't tend to make 'em like that anymore. When he spat in my face, I could have killed the bastard. Could have…but that would have been too easy, for him.

Soon I decided to go with a different tactic. My contact had just messaged me telling me there was at least one more gang member with that tattoo still alive. I cut the guy loose, and he lay there on the floor panting hard.

"Don't miss me too much. You might see me sooner than you think," I said, and with one punch he was out cold.

It didn't take long before I knew where to find this guy. I'd bugged lucky man number one's mobile phone, and he had arranged a meeting with my next target.

I expected them to meet in a diner, a parking lot, something like that, but no. That night they met right at this other guy's house. That was fine by me, less people to witness, my work.

I followed the guy to his friend's address. Sitting in my car a bit further down the road I waited for my target to be left alone.

As soon as the other guy left, I headed for the breaker box outside the house. The guy, similar age to his friend, paced around the living room until…darkness. I'd flicked the switch in the box and that was my queue to enter the house.

As I entered the house, the guy was stumbling around with his arms out in front of him. During training in the royal marines, I'd spent a week in a pitch-black warehouse. It teaches you to trust other senses, develop your eyes and mind, at least it did for me. I came at him from behind and before he knew it, a needle sank into his neck.

A short drive to a secure location and the scene was set up. Clear plastic covered all of the room, things like this can get…messy. I sat the man in a chair in front of a mirror. I wanted him to see everything that I was going to do to him. Tightly fastened to the chair with rope, this old man with a scar across his lip was ready for…my methods.

"We're gonna play a little game," I said, crouching in front of him. "It's called, crunch and response. Let's see how well you do."

I started by bending his fingers back until the bones snapped and pierced through the skin. He screamed with each break and stared at the blood pool in the palm of his hand. Then I took a brick hammer and grinned. "This little piggy is going to the market," I said and thumped the hammer down onto his toe. One by one, his toe bones turned to mush. "Hey. Hey!" I yelled and slapped him, bringing him back into consciousness. "Did I say you could sleep?" My contact had told me about horrible, disgusting even, things these guys had done but he couldn't prove in court. As a result, I didn't feel so bad making it hard for this guy to shake a hand, or go for a walk any time soon.

21

"Now, this can all be over if you just tell me what I need to know. Four people on their way to Savannah, 1981…"

He growled at me. Literally, he growled at me… "Down boy," I told him.

"Fuck you, and your four people."

It's not his fault, he didn't know how this linked back to Nancy. I squeezed his broken fingers together, bone rubbing on bone.

"Fuck!" he screamed.

"Sounds like you're ready to talk." I told him all the details, showed him photographs of the victims' families and that's when I had a thought.

He sat there in silence, his head waiving around. *Tough old bastard.*

"You know…I'm not much of a surgeon, but…everyone's got to start somewhere right?" I said, grinning and looking into his eyes. "Now which body part of yours would get me the most money on the black market I wonder… You're pretty old though, maybe I will just keep it as a memento."

"You're fucking crazy!"

"They say there is a fine line between a genius and a "crazy man", care to see which side of the line I'm on?" I picked up a scalpel and headed for his kidneys.

"No, wait! Wait! I'll talk, I'll fucking talk!"

"I was only young when the killings were going on. Our gang was new to the scene. We discovered that lots of tourists drove through that area heading to Savannah. We thought it would be easy pickin…" he passed out. *Good job I brought this car battery.* I hooked him up, clipped it onto his nipples, and flicked the switch. "Ahhhhh! What? What the!? Where am I?"

"It's me, your best friend!" I said with a smile, which I then wiped off back into a glare. "You were telling me about your easy pickings. Now continue before I get creative."

"Fine…Well, we'd create a barricade in the middle of the road," he coughed, and blood flicked from his hands. "Once they stopped, we grabbed the people and drove the victims to a secure location off the road that we had set up. One of the victims you mentioned tried to escape, but he didn't get very far. Bullets travel 1100 feet per second, that man couldn't…" a grin formed in the corner of his mouth. "The rest of them were sliced up and had their organs packaged away for the black market."

The little brother was right… He knew this for thirty-four years. Thirty-four years. He waited all those long years, nobody believing him, no help. That sort of thing can eat at a man, but I guess his love for his sister kept him strong. I was still pissed at the guy for what he'd done to Nancy, but I respected his love and determination for his sister. I talked with my 'play friend' a while longer, and afterwards cut his ropes and left.

The next day my contact would receive something interesting in the mail. I sent a USB stick with audio recordings on it and several signed documents. I had left just enough fingers unbroken so that the guy could sign his confessions. I recorded him telling me everything. This included cases my contact had tried but could never pin him to over the years.

Along with this evidence, I left a simple note:

Thanks for your help. I don't know if this will stand up in a courtroom, but I felt it was worth a shot. Keep in touch.

I still couldn't bring myself to visit the therapist, so he too got something interesting in the mail. I sent him a video of the man, showing the damage I'd done to him. The video also showed the man explaining everything that happened to his sister, in case nothing came out in the media.

That night after talking to the other three "reincarnated" people, I had lunch with Nancy.

"Can't you stay, just a little longer?"

"I wish I could, but I've got cases to solve," I said. I gave her a kiss on the cheek and left.

The trip had been a whirlwind of a ride, but it's just another day in the office and another case... solved.

WANNA PLAY

Case #222

As smoke played around in my mouth and flowed down my throat, my muscles began to relax. This would no doubt kill me one day, but sitting there, completely relaxed, I couldn't imagine my life without it.

Having just got back from the states I was ready for a fresh case. The leaning tower of envelopes was a welcoming sight and soon the feel of fresh paper was between my fingertips.

Okay God, what have you got for me today?

The paper was crisp, eggshell white, with the company logo raised. This was no ordinary stationery. No, the people who sent this had money. I flipped the envelope over and there it was, the return address to a private hospital. '**The London Bridge Hospital**', interesting… They were brief in their message:

> **Three children are dead, all hung, and we need your help to solve this case.**

I let myself enjoy the last of my cigar, checked the time on my old grandfather clock, and headed to the hospital.

Standing in front of the building, clothes soaked through, I looked up, cursed the sky, and walked through the entrance doors. The now broken umbrella crashed inside the bin and I headed for the front desk.

"You must be Detective Banks," the receptionist said with a smile.

"What gave it away?" I asked, but she just gave a faint smile and picked up the phone.

I knew of course why, as she looked me up and down. This was a fancy, private hospital. Men wore the best suits on the market, Rolexes on their wrists. I on the other hand was standing there in a suit my father had passed on to me before he died. He was a great man. Wearing this suit made me feel like he was always with me.

The lady at the desk dialled a number and then tapped her pink fake nails on the desk.

I didn't have to wait long before a serious-looking manager appeared before me. Shaking my hand, a hint of relief appeared to wash over his face.

"Thank you so much for coming, detective. Before we start, I have to say that as you can imagine, we want to keep this case to ourselves."

"I never discuss my cases with anyone else and respect my client's privacy, don't worry."

"It is a most unfortunate incident. The cleaner found the children this morning. I took a video for you," he said, handing me a phone.

Three kids no older than eleven swayed side to side, bumping into each other like those metal balls people have on their desks at work. Newton's Cradle I believe it's called.

"We would like you to solve this case before mentioning anything to the parents. They're all away on business but will be checking in, in a week. Can you have this done by then?"

"Yes, it won't take that long," I assured him, again.

I asked him to take me to the scene of the crime. This didn't take long as it wasn't too far from the entrance. Useful location for a killer if this *is* a murder case.

Video footage was good, but I trusted my eyes more. There it was, high up, a long solid pipe crossed the ceiling, paint ground off where the string had been. The stench of cleaning products climbed up my nostrils.

"Was there a ladder by the children?"

"Urr no, why?"

"A child couldn't reach that high using a chair, don't you agree?"

"So, you think this is..." he said, leaning in towards me.

"Murder, yes."

"I see. I want this matter dealt with quickly, Mr. Banks, so you have the hospital's full cooperation. Tell the receptionist to make you a pass which will allow you to access everywhere in the hospital. Now, if you'll excuse me, I have to make some calls." He paced down the corridor into an office and I headed for the morgue.

I pushed the heavy morgue door open and felt a cold air chill brush over my face. There they were, three children laid next to each other, so small. The medical examiner showed me where the nooses had wrapped around their necks. They'd cut deep into the skin.

"Two boys and a girl, aged between nine and eleven, died approximately seven hours ago. The ligature marks on their necks indicate they have been hung..."

"Do you have the rope used to hang the children?"

"Sure," he said, handing me a clear bag, "but it's not ro—"

"Wait a minute. Are these—?"

"Red Yo-Yo strings? Yes. You spotted the finger loop at the end too, I see."

I never thought they could be so strong. I guess yo-yo fanatics want indestructible strings for competitions or whatever.

"I found something that will be of interest to you detective. Look," he said, lifting the child's head and pulling back her hair.

28

As I leaned in toward the child, he revealed behind the ear the word, "PLAYTIME" which was tattooed onto the skin.

"It's the same for each child. This to me points towards a murder."

"Any fingerprints, something to indicate someone else might have done this?"

Shoulders raised; he shook his head. With that, I thanked him and headed out of the morgue.

On my way back to the main desk I looked for who was in charge of the ward these kids had been on. What I had seen so far, pointed towards murder but I still like to cover all angles.

The person in charge was a woman, in her sixties I guessed judging by her appearance. After handing her the strings, she smiled.

"Have you seen them around here before?" I asked, no response. "Miss? Miss?" She appeared hypnotised. "Miss!"

"Oh, I'm sorry," she said, eyes wide open. "These yo-yo strings brought back fond memories from when I was a child. I haven't seen any in years."

"You're saying none of these kids here have them? Is there a chance you just didn't notice?"

"I'm very thorough Mr. Banks. Nothing gets past me. Plus, these are rich children, they probably don't know what a yo-yo is. When they're feeling well, they're on their phones and laptops playing."

"I see. Well, perhaps they only got them recently from someone with fond memories like yourself. Have they had any visitors lately? Parents or…has there been entertainment for the kids? A volunteer?"

"Actually, yes. We recently had a clown volunteer here called… Marbles."

"What did he look like?"

"I'm afraid he never had his makeup or costume off. Urm…he was about 6ft tall…average build. A bit creepy if I'm being honest. I could give you his address."

"Great."

With no kids owning yo-yo strings and a new volunteer in the hospital, it again pointed to a murderer. Address in hand, I headed out of the hospital and back into the pouring rain. "I freakin' hate clowns," I said as a shiver ran through my body.

When I arrived at the address, it wasn't a house or an apartment building in front of me but a Starbucks... Fake address. *Shit. At least I know I'm on the right track following this guy*, I thought. I lit up a cigar and headed home.

After shaking off the rain and closing my front door, I headed for a hot shower. Refreshed and sitting in my favourite chair, I looked up all the hospitals in London. I wanted to find out if there had been any new volunteers or suspicious characters visiting them. It turns out there are more hospitals than you would think. Whiskey hit the bottom of a glass, cigar smoke whirled in the air and I started dialling.

By call number thirty-nine, my eyes were starting to close, my grip on my glass was loosening…

"Hello how can I help you?" a pleasant voice said.

"Ye-yes, I'm detective Banks, I was just calling to see if you have had any new volunteers lately, entertainment, a clown maybe?"

"Actually, we have one coming in this morning."

Morning? I must've fallen asleep. But then how did I make this call? Hmm…

"Sir?"

"Sorry, yes. Can you tell me the clown's name?"

"Umm…you know what? I don't have it here. That's strange."

"Okay, I'll be right over, thanks."

I got dressed and headed for the tube. I didn't tell the woman on the phone that this guy could be dangerous. He could after all just be someone trying to make kids smile. There must be thousands of clowns around this city. That thought gave me the creeps, but that's just me.

It turned out one of the tube lines was on strike. Moans echoed throughout the crowd as I headed up the steps towards a bus stop. As I lit a cigar and sat down on a plastic bench, if you could call it that, the bus arrived. That delay saw me rush through the hospital and arrive just as the clown was packing up. I approached him casually from the side as to not alert him that he was a target.

With a fake smile painted on my face, I told the clown, "Great show."

"You just got here." He replied while tracing a scar on the back of his hand.

He had a good eye. Was it for looking over his shoulder?

"You got me. I'm just here to see if you've been to the London Bridge hospital recently?"

He threw his bag at my face and ran! I chased after him as quick as my feet would take me, but he had a head start. As he turned a corner, I shoved a trolley towards him, and it crashed into his ankle causing him to limp. However, as I got around the corner there was no sight of him…the stairs! I was only on the first floor, so had to be fast. Halfway down the stairs I jumped over the railings onto the other set and then smashed through the doors! I looked left, then right just in time to see him exit the hospital. By the time I got out there, I was walking amongst hundreds of people. *Shit.* I'd lost him. I punched the wall and headed back upstairs, right to his bag.

The bag contained red noses, coloured hair, make-up, and… wait…Yes! Right there in a zipped compartment was…the yo-yos and string to spare. I inspected every inch of the bag, for anything that would help with the case. And there, right in the corner of the bag was a coffee loyalty card.

I spent the rest of that day in that coffee shop, not a whisper of a clown. Nobody with a round red nose came flopping in with giant shoes on. Of course not. I was however hoping he'd come inside for a hot coffee, see me and run. After surveying the room one last time, however, I slugged the last of my coffee down.

"That's a mighty fine string you got there, if you don't mind me saying so," said the waiter as he collected my cup.

"You know about this string?"

"Sure do. It's a yo-yo string and an expensive one."

"Get this in a lot of places 'round here?"

"Only one I know of, over in Camden."

I thanked him for the lead, took the address, and tipped him well.

As I got to the store, cigar in hand, the owner was locking up.

"Shit," I said under my breath. "Sir! Hold on."

"We're closed."

"I can see that, but I would appreciate it if you could just do me one favour."

"Look, man, it's been a long day. I'm tired."

"I understand so I won't take up much of your time. Name's Detective Banks," I said, shaking his hand which left a twenty-pound note in his.

He put his hand back in his pocket, looked at me and then gestured towards the door.

I followed the old man into an antique store, his cane clinking on the old floorboards. Violins and old trumpets hung on strings from the ceiling, classic typewriters lay on small tables and, "Ouch!" Something hit me in the eye. *Wait...it's an old yo-yo.*

"So, you do sell yo-yos and strings here."

"If you want something, I'll usually find it." The man said, sitting in a wooden chair behind a desk.

"I'm running an investigation regarding a possible homicide and these strings are my main lead at this point. Look familiar?"

"Why yes. Good quality strings, don't come cheap."

"Has anyone come in here for this type of string?"

"Umm, no, I don't think so...sorry." He said and scratched his head.

"Shit." I was tired of dead ends.

Suddenly I saw him take a book from his desk drawer and flick through it. His eyes widened. "Aha!"

"What?"

"I knew something was ringing in my ear for a reason," he said smiling. "Like I said, nobody has come *into* the store for this item but about six months, two people ordered some for home delivery." My ears pricked up. "I don't usually do deliveries ya see, but both these guys were willing to pay double. They wanted it urgently and both valued their privacy."

I was happy to see this lead was a solid hit. I'd already received two strikes with the coffee shop and false address, and three strikes make me mad.

After being haggled for a little extra money for the addresses I headed out. My instincts told me to check the most recent purchaser of the two, closer to the crime scene.

After making a quick pitstop, I arrived at the apartment block and climbed the outdoor rickety fire escape to the tenth floor. Customer number one was sitting watching television in his living room. I struck a match and watched the flame dance in the breeze before lighting up my cigar. Blowing the smoke into the westerly wind, I continued to watch him. No clown make-up on, hmm. He started to get undressed, and after seeing no clown shoes on his feet, I looked away. It was a sight I didn't care to see.

Sitting down, I caressed the cigar with my mouth, inhaled and inside the smoke band began to play. After several minutes I checked back in. Dressed in a sharp suit, flower in his lapel, the man threw a satchel filled to the brim over his shoulder. He soon left, and that was my cue to enter. Using a screwdriver, I pried open the window and entered the living room.

There were university certificates on the wall for a Michael Rodding. He was highly qualified when it came to computers. After noting down the name, light bounced off a photo and into my eyes. In the frame was the suspect with his parents as a child. They were stood next to him as he sat at the piano on a stage. Couldn't have been more than thirteen years old. A great day of his life and yet his eyes told a different story. I headed for the door to the next room and eased it open. Shelves and window ledges were all covered with toys. Each one methodically placed. An O.C.D. kid's room perhaps. Strict parents who wanted order or...a cold-blooded child-killing clown. Speaking of clowns...there was one in the corner of the room staring right at me, creepy bastard. As I headed towards it and had thoughts of destroying it limb by limb, something caught my eye.

I glared at another clown on my left...but I noticed his jacket was swaying as if caught in a breeze. With the window shut and the door closed behind me, there was no reason for there to be a breeze. As I edged closer and looked more sharply, I noticed a fine line in the wall. I placed the back of my hand in front of it and a breeze tickled my skin. I checked over my shoulder and pricked my ears. Nothing. I put my fingertips into the fine line, pulled, but nothing. I knocked up and down the wall 'til I heard something different. Nothing to hold on to, pulling had to work, and so I pulled and—

Shit! He'd come back. Not much of a party or he'd forgotten something. I was hoping for the latter. Through the doorway, he started to walk towards me but stopped and gazed at the picture of his piano recital He clenched his fist, and the sight woke me out of my daze. I needed to move! He itched the back of his hand, then turned and I quickly ducked behind the door, praying he hadn't seen me.

He entered the room, turned to the clown in the corner, and smiled. Then he turned his attention to one of the shelves, took out a small box, and went to open it. This was my exit chance. I slipped from behind the opened door and went into the living room. I headed towards the window, before glancing back over my shoulder, "Ouch!" I said after I'd banged my knee into the coffee table.

Rapid footsteps echoed off the walls and were getting closer. Time to make a move. The door flew open and I dived through the open window, crashing onto the fire escape. The man leaned over the window ledge. He looked left and right, while I glued my body to the wall, praying he didn't look down. "Weird," he said and pulled his head back inside. The cold air danced in and out of my clothes as I lay waiting. When enough time had passed, I peeked over the edge of the window. He was looking towards the kitchen now. I couldn't know for sure this man was the killer, but I had to see what was behind the secret door.

After a couple of hours, it was clear the man was staying home for the night. I headed back to mine, making a call to my contact along the way.

"Stan, what have you got for me?"

"I ran the name, Michael Rodding, through our database as you asked."

"And?"

"He's clean. No criminal record, no history of abandonment, or abusive foster parents as a child. He hasn't even had parking tickets."

"So, there's nothing on this guy, nothing out the ordinary?"

"Well…he lost both parents at aged 13 and went into the system."

"What was the place he went to live like?"

"It was a low budget place, not much to do. Not much to entertain the older children. Any toys or activities tended to be for babies. He never got adopted or stayed with anyone else."

"Hmm…thanks Stan. Say hi to the kids for me". My mind wandered. "Oh Stan, Stan. How did his parents die?"

"I'll look into it. It's not on the system at my end for some reason."

No record. No abusive foster parents. No speeding tickets... Pretty clean, hmm…my fingers and thumb massaged the stubble on my face. You don't need a record to kill, but usually, these killers do, an early warning sign. Maybe that secret room would help me decide, or perhaps it's the other string customer. Still, for some reason, I couldn't get that photograph out of my mind of the man's childhood concert.

I went to the other customer's place, 8th floor. *Don't suspects live in houses anymore?* A willow tree swayed in the wind as I climbed the stairs. Once at the suspect's window, I peered through the gaps in the blinds. A man stood there teaching his lover how to do yo-yo tricks. He held the man's hand while standing very closely behind him and taught him how to walk the dog. Yo-yo medals were hung on the wall next to photos of the young men on vacation. Some people would still entertain that this could be the killer, but I knew in my gut that this was a dead end, another fucking dead end. I pinched the bridge of my nose. Still, this meant that suspect number one, Mr. Rodding just went up on the ladder. Dark clouds rolled through the sky as I left the building and headed to his home.

The London underground was dimly lit, with steps in much need of repair. As I headed out the exit, the scenery hadn't much changed. Cracks filled the pavements, potholes in the road and those dark clouds now filled the sky. I checked my phone for messa- "Hey watch it!" I yelled after someone bumped into me. I looked up and was pleasantly surprised.

"Arlo!" I said with a smile. I tried to meet his eyes. "Everything okay their buddy?"

"You nearly gave me a heart attack, John." He said panting.

"What can I say? Reflexes. So, how's the cigar business. Been a while since I've been to your store."

"That's what happens when you buy so many boxes," he said with a smile, straightening up his back. "On a case?"

"Yeah," I said rubbing my forehead.

"How's it coming along?"

"Slow, but I'll solve it."

"You always do," he said with a smile. "Listen John, I've really gotta run. Come by the store sometime, I've just got a new batch of cigars I think you'll like."

"Sounds like a plan," I said, tapping him on his shoulder.

With a smile, he turned. "I'll be seeing you," he said raising his cane and beginning to walk.

I thought back to the day I first saw him with that cane. Fresh out of hospital after refusing to hand over money to an armed thief. "Don't say a word," he'd told me pointing his finger at me, "I can still kick your ass." I'm sure he'd have given me a good go. That's what years in the military does for you, *and a tour in Cuba will have you becoming a cigar store owner*, I thought and laughed to myself. Then, I put my personal life on pause and got back to business. There was still a killer to find, and so I continued on to Mr. Rodding's building

I arrived at Mr. Rodding's building, ready to climb to floor number six but took a second for myself. This could be the killer, and so I needed a smoke and some mental preparation. After striking a match against the wall, I watched the flame turn my cigar to a bright orange as I inhaled. I went over everything in my head and focused on what I needed to do. *There's still a chance this might not be the killer and just another yo-yo nut*, I thought. Focus…focus.

Cigar ash ground into the wall, I was ready. I climbed up the fire escape as rain started to pour, and with nobody home, I entered. The hidden door was the main focus now. *What was behind it? A body? Plans? Or merely some rare Lord of the Rings collectables.* The room's door handle turned with ease and I pushed it open. There it was, I could see the outline of the hidden door much clearer now. Edging closer, and closer, I placed my hands onto the secret door and—

RING!

My heart skipped a beat as my phone rang loud from my chest pocket. I muted it, saw who it was, and answered.

"It's me, Stan. Not interrupting, am I?"

"You could say that. What is it?"

"I managed to find out about the dead parents..."

"And?"

There was a loud crash of thunder.

"Did you hear me? Hello?"

"I'm here, what did you say?"

"I said both his parents hung themselves," he said. I pulled on the door. It creaked open, and I reached for a light...

"Banks? Banks, did you hear what I said?"

I pulled down the cord, and the light blinded me for a moment. When my eyes opened and the floating spots began to fade, I saw it all. A map pinned to the wall with hospitals circled in red clown make-up, yo-yos and all the fancy strings to go with them. He even had locks of hair...the sick fuck.

"Wait...what's that?" I said, brushing some dust off some sort of cloth.

"What's what?"

"Fuck. I've found our guy. I know who the playtime killer is, and I also think I've just found..." I said, unravelling the dirty cloth.

"Found what? Banks! Found what?"

"I've just found...shit..."

I went quiet. My brain needed time to process what I was seeing.

"Banks...are you still there?"

"The parents' graves."

"What?"

"The parents' graves. Was there ever a report of a disturbance of them?"

"Let me check, hold on...Yeah, someone reported a person messing by the graves, but nothing came of it, why?"

"The sick son of a bitch. He took them…"

"Took what?"

"He took their heads. They're right here."

I took photos of everything and took strands of hair for the lab guys. I placed everything else carefully back in place and closed the door. I sat in the living room and waited. I wasn't going anywhere. I wanted to catch this guy, and giving people his details wasn't enough for me this time.

I stayed there for twenty-four hours, but he never showed.

I went downstairs, spotted a young receptionist reading a book behind a desk. "Hi, I'm John. I'm looking for my friend Michael. Do you know where he might be?"

She pushed up her glasses, looked up, and gave a smile. "Mr. Rodding? Yeah, he's gone away for a few days. He does this every now and then. Tells me 'It's Playtime', though I'm not quite sure what that means."

I thanked her and left. This must be his M.O. Goes away, executes his kill, and hides out with his newly acquired trophies in a hotel, using a fake name. This meant he was about to kill again!

Luckily, I now had the killer's list of hospitals after discovering his secret map, and so I began calling them one by one. It was important they didn't cancel any volunteers. There could be other friendly…clowns, and also, I wanted to catch the bastard, not scare him off. I made a point of talking in person to the security guards who worked in each control room that contained all the security screens. "I want you to be on the lookout for a man dressed like a clown. Here's a photo of him without the make-up as well. Do not approach him. You see him, call me." After that, all I could do was wait.

I wanted to be central to the majority of the hospitals on the list. That place just so happened to be by one of my favourite bars,

O'Rourke's. I was on a serious case, but a glass of whiskey calmed me and kept me on track. The bell above the door rang as I headed inside, and the bartender looked up and gave me a nod. A few of the regulars occupied the dark leather booths under the dim light, but as for the bar, I had it all to myself. I folded my coat, laid it on the bar, and sat down.

"Whiskey, no ice."

"Same as usual then?" The Irish barman said, with a hint of a laugh.

"Yeah. You wouldn't believe the number of places that get it wrong."

Sitting at a table, drink in hand, I sipped the whiskey which caressed my throat on the way down to a well-used liver. As I placed the glass onto the table my phone rang. It was the London Bridge Hospital.

"Detective Banks?? I think he's here! Shit! The other guard was throwing up in the toilet, and I, I, I waited as long as I could, but I needed to pee so bad... I missed him coming into the building, but I've just seen him in the corridor!"

"Okay calm down. Keep an eye on him. I'm on my way."

The hospital was about a five minute walk away. I threw the last of the whiskey down my throat and ran for the hospital. I got there in two minutes.

I called the guard. "Where is he?"

"I don't know! He's knocked out the cameras!"

Why had he come in secret like this and to here? This wasn't his M.O. Had he found out something about me? About people watching him? Either way, the children needed to be found. I ran so hard my thighs burned and my breathing went as rapid as a turbo engine.

I got to the children's ward and looked around quickly — three empty beds where children should've been. I looked left and right, left and right. Then I spotted something…a child's teddy bear in the distance on the floor. One of the children must've dropped it. I ran, grabbed the teddy without breaking my pace, and drifted around the corner. There, at the end of the corridor were the three children, nooses around their necks and a high table that their tip-toes barely touched!

The man leaned in towards the children and whispered something as I ran towards him. He smiled but then spotted me.

"Playtime!" he shouted and kicked the wheeled table from underneath the children.

I ran and dove for the table that was sliding down the corridor. The edge of it hit my stomach, winding me. *No time to stop.* I ran it to the children's feet and jumped on top of it. After cutting them down I shouted down the phone.

"Lock this fucker in! Lock him in!"

The children now safe, I ran down the corridor after the killer. There was silence… No noises. No signs of light from open doors. The lifts and stairs were behind me. *Where is he?* I thought.

I sat on a nearby bench and began to meditate. Deep breath in, 1, 2, 3, 4 and out 1, 2, 3, 4. My heartbeat and its heavy beating sound lowered. I focused on nothing but my hearing. *Where are you?* I thought. And then…I heard him breathing. He wasn't too close, but he was close enough.

I stood up, still keeping my meditation going, eyes closed, I followed the sound. Each step I took was taking me a step closer to him until I turned and the sound began to get weaker.

I turned back, opened my eyes, and saw a door. As it swayed open, the breathing became louder. He was hiding, but he wouldn't be safe for long. There was a curtain around a bed and shoes at the bottom. This was it. I walked over, threw back the curtains and—

"What?" I asked, with nobody there, and then *BAM!* He was on my back! A scalpel edged towards my throat! I managed to grab his hand, but his arms weren't letting go. I rammed him back into the wall, then again and again until he fell off. He turned quickly only to be greeted by my fist! Flying back into the wall his body slumped to the ground and I placed my boot on his throat.

"Playtime's over," I said as I looked down at him. When he had nearly passed out, I restrained myself and then tied him to a chair.

"So, why'd you do it. What's the reason, you sick bastard?" I said, trying to calm myself down.

"I'm ain't telling you shit," he said, which earned him a broken nose.

"Tell me!"

"Fuck you!" he yelled and spat in my face. Big mistake.

I took a handkerchief from my pocket and wiped off the mess; he saw a grin on my face as I removed it and he looked confused.

I booted him in his broken nose which crunched as he went flying to the ground. Standing over him and the broken chair I told him, "Time to have a little fun." I spotted his bag in the corner of the room and brought it over. "There they are," I said and grinned as I pulled a couple of yo-yo strings out.

"What are you going to do?" he said, raising his head. I looked him in the eyes but said nothing.

I threw the strings over a steel pipe and headed towards him. "You're not seri-"

"Shut the hell up," I said and tied the string around his neck. "Since you don't want to talk, let's see if I can make you scream." I walked to the other side of the room, grabbed the other end of the string, and began to hoist him up. Feeling the string slowly sinking into my palms, I grabbed a doctor's coat and wrapped it around my hands. With a few big pulls, his body started to leave the ground.

"St- stop," he squeezed out of his mouth.

I pulled harder and a drop of blood trickled down his neck. Once fully off the ground, I tied the string up, still amazed how strong it was.

"Ready to talk yet?" I asked.

He managed to get out enough noise and said "yes."

"Well I'm not quite ready," I said and reached for the surgeons' tools I'd pulled out the drawers earlier. "Have you heard of a procedure called the twister?" I said, holding up the pliers. "No? Well, you'll go nuts for it!" I yanked down his pants, grabbed his testicle between the pliers, squeezed, and twisted hard." He screamed out in agony. "Like to kill little kids, eh? Don't have the balls to tell me why? Well, one ball, now," I said, taking the pliers away. I looked at the other tools and heard a thud. As I turned around, I saw him wriggling on the floor. "I guess the string wasn't as strong as I thought."

With a blood red scarf forming around his neck, I knew things needed to speed up. I yanked him up onto another chair and dangled some of the yo-yo string in front of him. I whispered in his ear, "Want to go for another ride?"

"No!! Please!" he yelled.

"Then tell me everything before I get *really* creative."

"Okay, okay! I'll tell ya," he shouted and put a hand to his throat as he regained his breath. "My parents. My *bastard* parents were strict, super fuckin' strict. They wanted me to be perfect every fucking second of the day, there was no time for toys, friends, or "playtime". They had me hammer that frickin' piano for hours," he said tracing the scar on the back of his hand. "When I wasn't on that, I studied or tidied like a fucking maid. I had no childhood and I hated them for it! The closest I came to playtime was watching other kids do it in the street, running around smiling. There was no playtime for me, why should anyone else have it?!"

"Your shitty childhood doesn't warrant death sentences!" I yelled, inches from his face.

"I'm not finished!!" Veins throbbed at the side of his head. "I-I…" he fainted and fell to the floor.

"Oh no you don't, you fucker." I said and slapped his face hard. No good. I poked my head out of the door, nobody there. I looked for the medicine storage room in the corridor and as luck would have it, the card given to me really *did* open everywhere. A mistake by the hospital, but a gift I was thankful for.

I grabbed a syringe and a small bottle of adrenaline. Back in the room I knelt over the man. I inserted the syringe into the bottle and pulled it back. The fluid trickled in and then I pushed it up, squeezing a small amount out to test. "One, two, three!" I stabbed it into his heart and his upper body flew upright.

"What the ?!" he yelled and then lay back down.

"Remember me? Time to finish your story" I said and shoved him back up onto his chair. "I was saying your shitty childhood didn't warrant child death sentences. Still don't agree?"

"What I said was that I wasn't finished, ok?!" his eyes were wide open now, the adrenaline coursing through his veins. "Like I was saying, I thought all I wanted to do was play in the street, but then I saw it. A yo-yo." He looked to the ceiling in a daze.

"Stop your fucking fantasising and get to the point, asshole."

45

"Fine," he said with his eyes coming to meet mine. "The kid holding it was a yo-yo champion, you see. The tricks he did mesmerised me, I'd never seen something so beautiful… I asked my parents for one on my thirteenth birthday and what do you think they told me?"

"That you're insane?"

"No!" he yelled with fire burning in his eyes. "They told me fucking no! Just like they did for everything else. But don't worry, I got my revenge. I hung those bastards up in our basement and it made me feel *alive*. It set me free." He smiled as his breathing got heavier. "I never want to lose that feeling, and who better to do it to than those punk kids who get to play all day long? I never got a childhood, and neither will they." He tried to hide laughter that had begun to form, "The cherry on the cake was the yo-yo strings. A symbol of what I wasn't allowed to have, resulting in breaths they would never have again." He rocked back and forth with a twisted grin on his bloody face. "I hung them up and they squealed like little piggies. When their life tank emptied, mine filled right up!" He grinned from ear to ear, with a crazed look.

"Say goodnight," I said and booted him in the face. He slid slowly down the wall, the smile going back into its cave and the lights in his eyes turned out. I resisted the urge to break some more bones to the sick bastard, turned away and called the police.

I watched as they threw him into the back of a police van and then stood there for a while looking into the river Thames. The water was a little calmer now. One more killer off the streets and one more case…solved.

ITCHING TO KILL

Case #223

The door to my office swung open as water dripped from every inch of my clothes. *Thank you, London...* I grabbed a case file to warm my blood and lit a fire. Soon, the logs crackled and steam rose from my clothes. I hung up my jacket near the fire, rain still falling from its sleeves, and sat down on the leather chair.

What have you got for me today, God?

I sliced the envelope with my letter opener and read,

"Detective Banks. Five of my CEOs have been found dead in their offices, supposed heart attacks. I don't buy that, and it's up to you to prove me right and give me the answers. Accept this case, and you will be handsomely rewarded."

I threw some more kindle into the fireplace and lit a cigar, mentally preparing myself for the case ahead.

The name on the letter, a Miss E. Blake was not at her office; in fact, she was not even in the country. Her well-spoken receptionist informed me that her boss would Skype me and to expect a call at 12:30 sharp.

The call was short, but enough to express how important the case was and to reassure herself she'd chose the right man for the job.

"My receptionist will send you an information pack within the hour. This will contain all the information you'll need about the dead CEOs, office addresses and so on. Goodbye." Before I could reply she'd ended the call.

An hour later, and with the information pack in hand, I headed for the tube. As I skimmed through the pages, I noticed a lot of blacked out areas. *What was it that they didn't want me to see? Was it secrets to Miss Blake's success? The success which has granted her five very successful companies below her? Or simply secrets that she wouldn't want anyone with connections to the law to know?* Either way, it gave me enough to go on for now. If I needed more, I had a way of finding what was hidden in the black mist.

Out of the tube and then under the dull clouds of London, I headed to the morgue to speak to my coroner contact and explain about the case.

I walked down the bland corridors of the hospital, nothing but grey walls and signs. I arrived at the lift, to find an out of order sign, "great..." I said with a sigh and headed for the door to the stair well. The echoing of my shoes bounced around as I descended downwards to the morgue, walking towards death.

I pushed both doors to the morgue open. "I didn't know Tetris was part of your work now, Charlie," I said, causing him to throw his phone up into the air. I caught it and told him about the case.

"Sounds like another crazy case you've got there," he said, moving his glasses back up his long nose.

"Listen Charlie, I need you and you alone to do an autopsy on five bodies for me," I said with a hand on his shoulder. "Afterwards come straight to me, nobody else. Can you do that? I don't trust the companies' own people to do it or to receive the information first."

"Well…okay J-John. Only because it's you. Oh, and John?"

"Yeah?"

"Go easy on those cigars. Smoking k-kills and I don't want your ugly ass on my table." He grinned and went back to work on a body.

"I'll see what I can do. Goodbye Charlie."

Next, I headed to the buildings of the five CEOs' offices. I wanted to check for similarities, talk to the receptionists and see if I could gain more intel. After visiting four of the offices, I'd noticed similar things but nothing that stuck out too much. Bottles of refrigerated water, a bottle of whiskey, cologne. I asked all of the receptionists about anything out of the ordinary that had happened lately. But besides the usual about competitors being possible enemies, there wasn't much to go by.

The skies had turned black by the time I got to the last CEO's office, rain threatening to hit my hard. I expected a similar result but kept an open mind and headed inside, up to the 40th floor.

"I'm—"

"Detective Banks, yes I've been expecting you," the receptionist said with a smile.

I'd seen that kind of smile before, but hadn't gone there to get a woman's number, I was on a case. So, I gave a polite smile and asked if it was okay for me to look around.

"Sure. Anything you need just ask."

Again, there were the same similar things; water, whiskey, a bottle of… I turned away and tried to focus on something else, my hands clenched. That bottle of cologne… the same one that happened to be the last thing my wife bought me before…the accident.

"So…"

"Kate."

"Kate. Have you noticed anything unusual this past week? Anything at all? Meetings that got heated? Your boss being more stressed than usual?"

"I'm afraid not, I tried to rattle my brain for you while I was waiting, but I couldn't think of anything."

"I see."

"Oh! But Miss Jenny might be able to help."

"Miss Jenny?"

"Yeah, she's a reporter, and she's always interviewing Mr. Black, sometimes in the office, sometimes out. I bet *she* would know if there was something worth mentioning," she said, handing me a business card for the local paper. "I could take you there...if you want?" she said, looking me up and down.

"I'm afraid I try not to mix business with pleasure. Rain cheque?"

"Sure." She smiled while playing with her long brown hair, I smiled back and left.

On the way to the reporter's office I called the number on the card and arranged to meet Miss Jenny, for a cup of coffee near her work.

There was no flirtatious smile when I met Miss Jenny outside her tall office building, but she gave me a pleasant one still. A smile which in the right circumstances, would allow her to get information from people for stories she wanted. We headed to the coffee shop. It was a basic place, a few round tables and an I love NY picture on the wall. I insisted Miss Jenny sit down as I got us both a drink. This worked well to make me look kind but also gave me a chance to study her body language for a while. She appeared calm as she looked at some papers while she waited. A reporter never stops, I guess. Drinks in hand, I headed over to the table.

"So," I said, sitting down and placing the drinks onto the table. "How long have you been talking to Mr. Black?"

"I've been speaking to James- I mean Mr. Black, for eight months now," she said, twirling a pen through her fingers, "Terrible thing what happened to him. A heart attack wasn't it?"

"That information wasn't released to the media." I leaned in closer. "How did you come about that information?"

"Oh, urm..." she put the pen down, "he told me about his bad heart. He was taking pills for it and with the stress of being a CEO of a big company I guessed is all. Is there anything indicating it was something else?" she said and began twirling the pen once more.

"No." It was always easier to stick to a simple rational story for the public while I was investigating. "Had Mr. Black acted any differently lately? Did he talk about possible enemies? Had any business deals that went sour?"

"No, not really," she said, tapping her pen on the counter. "I know both Mr. Black and another CEO, Mr. Red were highly competitive. My bet though, is a heart attack for sure. You see it all the time with these office types, working god knows how many hours."

"I see," I said studying her face. "Do you know of any unusual mee-"

Her phone rang, "Sorry, I have to take this," she stood and walked over to the toilets. She tugged at her ear as the call continued and then smiled. *Wow, nice smile.*

She soon hurried over to me and grabbed her jacket, "I'm sorry, but I really have to go. Rain check?"

"Sure," I stood and shook her hand, with a smile, "I'll be in touch." I said and watched her walk away. She hadn't given me much to go on, but it was a nice meeting and it put Mr. Red in the spotlight.

I lit up a cigar and stood under a bus shelter out of the rain. With smoke fogging up my view of the world, I messaged a contact about Mr. Red, the competitive CEO and what he messaged back was very intriguing.

It turned out Mr. Red had been previously linked to drug use, drug sales, drug importation, the lot. Whenever there was a hint of this information being discovered however, it was soon undiscovered, most likely by dirty cops. When it did slip through the cracks and go to court, the witnesses brave enough to take the stand, never quite made it...

Being that high up in the drug world is a good motive for wanting the CEO dead. Drug dealing competitors could also kill the others under the umbrella. A message to say you mess with us and we kill your family, well…in the business sense.

While waiting on the autopsy reports from Charlie, I headed for the highest competitors in the drug world. I wanted to investigate who would benefit the most from Mr. Red's death.

Standing on the border of Peckham, I took a longer inhale of my cigar than usual, closed my eyes, and began to meditate. This was one of the roughest neighbourhoods around London and home to the Peckham Devils. If you've ever walked through this area, then you'll know it doesn't take long to find some troublesome characters. You can even feel the winds change when you step over that border line. I opened my eyes, it was time.

I couldn't just walk up to a drug lord and ask him if he'd decided to kill some people. The answer would be yes regardless of my case. That's what you sign up for when you become a drug lord. No, it's always easier to start speaking to people near the bottom. They are paid less, less respected and with some persuasion, will tell you what you need to know.

As I walked down the streets, I could feel eyes on me, a stranger in their land. Graffiti of devil's and "fuck the police" filled the walls, the smell of weed slapped me in the face every five minutes. Soon I spotted a small newspaper shop and went inside. I grabbed a box of matches, placed them on the counter and put down a ten-pound note.

"Would there be anything else sir?" a man said who smelled like he'd taken a bath in a pool of curry.

"Yes actually," I pulled out another ten-pound note and laid it down on the counter. "Could you tell me where I could get some...devil-ish drugs tonight?"

The man looked me up and down, trying to use his instincts to see if I was a cop. After caressing his cheek with his thumb for a while, he gave a nod. On a piece of paper, he wrote down an address and phrase, slid it towards me and put the money in his top pocket.

The temperature had dropped a lot by the time I arrived at my destination. The house's windows were bordered up and the bricks on the walls were crumbling. This place looked like it had been abandoned for years, home only to the pigeons. It was the perfect cover for a drug dealer's business. I gave a few knocks and waited, and waited. A few minutes went by, and as I edged my ear closer to the door, a little slit opened.

"What the hell do you want?" a voice from behind the door asked.

I looked down at the piece of paper. "Niech żyje diabły."

Click, click, click, click. *Four locks; smart or paranoid?* The door creaked open and revealed a dark, smoke filled corridor. A man in the shadows pointed me in the right direction. I strolled, allowing myself to mentally photograph everything. To my right, a man was tied in a chair receiving a blow to the head. To my left—

My back got pushed. "Move it!" the shadowed man said.

Edging closer to the lit-up room at the end of the corridor, I went over my plan. Buy a small amount of drugs, spot the weakest guy, and later follow him. I walked into the room where a tall, lean man was staring out of a window. He slowly turned, and when his eyes caught mine, they twitched and then looked at a man behind me.

"Please, sit. How can I help you?"

"I'd like to have some snow," I said, placing fifty pounds on the table to show I wasn't playing around.

"No problem. I can make it snow for you. I'll be right back."

He stood up, walked past me, nodded at the tall, well-built man and left. The man remaining in the room locked his eyes on me. The door lock clicked, and he headed towards me.

"What's this? Three minutes in heaven? Cos you're not my type," I said which made a vein on his forehead throb.

"You may not know me, but I know you...pig! You put my brother away for a long time and now it's my turn to put you under the ground" Vengeance was in his eyes. This was going to get real' ugly, real' quick.

I briskly looked around the office as he came towards me. "I thought you left boss man," I said, looking over the man's shoulder.

As the man turned, I smashed a snow globe over his head. He stumbled backwards and reached up to his head which still had half of the globe in it. I took my chance and went for the door only to be met by his large hand which wrapped around my throat. I grasped his hand, but it was as stiff as a statue, I was going to have to think of something else. The room started to get blurry as he squeezed tighter. Reaching out with both arms towards the desk, my fingertips reached a tall glass, *easy does it* I thought. I edged it closer, closer…but then it fell. *Shit. Time to go old school on this turd'.* I pulled back my leg and kicked his balls right out of the park! He fell to his knees and finally released his grip. I had to be swift. I took a lamp and smashed it over his head. This time he fell to the ground, knocked out cold.

He awoke to a chair over his throat and me sitting on it.

"Now here's how it's going to go. You're going to tell me what I need to know, and I *might* let your ugly ass live."

He spat at me. I hate that. It really grinds my gears.

I pulled a pen out of my pocket. "Now usually I would use a knife," I said rotating the pen, "but you've pissed me off. This will be harder to pierce the skin you see, take a little longer and hurt like fuck." I turned on the chair and stabbed it into his thigh.

"Jesus!!!"

With a grin I asked, "Oh by the way, did I mention ink poisoning?" I twisted the pen while clicking the end.

I worked on this guy hard and showed no mercy. By the time I was finished, the guy looked like he'd been to a lousy acupuncture session. The one thing these guys had got right was to soundproof the room. This is where they spent the most time with people they disagreed with.

He told me that his gang had nothing to do with the murders. Everyone, not only his gang was too scared to even try to touch this CEO drug lord. After the number I'd done on this guy, I believed him. Now my problem was how I was going to get out of this place, preferably not in a body bag. A swift punch to the side of the head and it was lights out for Mr. Muscles. Inside his jacket was a gun accompanied by a silencer, *nice*. I didn't know how many of these guys were at home to play, so a silencer fit the bill.

I steadily opened the door, standing behind it in case anybody was waiting outside. The coast was clear, for now. I pointed my gun out the room, better they shoot for that instead of my head. Silence... I stepped out and turned to the front door just in time to see a guy putting out his cigarette as he turned towards me. He quickly drew his gun, and I put a bullet right in his eye. His body stayed upright for a second, it flinched and then hit the ground like a sack of spuds. I moved the body out the way and left the building lighting a fresh cigar, which I always did after a kill. I don't like to take a life, but I do it when necessary.

I didn't have to wait long for the train to arrive and managed to get on despite it trying to decapitate me in the process. A woman pierced in every face hole possible had grabbed me by the tie and pulled me in as my balance swayed. "You saved my life, thanks," I said with a smile, but she just looked at me and turned away, revealing air pods in her ears.

When I got out of the tube, there was a message on my phone, the autopsy and toxin reports were in. The samples from the bottles of water and whiskey I'd sent in revealed nothing. It was a bit of a long shot, but they all had the same items in their offices. This was a perfect place to hide something toxic without it looking new or out of place. There was nothing suspicious found in the bloodstreams. I wanted to know more, so I called Charlie.

"Hey Charlie, I got your message. I've got another question; did you notice any strange markings on the bodies?"

"Actually, on the necks there were heavy scratch marks, thought t-to be due to the heart attack. People can g-get sweaty and itchy as a result."

"What else could make someone scratch like that?"

"Umm, bug bites, allergic reaction, bad cologne; I've had my fair share of those. This one time in Africa I b-bought this—"

"Wait a minute! Did you say cologne?"

"Yeah, why?"

"Just be expecting something in the lab which will need working on right away."

"Sure thing."

"I owe you, Charlie. Your father would be proud of you."

I got back on the tube where the stench of sweaty people in the air was more toxic than usual. I was heading for all the offices, again. There were samples to collect. I kicked myself for not spotting this clue earlier. My emotions linked to that last cologne bottle name got the better of me, never again.

After many tubes, elevators, stench, and stairs, I finally reached the last of the five offices, four cologne bottles in hand. After reaching the twentieth floor, I headed to the CEO's office and sat at the desk. Putting bottle number five next to the others, I began to inspect them. As I lifted each bottle up to the light, I could see the tiniest hint of purple floating around inside the orange liquid. *Poison or just something to catch the customers' eye.* I wrapped each one carefully and placed them into a box. After handing them to the receptionist, I asked her to send them off to Charlie immediately for an examination. With a good day's work done, I headed home.

✶ ✶ ✶

The next morning, Charlie called. Multiple tests had been done on the colognes, he even managed to abstract the purple substance. It was a poison and very sophisticated. He imagined the killer would have anticipated it disappearing before anyone noticed it like it did in the bloodstream. We caught it just in time.

I got on the phone and asked all the receptionists about the cologne. Where did it come from? Was it delivered? When was it delivered? By who? The answer from each receptionist was the same.

"They received it from their wives and on the same day as the heart attacks."

Were they all married to the same woman? I thought and laughed.

I asked each of them if they still had the notes that came with the colognes, and did they recognise the brand. They said they would check and said I was welcome to come over. I emailed them the photos of the colognes to jog their memories and headed out.

Each office I visited had the same note by the cologne:

A gift just for you darling, please wear it for when you come home.

It turned out to also be the same handwriting... One thing I didn't understand is why one of the cologne bottles was different, yet they all had the same poison inside. The first couple of receptionists couldn't help me with the identification of the cologne. On my next office visit, however, I was in luck.

"I looked hard at the photos of the cologne for you Detective. I realised they were the same as the one my friend had shown me. He works in the CEO's company that produces beauty products. They produce perfume, skin creams, foundation, you know stuff like that."

One thing that bothered me was that if it was from the CEO's company, surely he would notice that when he received it. *Did he not pay much attention to the products?* Then it clicked, one of the bottles had a different label...I called up Charlie and had him examine it. Without too much trouble he was able to scratch at the label and remove it, revealing the same name as the rest. I checked with the receptionist. She said that the CEO who'd received that bottle was from the company she was talking about. It was his product, one which hadn't been launched to the general public yet, that had killed him. I had my next destination, the beauty products company.

Everything was white and pristine at the beauty products factory. After walking through security and seeing some modern art on the wall, I asked who was in charge now. A lady asked me to take a seat. I waited in the lobby for twenty minutes studying the receptionist and the people coming in and out. Soon a tall, slender man in a blue suit with a red tie greeted me.

"Hello Detective Banks, I'm Mark Bossnan. If you'd care to follow me to my office, I will answer any questions you may have."

I thanked him, and we walked to his office. When we went inside the room, serious-looking men in expensive suits were standing around a tray of tea and coffee. *Solicitors? Hmm, maybe advisors.*

Sitting down in his chair behind an oversized desk he asked, "So, how can I help you today?"

"As you may know I am investigating the deaths of the CEOs. I recently came across one of your company's products and was hoping to gain some intel about it."

He looked at me and then the other gentlemen, "Ask away, and I will see if I can help you."

"Can you tell me about who was in charge of making the cologne? Who had access to it and who shipped it?"

"We have a set group of people who make the cologne in a large room in the factory. They and their manager would have access to it in there. Then it would be packed up and given to the drivers. We don't hire a third-party delivery service, everyone involved is our own people."

"Were employees allowed to take the products home with them, free samples perhaps?"

"No, definitely not. That is strictly forbidden," he said, adjusting his tie.

"I would like to speak to all these people. That wouldn't be a problem, would it?" I raised an eyebrow.

He looked at the suits and a few moments later, they nodded. "Yes, that will be fine detective."

The trouble was that with every person I went to see, the suits were sure to follow. So, I got my basic info, they ran quite a tight ship. Nobody tended to be left alone with the product and so on. With the suits there though I knew I couldn't get any real dirt. I got the impression that one wrong word about the company or how it's run would get you fired. By the end of my walk around the place I was frustrated, heck, I was pissed.

After stepping outside through a side door of the building, I struck a match and lit up a much-needed cigar. I took a deep breath and blew a cloud of smoke in front of me a second later. When the smoke cleared, however, there was a man standing in front of me. Thankfully, he *wasn't* another suit.

An employee who had caught my eye earlier asked, "Got a light?"

"Sure." I threw him my box of matches. "Have you got something for me?" I asked with my eyebrow raised.

"I might have…for the right price?"

I'd met guys like this before, low wages and after a quick buck. I didn't mind what he was asking for, crime pays but so does good information at times. I slipped the guy some notes, and he grinned.

"Half the time the stuff that goes through here isn't officially checked by the regulators. There's a few handshakes and one guy leaves a little bit richer if you know what I mean. Big boss man was very competitive. He wanted his stuff made yesterday and to win today, no matter what."

"I see. Are the employees here happy?"

"The pay is shit. Like I said, the boss man liked to win, that meant higher profit margins which meant lower wages."

"Any employees extra unhappy? Angry? Violent?"

"There was a guy, Jimmy Ratchard."

"Was?"

"Yeah, he spoke up to the boss, ran straight into his office. We never saw *him* again." He looked to the ground as he flicked some ash from his cigarette.

I got an address from the man, and he vanished back inside. I now had a good lead with a motive to kill. It was time to pay a little visit to Jimmy Ratchard's place, although he would never know about it.

Before heading over to Mr. Ratchard's however, I paid a visit to the reporter 'Miss Jenny' at her work, to see if she could verify anything the employee had said.

"I've reported on that company several times, although the stories never made it to print," she said and almost snapped her pencil.

I was intrigued, "Why's that?"

"Let's just say they either have a lot of cash or friends in high places," she said, rolling her eyes.

"What had you found exactly?"

"My sources told me about secret meetings, and apparently the boss of the company bribed the guy who was due to do lengthy safety checks on his products."

"Anything else?"

"Well…" she picked up a pen and began twirling it around her fingers, "I know they didn't pay the employees well, didn't even give them free samples of the products." She gave a faint laugh.

"I see," I said, tapping my foot. The employee had been telling the truth. Good to know it had been money well spent. "Thanks again for your help Jenny, I think I have everything that I need."

"Anytime, I'm glad I could be of assistance. Maybe give me the whole story after it's all over?" she said, and began chewing on her pen.

I smiled, "See you around."

The address the employee gave me led me to a block of flats in a neighbourhood you wouldn't want your mother walking through. A poor area however, usually meant poor security; this would be easy.

The buzzer on the entrance door made a horrible sound, like a mosquito being squashed as I pressed it. No answer. The door was loose and cracked, so with ease, I managed to move in and enter the building. I walked up five floors of stairs due to the lifts being out of order and finally reached Jimmy's door. I banged my fist on the door, and I walked away down the corridor. Nobody came. Lock pick in hand, I went to work on the door. *Click, click…click. Piece of cake.*

There wasn't much to this guy's place. It was small, empty takeaway boxes everywhere and what furniture he did have was mismatched, most likely from Ikea or charity shops. I looked around for any evidence of laboratory work. Was there something there that the poison could have been created with? After a while, I still had no luck. I felt sure it would have been too risky to make the poison in the company labs, so continued looking. As I opened the bedroom door, I spotted a dartboard with a photo as its bullseye. It was the face of the company's boss.

Suddenly, the front door creaked open. I swiftly moved into the walk-in cupboard and closed the door. My feet bumped into a box which made a clinking noise. I reached down and picked up an item from the box. It was the cologne! In the darkness I couldn't see the colours, but knew the shape and feel of the bottles used in the crime and this was it.

The door opened, and an angry face greeted me. His fist came towards my head, so I blocked it with the box of colognes. Bottles now everywhere, I scrambled out of the cupboard. I swung my first hard into his stomach and he slowly collapsed. Reaching down, I grabbed the man by the back of his hair. As I started to slowly pull him up, he smashed a bottle of cologne over my head; the liquid cascaded down my face. The man fled, and I ran to the bathroom faster than ever before! My heart was pounding. *Gotta get this shit off, gotta get it offa me!* I turned on the shower and jumped in, scrubbing my face urgently with the soap. I prayed that my racing heartbeat was down to my slight fear and not the poison.

After five minutes my heart rate started to lower, I was alive, drenched, but alive. I stood up and headed out of the flat to see if there was any sign of where Mr. Ratchard had gone. As I walked through the fire exit at the end of the corridor, my phone rang.

"Detective Banks." I said, flicking water off my hands.

"I'm calling to let you know that we've looked through hours of CCTV footage. We looked into where the parcels could have come from, and we've had a hit."

"I think I know who you're going to say. Jimmy Ratchard, right?"

"Actually, no."

"You sure?"

"Positive"

"Is it someone working for the company then?"

"No sir."

"Then who?" I said with a lack of patience.

"It's that reporter friend of yours."

"You're kidding?"

"Not at all. We managed to track the parcel to a post office in Bethnal Green. The reporter had been careful to keep her face hidden, that is until she dropped some money onto the floor. When getting up, she looked right at the camera that she was trying so hard to avoid. I took the liberty of calling the newspaper's office to see if she'd been working on a story in that area or lived near there. Turns out she'd told her boss she was doing a story down there, but didn't deem the story worthy of putting in the paper."

"What's her address? I'll head right over."

"That's the thing…the boss at the paper said that she'd moved place recently, but hadn't given them her new address."

"Thanks for the information. Let me know if you get anything else."

I grabbed my phone and rang Miss Jenny. It went straight to voicemail…

"Hi, this is Jenny. I'm on holiday right now. See you when you see me."

Shit. She'd done her dirty work and was fleeing the country. I called the boss at the paper on my way to the airport, explained the situation and asked if he knew about her flight.

"Miss Jenny has never interviewed the CEO, at least not for this paper… I saw her leave for the airport about…thirty minutes ago but she didn't say where she was flying to, I'm afraid."

She had a head start and so I needed to act fast or this killer would be lost forever. Who knew who she would kill? I ran outside and hailed down a taxi.

I was getting close to the airport and was itching to get out and catch this woman. "Here's an extra twenty. Pick up the pace," I said to the driver. The driver put his foot to the floor. We arrived at the airport and the driver slammed the brakes. When I looked up, there she was, entering the airport. I threw money at the driver, opened the door, and hit the ground running. I ran through the airport door and stopped to look left and right. Then I saw her, but she also saw me. She paused for a moment, and then bolted. This girl was fast.

I ran through the crowd dodging people and shoving them out the way when necessary. I saw her about to leave through an airport exit door, so I dove through one next to me. She was heading for a taxi; she opened the door and *BAM!* I tackled her to the ground, only to be pulled off her by some men as she smiled and jumped into the taxi. I shoved the idiots off me, knocked them to the ground and scrambled over their bodies and into the next taxi before they could get up.

"I'll give you a hundred pound if you stop that taxi," I said, showing the money to the driver.

He put his foot to the floor as I kept my eyes fixed on Miss Jenny through the taxi window. The lights were about to turn red, and she had just gotten through.

"Time to earn your money," I said as the lights turned red.

He nodded, accelerated through the lights, swerved out the

way of a car onto the pavement, gave a cat the fright of its life, hit the handbrake and drifted in front of Miss Jenny's taxi. This was my chance. I threw the money at the driver, jumped out of the taxi, and dragged Miss Jenny out of hers. Grabbing her by the wrist, I pulled her away from the crowd and into the nearby park. She tried to break free but failed.

"Alright talk!" I told her while throwing her onto a bench.

"Okay! Okay! I did it. I stole her jewellery."

"What??"

"The CEO's wife's jewellery."

"I don't give a rat's arse about the jewellery! What I do care about is the cologne."

"What about it?" She looked puzzled.

"Don't play dumb with me. That cologne that helped you kill five men!"

"What?!" she said, shocked. "She said it was just to remind them of her!"

"What?! Who?"

"Nobody…"

"Who?!" I shouted, shoving her shoulders against the bench.

"The bitch who hired me, okay?! She hired me to have an affair with the CEO and make him leave his wife."

"But he didn't leave her, did he?"

"No, but she seemed to accept it, accept that it was over. Then she asked me nicely to do one last thing, send the colognes to all the CEOs with notes from their wives."

"And you just went ahead and did it, didn't you? Didn't bother you whether any of her tales made sense or not. You just did it, and now five men are dead!"

"I'm sorry! I didn't know. I didn't…" Tears rolled down her cheeks.

"If you're truly sorry, you'll help me catch this bitch. Tell me everything. Then, maybe, *just maybe* I'll leave your name out of this when I write my report."

"Okay. I met her at the hospital. My brother has been ill for a long time. The doctors told me he needed an operation and would have to go private, but we couldn't afford it. That's where she came in. She found me crying on the stairs. I wanted to be strong for my brother when I was in the room, but outside I needed to release the pain. She came down the stairs with a cup of coffee, black, no sugars. I don't know why that's important umm, yes so she came, gave me the coffee and comforted me. She offered to pay for the operation and said all I had to do was make a man sleep with me. I was desperate and so couldn't refuse. But…it turned out the woman didn't have as much money to give me as initially promised. That's why I stole the jewellery. After speaking with you a couple times, talking about the case, I panicked. I was convinced you'd find out about the jewellery and come after me."

"And what had this man done to deserve all this, huh?"

"She didn't say too much. Just that he was a bad man, who'd ruined her life and now it was his turn."

"And that was enough for you, wasn't it?"

"I told you, I was desperate. I don't know what more you want from me."

"I want you to arrange a meeting with her. How did you two communicate?"

"We put notes in a letterbox outside an abandoned house. Red tape is then put on them to indicate there's something to read inside. But she's probably left the city, right? She thinks her job's finished."

"It's our best shot, get writing."

I borrowed a car and parked not too far away from the letter-box. Miss Jenny then proceeded to put the letter inside it. She walked up to my car window, and I rolled it down.

"Okay I did what you asked, now I'm going."

"You're not going anywhere, get in. We're on stakeout duty. Pray you don't need to pee much."

"Why?"

"Cos this is your toilet," I said, pointing at a bucket. "No toilets or bushes here for miles."

Hours passed as we watched the letterbox and snacked on nuts and crisps. I was now onto my second cigar; Miss Jenny was on her fourth cigarette. The street had been quiet, but just as I was putting out my cigar, a figure approached the letterbox.

"Is that her?!" I whispered urgently.

"I can't tell. It's dark, and she's got her hood up."

I took slow, deep breaths, readying myself for action... She opened the letterbox! I stepped out of the car and closed the door a little too hard, so she turned towards me. *Shit.* I ducked down for a second, and when I stood up, she'd already walked to the other end of the street. I walked as slow I could as not to spook her, but just as I was making progress, she saw me and ran. The chase was on, and I was ready.

She turned a corner or two, crossed to the other side of the roads but she wasn't getting rid of me that easily. I was close, very close. I reached out my arm to grab her...but she turned. My brain showed her in slow motion revealing one of the bottles of cologne, and a spray of it came my way. Managing to dodge some of it but not all, I fell to my knees, my heart raced. The veins in my body were on fire. As my skin became insanely itchy, I resisted the urge to scratch and called 999. "Ambulance! I need an ambulance...ambulance..." I managed to give a rough location but then passed out.

69

August Lee

★ ★ ★

When I opened my eyes there was a bright white light. The bitch had killed me.

"Sir? Sir?" a voice said. "You're okay sir, you're in an ambulance."

The man had been shining a light into my eyes to check for a response.

"You're very lucky."

"I sure as hell don't feel like it."

"Well sir, another small amount of that stuff squirted on you, and you'd be dead for sure."

"That bitch is gonna wish I was after I'm done with her."

I tried to get up, but he pushed me down and told me how they need to check me in the hospital. I wasn't out of the woods yet.

As soon as I was able to use a phone, I was on to my contacts. This was now a very personal matter. I gave a description of the woman in great detail.

It took several hours, but my contacts got what I needed to find her. I had called up people I knew in train stations, airports, coach services and sent her photo to each. If she went anywhere near those places, I would know about it.

Later that morning I got a call. She'd been spotted getting onto the express train to the city airport. I called my guy at the airport and told him to stall her.

On my way over there I pictured all the things I could do to her; torture was my speciality. But as I got closer to the airport, I calmed myself down and put my detective head back on. I wasn't going to be brutal with her, but that didn't mean I had to play nice.

As I was about to enter the airport, she was being padded down by my friend. He would have told her that she'd been randomly selected for a security check and then took his time about it.

I walked into the building nice and calm. I got closer to her, closer, closer, until my friend made the mistake of signalling hello to me with a nod. She took one look at me and ran again.

The crowd was big, and she was slimmer than me, which gave her a slight advantage, but I wasn't letting her slip away this time. After pissing off several people who I shoved aside, I was finally free to run. My determination made me go faster and faster. She ran outside, and I was close behind. I grabbed a baggage trolley and hurled it her way and *BANG!* It crashed into her ankle and down she went. She tried to stand up, but I stamped on her ankle. She screamed hard, and it didn't stop once I removed my foot. She was breathing hard, and as I leaned in closer, I noticed broken glass and a huge puddle of fluid underneath her. *Shit, that must be the cologne.* I knew I didn't have long.

"Tell me why! Why'd you do it? Why?!"

"Because, because…because that bastard, *that bastard* left my mother and me all alone. She had nothing, NOTHING!! Just a crying baby to feed and bills she couldn't pay. We had to choose which days we would eat and which days we wouldn't. We wore clothes until they had more than three holes in them or until they were so tight, we'd almost burst. In the end, my mother's body and mind couldn't cope, and she died. That bastard caused all this suffering, and I planned to give it right back at him," she replied when her breathing permitted her.

"But why kill the other guys?"

Her eyes started to flicker fast. "Hey! Come on, stay with me."

"Wh-what?" Her eyes attempted to widen.

"Stay with me."

"I'm okay." She gave a faint smile.

"So, tell me, why'd you kill those other guys?"

"Well—" she coughed. "I dug up dirt on him, but while doing so my P.I. discovered all kinds of shit that these other guys were doing." Her eyes became bloodshot as the coughing continued. "One was a drug lord using kids to do his work, another bribed a medical examiner after he raped a girl. There were pharmaceutical test bribes and a guy who fucking killed the last CEO before him. Why kill one evil bastard when you…when you can…kill…kill them…all…" her eyes glazed over.

Those words turned out to be her last. More poison meant less time. Five minutes later the ambulance came. I never like to see a person killed, but her story especially tugged at my heartstrings.

She had gotten what she wanted but fell at her own doing. The poison that she had created had been the last thing she'd felt.

I wrote up a report for the company while in a bar having a whiskey with no ice. I walked out of the company's office later that day, lit up a cigar and headed home. Another case…**Solved**.

THE RED KITCHEN

Case #224

The office chair creaked as I sat back, brought a cigar to my lips, and reached for the matches. My hand walked around the table, like a blind man, for a while, but it never found them. Looking down, I discovered it was because there weren't any there. I proceeded to check my desk drawers from top to bottom. No matches. Next, it was onto my pockets both in my trousers and suit jacket. No matches. Then out the corner of my eye, I spotted them. They were in one of my spare shoes. *How did they get there?* That mystery would have to remain unsolved however, as there was important business to take care of.

A smoke cloud danced around the office.

What have you got for me today, God?

I grabbed hold of the new samurai sword letter opener my niece had sent me. It cut through the envelope like butter. I pulled out a letter and a file labelled 'Jacob Ayres'. I placed the file to one side and read the letter about my latest case.

> **"My name is Neil Ashley, and I am the owner of a luxury hotel in Romania. I'm afraid I have received some rather unfortunate news from the hotel manager. After recently procuring the most coveted sous chef job in the city, Jacob Ayres has turned up dead. I need your help to shine a light on the killer."**

I grabbed my passport from the desk drawer. Time to visit Romania.

Much to my annoyance, the train to Gatwick airport was delayed. As a result, I had to sprint to the plane once at the airport. I couldn't remember the place being so big. Perhaps because I normally strolled through the airport with a case running through my mind and a coffee in my hand.

After boarding the plane and taking my seat, a young male flight attendant came towards me and smiled while playing with his hair. I'd seen that look before and wasn't interested. On the plus side though, I would be getting the best service on the flight—pillows, drinks, you name it. I gave a polite smile and got comfortable.

I pulled out the case file from the thick envelope in my bag. There was a photo of Mr. Ayres, average height, brown side-parted hair, no smile. The file also contained information about where he was, where they found the body, *the chef's office, interesting—*

"I'm sorry cutie but we're taking off now," said the steward, placing a hand on my shoulder. "You're gonna have to lift up that tray of yours."

I gave him a closed smile, lifted my tray, and put the file back into my bag. I would read more at the hotel.

After six hours, the plane landed in Sibiu airport. I stretched my legs, and once I claimed my baggage, headed outside the airport.

The warm morning air brushed over my body, and I found some shade to stand in. Cigar lit and drawn to my lips, I slowly inhaled. *And breathe.*

As the last cloud of smoke washed over my face, a taxi rolled up in front of me. "Take me to Bălan Castel," I said, crushing my cigar into the ashtray on the bin.

After a short car journey through the countryside, the taxi turned left and drove up a long winding path. Soon, a castle came into view on the horizon as if rising from beneath the ground. It was stunning. It consisted of Romanesque, Gothic and Renaissance styles, which I had never seen before, despite all my travelling. I felt like I was in some sort of Dracula novel. As we got closer to the castle, the smell of Brugmansia flowers filled my nostrils. Those creamy orange 'angel trumpets' as my mother called them, filled the fields around me. I felt, however, they might be the last angelic things I would see for a while.

After pulling into the hotel car park I paid the driver and headed towards the lobby. Along the way, there was a sign revealing a five-star award for the restaurant. That would be my primary place of interest, where the sous chef laid his head to rest.

Once inside the hotel, I pressed the call bell at the desk and waited. Leather chairs nestled near a roaring fireplace, *a perfect place to smoke a cigar...* Swords crossed each other in front of shields, a murder weapon? I doubt it but—

"Can I help you, sir?" a young man in a maroon and gold uniform asked.

"Name's Mr. Jones. I have a reservation," I said, not revealing I was a detective yet. I sometimes do this to get a more honest judgement of someone's character. The man behind the desk would know many people and see a lot of things happening. He would also know how to do things without being noticed, hmm...

He flipped through the pages of the logbook, then looked up at me and smiled. He had a bellhop come over to take my overnight bag. I declined, but he insisted, and we headed to my room. The room had an inviting and expensive looking four-poster bed inside, but I wasn't interested. After a flight, it's a hot shower that I crave.

After a shower and a glass of water, I was ready to start the case. Door locked, notebook in my pocket, I made my way to the lift.

As I walked down the corridor; a man with a striking resemblance of Mr. Ayres walked past me. I went to say something, but then shook my head and headed inside the lift. There was no point in wasting time on thoughts of the walking dead. The doors shut, and the lift moved. Romanian folk music played in the dim lit box which I had never heard before but in a strange way kind of enjoyed. I reached the ground floor and headed for the reception desk. Along the way, however, I was stopped in my tracks.

"Is everything okay sir?" the tall, well-built, man asked. "I'm the front of house manager, any problems, you can come to me." He said as he shined his gold pocket watch.

"I'm Detective Banks. I'm here about the death at the restaur—"

"Shhhh!" he said. I gave him a stern look. "Oh, I'm sorry, detective. It's just this is a very sensitive subject and one we don't want people hearing about."

He waited for me to say something, but I remained quiet and simply gave him a small nod. He pointed towards the restaurant.

"Actually, I would like to ask you a few questions, if you don't mind that is."

"Me? Umm…" he said with his hand pointing to his chest.

"Problem?"

"N-no, of course not. Go… right ahead," he said, brushing his hand through his hair and then scrubbing his pocket watch hard.

For a front of house manager who was so together before, he suddenly looked like he'd seen a ghost.

"Do you need some water? Do you need to sit down?"

"No, I'm fine," he said and scratched the back of his head. That meant he was lying — not a good start for him.

"How is the security camera system in the hotel and restaurant?"

"State of the art, sir." He said and began to mumble something, *numbers?*

"Are you late for something?"

"What?" he asked, eyebrows raised. "Oh...you noticed my counting?"

"Yeah, and I've never saw a pocket watch shine so hard."

He gave a tight lip smile.

"Are there any places you don't have cameras?" I asked, sensing his mood dropping.

"Well, inside the rooms we don't, to give our guests privacy, same for the toilets and showers around the castle. And the kitchen, unfortunately. Oh! Also, there isn't one in the head chef's office." He said and tapped on the watch which he'd placed in his breast pocket.

"How about cameras outside the office and kitchen. Do they catch people going in and out?"

"I'm afraid our cameras don't face towards those doors. You could perhaps see people going down the corridors of the hotel. I'm afraid, however, that there is no way to tell if they ended up in the kitchen or the office."

"Can you take me to see the camera footage now?"

"I'm afraid not..." he said, tapping his foot in counts of three.

"And why's that?"

"I...lost the key to the security room." His counting got faster. "The locksmith is fitting a new lock in the morning."

"I see," I said, scratching my forehead. "Tell me, who usually has access to the chef's office?"

"Well...the head chef of course and the owner."

I focused on his eyes. "Not yourself?"

He attempted a smile. "Oh, did I not mention that? Yes, I have a key, part of being the front of house manager." He said and stared intensely at my shoulder.

"I will need to see the head chef, of course. Can you tell me where he is?"

I waited for a response, but noticed his eyes still focused on my shoulder. "Actually" he said and lifted his head up for a moment, "I'm afraid he's not here, he left a couple days before…the *incident*." He said, leaned forward gently and brushed something off my shoulder.

"You're kidding me?"

"No." he replied straightening himself up.

"Does he often take time off?"

"Don't be absurd," he sniggered, then caught a glimpse of my face, and realised he'd made a mistake. "I'm sorry. I shouldn't have talked like that to you Mr. Banks," he looked to the floor and mumbled 'sorry', under his breath three times.

"So why take the time off then?"

"Family emergency." He said staring at something on the floor.

"At the time of the…incident" I said. "You were…?"

He lifted his head. "I was…running some errands, yes, running errands far away from the kitchen. I was gone for…I'm not sure how long."

"Can anyone verify that?"

"I was alone. I assure you I was there though," he said, looking around the room.

"I see." I glanced at him and then my book.

I wrote any useful information down as I continued to ask him questions. "Who else was working at the time? Did you see any guests walking around near the time of the incident? See anyone acting suspicious?"

"I'm afraid n-not. Everyone, as far as I know, were in their rooms. The restaurant was closed as it was late and only a few of the staff were around here at the time." He wrote on a piece of paper the names of the staff members who had been present and handed it to me.

"You don't need to check the books first?"

"No. Lists, names, numbers. I remember them all well."

"Very well. Oh, one last thing."

"Sure." He said, pulling his pocket watch out.

"Can I have the key to Mr. Ayres' room?"

"Umm…sure." He put the watch back in his pocket, went behind the reception desk and bent down. After a few seconds, he popped up. "Here you are, room 406."

"Thanks," I said while rubbing the key with my thumb.

I now had a list of people to look into, Mr. Ayres' room key and an ancient castle to explore.

Before I spoke to anyone from the list though, I wanted to see the scene of the crime.

I walked into the kitchen of the restaurant, which was so clean I could see my reflection on every surface. Not a spot of dirt anywhere. This was a clear sign of a five-star restaurant. Those stars are not easy to come by. I opened the case notes of the death, which helped paint a better picture of the crime. Flipping through the folder, I came across a photo of a coffee cup found on the floor near the body. Before I arrived at the hotel, I'd asked the hotel to send the contents over to my lab contact in Romania. He is very fast and thorough. The results were already in as I strolled around the kitchen. There were traces of cyanide which you would usually find in pill form. *In the cup and not a pill in the mouth…* This was looking like a murder case indeed. As I looked around, I came across a box of blue gloves, a way of keeping food and surfaces extra clean I guessed. With such easy access to gloves, a smudge, and no fingerprints, therefore, was all that was found on the cup.

I headed inside the office where the dead body had been found. Nothing looked out of place. Even the chef's notes where neatly stacked in an open box. I crouched down and studied the stone floor, expecting to find a patch of blood. There was nothing. I guess the guy who cleans the kitchen so well came to the office after the police had left. As I was about to stand up, however, I spotted something on the fringes of a small rug. With a pocketknife, I scraped the substance onto a piece of paper. Inspecting it carefully, I found what I'd been looking for, blood. This could be the victim's, but I was hoping it would be from the killer. I placed it into an evidence bag and would send it to the lab as soon as possible.

After leaving the office, I felt something digging into my leg. I put my hand in my pocket and revealed the culprit, Mr. Ayres' room key. *Wanting me to go to his room next, huh God?* I thought, then smiled.

I headed for the lift and once inside hit the number four button. Turned out they didn't have a big playlist for the elevator music. After beginning to almost hum the familiar tunes, I arrived at the fourth floor, and headed for room 406.

As I slid the key into Mr. Ayres' door, I took a deep breath, then turned it. The first thing I saw was the bed. The quilt was ruffled, evidence someone had once slept there and forgot to fix it. As I looked around the rest of the room, nothing appeared to be out of place. Mr. Ayres didn't have many belongings. *A minimalist?* I thought while flicking through his wardrobe clothes, or lack of. After looking through the wardrobe, I pulled out all the drawers in the room. There was no sign of a phone, no laptop, nothing. Just an impression of a man who lived a rather simple life. That's nice, but I wanted evidence, a lead, *something*.

Disappointed with the lack of findings in the bedroom, I headed to the lobby where I sat in a chair by a roaring fire. The logs crackled and the heat caressed my skin. Pulling out the phone from my pocket, I called my contact and asked if there had been any forensic developments. I also informed him that a blood sample would be with him shortly. It helps with getting things done quickly when you have contacts within the police and courier services. Your items are always a top priority. He said he was afraid there was nothing new to report but would keep an eye out for the blood sample.

I walked over to the reception desk and asked for the hotel's records for the employees who were around at the time of the crime. I sat back down in the chair and flicked through the pages. Leaning back, I struck a match against the nearby brick wall and brought it towards my cigar. I inhaled and—

"Sir?"

"Yeah?" I replied without turning, irritated for being interrupted.

"I'm afraid there's no smoking in the lobby."

I looked to my side and gave the tall, skinny employee a hard stare and distinguished the cigar on the bottom of my boot. He smiled and walked away, looking over his shoulder several times along the way. Once he was out of sight, I stood and put on my heavy coat, which I'd purchased, anticipating the cold weather of Romania. Wrapped up, I headed outside to finish my cigar. It was late, and the moon was out, a perfect scene for smoking in.

I struck a match, brought the cigar to my lips, and dragged the smoke into my lungs. What smoke remained slithered out of my mouth and made its way towards the sky. One foot in front of the other, I took a walk around the castle's grounds, making footprints in the soft snow.

After walking for a while, I came across a manmade path. Even with all this snow, it was still visible, part of the five-star service, I guessed. The hotel made the extra effort to give you somewhere to walk even in the heavy snow months.

The castle was high up, and so there was a panoramic view of the area below including a little town nearby. This would be where people of the hotel would go to buy the necessities, socialise with friends, or go on dates with their lovers.

After walking a while, I spotted a trail of boot prints in the snow to my right, size four, female. The trees had protected the tracks to a certain extent, which was enough for me as a skilled tracker to follow. After a few minutes, a shadowed figure appeared in the distance, near the edge of the mountain. I was far away, but I could see it was a female, say...5' 4", around 130, 140 pounds. I approached slowly to not startle her.

"Got a light?" I asked.

"You've come a long way just for a light," she said and passed me some matches.

"Matches? Great." I said, smiling. "Few people carry them nowadays."

"Lighters affect the taste." She leaned her head back, inhaled her thin cigar and allowed the smoke to slowly slither out her pursed lips.

"It's a little dangerous being out this far on your own at night though, don't you think?"

"I can take care of myself," she said sternly.

"You work here?" I asked, but already knew after seeing her on the staff photo.

"Da, I am the chef de partie in the restaurant."

Looking for a reaction, I asked, "Not the sous chef?"

"Nu, I mean no. They shut the door on that the day they

promoted *that*— I mean, Mr. Ayres." She turned away, appearing unpleased with herself. I made a mental note. She dropped her thin cigar into the snow and crushed it with the heel of her boot. "If you'd excuse me, I must head inside."

"I'll be seeing you around," I said, looking into her eyes. She said nothing and left.

I finished my cigar and meditated while thinking of what I'd come across so far. *Breathe in, 1, 2, 3, and out, 1, 2, 3.* The front of house manager wasn't at his station and was unaccounted for at the time of the crime. The runner-up to the sous chef position was displeased with Mr. Ayres' promotion. And there was still another person on my list to say hello to. I bent down and picked up my finished cigar from the ground. Such a beautiful place didn't deserve to have things like cigar ends littered around it. I picked up Ms Constantin's cigar end too, DNA would be on it, and you never know when you might need it.

As I headed back from the woodland, images of a soft bed came to mind. It had been a long day, and my body was craving it.

A bell above the entrance door dinged as I walked inside and headed towards the lifts.

"Detective Banks!" a voice called out.

To my left, a man in an Armani suit sat by the roaring fire. The bed would have to wait. I raised my head to acknowledge the man and sat in the same chair I had before, this time without the cigar...

"I'm Stephen Singleton, the owner of the hotel. I thought we might get acquainted," he said and shook my hand. "Can I get you something to drink?"

"I'm fine thanks," I said, studying his face.

"Very well. I thought I could answer any questions you might have."

"You're from Liverpool. I didn't expect that. How did you end up here?"

"Actually, my wife's grandfather owned the hotel originally and his father before him and so on. The hotel was passed onto her and with my background, it seemed I was the perfect fit for the job. I'm experienced and although my wife is not with us anymore..." He looked to the floor. "I'm still technically part of the family."

"Well I have to say, it's nice to hear an English voice on my travels," I said, and he smiled. "What can you tell me about Ms Constantin?"

"Well, she's a hard, dedicated worker. She has continuously tried to show me how she would be a fabulous sous chef. It didn't matter to her if a sous chef was already working in the restaurant. Ms Constantin is the type of person who will do almost anything to get what she wants. That's why I hired her in the first place. Still, when the job did come up, Mr. Ayres was simply the best choice," he said, scratching the back of his head.

"Had you known Mr. Ayres long? Were the two of you close?" I asked, watching his eyes.

"I didn't know him too well...only enough to know his talent in the kitchen was first class and he was a good man."

"I see." Something was off about him when he talked of Mr. Ayres, but I couldn't put my finger on it. "Did Mr. Ayres have any siblings?"

"Umm, not that I know of."

"I see. What can you tell me about your front of house manager?"

"He's been with us for almost fifteen years now, a loyal man who treats this hotel like his child."

"Has he caused any trouble before?"

"There have been several...minor incidents where he hadn't been pleased with how some of the staff were working. He actually punched a staff member once after arguing they were damaging the hotel's reputation. But he's a good man, usually professional to a T, a solid worker. Maybe a bit of a perfectionist but that can't be bad, right?" I wrote all this into my book.

"Did Mr. Ayres have any lovers? A woman he was seeing or sleeping with?"

Mr. Singleton's right eye twitched involuntarily before his eyes glazed over.

"Mr. Singleton? Mr. Singleton??" I said, snapping him out of his trance.

He stared at his hand while twisting a ring on his finger, "Oh, sorry. No, he wasn't seeing anybody or sleeping with any woman around the time of his death."

"And your bellhop. Tell me about him." I said, pen in hand.

"He's been working here for the past nine months. A young man who's always asking questions, an inquisitive person. This was one of the reasons I hired him. I figured, if he was always asking questions, he would learn a lot and be a great employee."

"I see. Thank you for answering my questions, Mr. Singleton.

"No problem."

"Oh, one last thing. I noticed Mr. Ayres didn't have a laptop in his room."

"That's right. He just used the staff computer."

"Can I see it?"

"Sure. It's behind the reception desk."

We walked over to the desk, and Mr. Singleton walked around it and disappeared as he crouched down.

"That's strange," he said.

"What's that?"

Mr. Singleton popped up. "It's not here." He scratched his head.

"Stolen?"

"No, I doubt that very much. A staff member must have taken it somewhere, though that's not really encouraged..." He tapped his lip. "Don't worry Mr. Banks, I'll find it and get it to you as soon as possible. It's been a long day for you; I'm sure. Why don't you get some rest and meet me here in the morning? Sound good?"

I nodded and shook his hand, "Goodnight Mr. Singleton." And on that note, I left and finally headed to bed.

As I got to the room, my body felt heavy, but my brain was still wide awake with all the information I had received in the past few hours, and as a result, I couldn't sleep... I opened my book and reviewed what I had written.

Suspect number 1: The front of house manager.

Loves the hotel and restaurant. Loves it so much, he once harmed a staff member because he thought they weren't doing the place justice. Also, he was unaccounted for during the crime with nobody to verify where he was.

Suspect number 2: The chef de partie, Ms Isabella Constantin.

A runner-up to the sous chef position. Very determined and in Mr. Singleton's words, 'would do almost anything to get what she wants'. She appeared robust and more than capable of taking care of herself when I spoke to her in the woods. She clearly did not agree with the appointment of Mr. Ayres as sous chef. Would this be reason enough for her to kill him?

On top of those two suspects, there was still the question of why cyanide was in the cup. Usually, it's taken in pill form. Also, whose blood was on the carpet?

The hotel, it turned out, makes employees take a blood test and even urine tests from time to time, the hotel boss included, as to lead by example. They were almost to a point obsessed about having the perfect staff which meant no junkies or steroid takers. A bit extreme, but I didn't care. If the blood sample I sent was from the killer, tests by the hotel would surely lead me to the killer.

Reviewing done and with my eyelids getting heavy, I laid down and fell asleep.

✫ ✫ ✫

After a night of tossing and turning, I was awoken, not by an alarm, I realised after reaching for something to hit, but my phone ringing.

"Hello?" I mumbled.

"Hi detective, it's Ştefan with the blood result."

"That was fast, even for you. Good news?"

"The blood sample you sent is the victim's. I know it's not the news you wanted, sorry."

"No need for apologies. Thanks for your help, I appreciate it."

After I got off the phone, I brushed my teeth, splashed some water on my face and readied myself for the day.

I'd forgotten to charge my laptop, so plugged it in and headed out the room, towards the lift. Unfortunately, as my bedroom door closed, so did the lift's. I headed for the stairs instead. A little exercise never hurt anyone, well...

After walking down a floor, I spotted a man on a lower set of stairs. *Why does he look so familiar?* "Excuse me, sir?" I said, to which the person ignored me and walked a little faster. "Wait," I shouted and moved faster myself. The man moved quickly and soon exited through a door while I was still two flights above him. I skipped steps, jumped several, and eventually burst out through the door—

"Watch it!" A female guest yelled, with a hand on each of my arms.

"Did you see a man exiting here?" I said, chest panting.

"A man? Nobody has come out no door, except you. Scared me half to death."

"What?" I said, bending over and catching my breath. "But I just saw…"

"Are you feeling alright? You know, I read somewhere that people don't sleep properly in hotels. Maybe you're seeing things. You should get that checked out."

What's going on? I didn't sleep well last night, but could it really affect my vision that much? Is she right? Am I seeing things I want but aren't there? I shook myself. Get it together Banks.

"Sir? You're looking kinda funny. Do you need me to call you a doctor?"

"I'm fine, thank you," I said and smiled.

I headed to the reception desk, but no one was there. I wandered around, trying to find the front of house manager, but it was a big castle… Eventually, while walking through a long corridor, I heard someone shouting. I turned the corner, and there he was, the front of house manager, two inches from the bellhop's face, yelling. I placed a firm grip on his shoulder and eased him backwards.

"Who the—?!" he said in annoyance, but then saw me. "Oh, Mr. Banks. My apologies."

I caught eyes with the bellhop and pointed at a chair to which he sat down on, "A word," I told the front of house manager.

"I heard about your 'dedication' to the job. I wonder how far you would actually go," I said and stared into his eyes. "Tell me, did you agree with the appointment of the new sous chef?"

"Of course!"

"Are you sure? You sure you weren't just a little unhappy? Your whereabouts are still unaccounted for at the time of his death."

"No no, I did nothing to that man. I can prove it to you."

"How?" I said with a raised eyebrow.

"Remember I told you about how the cameras are everywhere?" he said, polishing his pocket watch. "I checked on the footage this morning to prove I was nowhere near where Mr. Ayres died. The cameras don't lie, you can see for yourself."

"Why didn't you tell me this right away?" I said, slightly annoyed.

"I'm sorry, Mr. Banks, all this murder business throws me off. I never thought I would be in a place where this could happen. I'm still getting used to the idea." *That could explain the nervous behaviour...* I told the bellhop to sit tight and went with the front of house manager to look at the security footage. He was telling the truth. I viewed all the different camera angles from the time of the murder. The front of house manager left the restaurant and kitchen, then wasn't seen on the cameras again until hours after the death. He wasn't the killer.

I turned and headed back towards the bellhop when—

"OW! Watch where you're going!" Ms Constantin said, and turned towards me. "Urgh...I'm sorry, I didn't know it was you."

"I just needed to ask you about your whereabouts at the time of the crime, do you mind?"

"Yes, I do. I'm late to see my sister."

"I'm afraid this can't wait. Where were you when Mr. Ayres died?" This received a harsh stare from Ms Constantin. "I'm asking, Ms Constantin because I've been told you'd do anything to get what you want, including a job position. So, where were you when Mr. Ayres died?" Her phone rang.

"It's my sister. Here! You take it. Ask her where I was." She shoved the phone into my hand.

I spoke to her sister, who told me they were together at her house during the crime.

"But I was told you were working at the time of the murder."

"I sneaked out of work early. Please don't tell boss."

"Alright. I'll see you around Ms Constantin." I handed her the phone and turned away. Even though she was quite convincing, I still later checked the security footage. There she was, exiting the building a couple hours before the estimated time of death.

Later, I headed back to the bellhop who had been waiting a long time for me and was probably wanted elsewhere. I got a feeling from talking to him straight away that he was not capable of murder. Aged seventeen, he was still reasonably innocent to the world. Young enough that he could raise hell at times but still be a bit of a mummy's boy. Yet, I went through the questions, discovered his whereabouts and whatnot. *Not guilty*. Mr. Singleton had said this boy was inquisitive about everything though. Who better to ask about the happenings inside this hotel?

"Did Mr. Ayres have any enemies you know of? A former lover?" I asked with a raised eyebrow.

"Well," he said, looking around. "Don't tell anyone I told you this but…" He hesitated.

"It's okay. You won't get in trouble," I said, placing my hand on his shoulder.

"Well…one night I was working late. All the kitchen staff had gone home, and I was asked to collect something from the chef's office. It was there that I saw…Mr. Singleton and Mr. Ayres…having sex."

He failed to mention he was so…close to Mr. Ayres. "Were they still *together* at the time of the death?"

"Actually, I think not. I heard them arguing not long after Mr. Ayres was appointed sous chef. From what I could hear, Mr. Singleton was furious because Mr. Ayres said something like, let's part ways. I took that to mean that he ended it and Mr. Singleton wasn't best pleased."

"I see. I'm gonna go now but thank you for answering my questions. You were very helpful."

The bellhop smiled, then turned as he heard his name being shouted by the front of house manager. "Oh, Mr. Banks! I almost forgot. Here is the company laptop you wanted." He handed it over, turned and then ran off to the front of house manager. With the laptop tucked under my arm, I walked away. Thanks to the boy, I now had a lead suspect to talk to, Mr. Singleton. Love was at the heart of so many things in life. He had access to security cameras so no evidence would be there I assumed. He had given Mr. Ayres the prestigious job in the restaurant only to be tossed to the side not long after... Feeling used and heartbroken can make you do bad things, including lying to a detective.

I went to the front of house manager, where I saw the bellhop boy walking away with an envelope in hand.

"Where's Mr. Singleton?"

"He's in a meeting right now and won't be out for a while."

"Well when you see him, tell him I want to meet him in the head chef's office." A fitting place to talk I thought. The front of house manager nodded, and I headed to the office.

After I arrived in the office, I paced back and forth, awaiting the arrival of Mr. Singleton. After twenty minutes of waiting, I was growing more and more impatient. I decided to focus on something else and so pulled out the staff laptop and logged in with Mr. Ayres' details which had been written on a piece of paper for me.

There was no WhatsApp, Line, or any other messenger apps on the computer, so I checked his emails. I started to scroll through the usual junk, emails about enlarging... 50% off this and that—"Wait. What's this?" I clicked on an email with the subject 'I'll See You Soon'. *Could this be from the killer?*

I read the email which was about someone visiting Mr. Ayres. It said the person was coming back home, something about taking a break from a tough job in Germany. As I got to the bottom, I found out who it was from, his brother. *A brother?? Why wasn't I told? How could no one know he had a brother?*

I searched the email for any sign of an address or phone number. As it happened, I was in luck. Mr. Matthew Ayres had an email signature which showed an address. I wrote down the address and headed out of the office.

I spotted the front of house manager heading out the entrance door.

"Sir!" I shouted at him.

He turned around and gave a nod, "What can I do for you, Mr. Banks?"

"I was hoping you could tell me where this is?" I handed him the piece of paper with the address.

"Yeah. This is in the village nearby. I'm heading that way now; I can take you."

"That's very kind of you."

"It's no problem, really."

As the car pulled away, the wind danced all around us, and once again, the smell of Brugmansia flowers filled my head. I took a deep breath and relaxed back into the seat.

"Mr. Banks...? Mr. Banks."

"Wh-what? What?" I said, blinking my eyes.

"We're here. You fell asleep..."

"Sorry. Long couple of days."

"You will have to make your own way back to the hotel Mr. Banks, you understand?"

"You're a busy man, I get it. Thanks for the lift." I opened the car door, and as soon as it closed, the car pulled away.

The house before me was an old, modest sized bungalow painted white with red trim at the bottom. Red exterior window shutters blew in the soft breeze, as the apples in the trees danced in the wind. I opened a creaky wooden gate and walked down the path to the front door.

I grasped the cold door knocker in my hand to hit it against the door. Out the corner of my eye, I saw net curtains moving in the window.

"Hello?" I called to the window. A few moments later I heard the front door unlock and a man stood— "Wait! Jacob Ayres?" I said, wiping my eyes in disbelief.

"I get that all the time. No, I'm his brother, twin brother, Matthew," he said with a closed smile.

"Right…" I said, looking his face all over.

"Can I help you…?"

"Sorry, yes. I'm Detective Banks. I'm investigating the death of your brother Jacob."

"Oh. I see," he replied, scratching the back of his ear.

"Kann ich reinkommen?" I asked.

"I'm sorry?"

"I read you've been working in Germany…I just asked if I could come in," I told him and stroked my chin.

"Oh, of course. I umm…just didn't expect to hear German here," another closed smile. "Come in."

As I walked inside the house, I saw pictures of the Ayres brothers and parents on the walls. There weren't many photos of the brothers in the same photographs, however.

"This was my parents' house," he said, ushering me to a living room.

"It's very nice. Are these all handmade throws?" I asked, pointing towards the throws over the couches and chairs.

"They've been here as long as I can remember. Perhaps my grandmother made them," he replied as I sat in a chair and he on a sofa.

"How long have you been working in Germany?"

"Good question. Umm...coming on eight years now."

"And you enjoy your job, at...?"

"At? Oh! Um...at Kütchenhaus. Yes, very good."

"Can you tell me about your brother Mr. Ayres?"

"Sure. What do you want to know?" he asked, rubbing his knees.

"What was he like? Did he have many friends? Enemies?"

"He's always been a dedicated, hardworking man. If he wanted to do something, he did it. I admire that about him, sorry, *admired* that about him. He was always in the company of people, especially at the hotel, but they weren't his friends."

"You seem to know a lot about him, considering you've been away so long," I raised an eyebrow.

"Oh, hunny!" he said, looking over my shoulder. "This is Detective Banks. He's here about my brother's death."

I turned to see a beautiful, tall woman, with red curly hair flowing past her shoulders. Standing up, I shook her hand and smiled. "Guten Abend."

"Guten Abend Herr Banken."

"You speak perfect German Mrs Ayres."

"I should think so. They don't speak much English where we live now, so we really need to know the language."

"Is that so?" I said, glancing over at Mr. Ayres and then back.

"If you don't mind, I just have a few more questions for your husband."

"Of course, I'll go make some tea." She turned and left for the kitchen, rubbing her hands together as she walked.

95

"So, Mr. Ayres, like I asked before, did your brother have any enemies? Anyone who would want to harm him?"

"Not that I can think of. I suppose getting a promotion can annoy those who don't. I also know love makes you do crazy things too, but he had no partners that I know of. My brother was a great man, Mr. Banks," he said, turning his head to the bay window.

"I don't doubt that. Sorry to ask, but has your brother ever been known to be...violent? Or provocative?"

"Like I said, my brother was a great man."

"I'm sorry, but that doesn't really answer my question." He glared at me.

"No, he wasn't. He was a hard-working, dedicated, and brilliant man. Nothing less."

He certainly held his brother in high regards.

"Let's move on. So, how long have you been back?"

"Just a week. I came to visit M—Jacob. Got here a few days before he died. I still can't believe it. My head's been spinning."

"I understand. Can you tell me where you were at the time of Jacob's death—?"

"He was with me!" Mrs Ayres said, walking in with tea on a tray. As she came closer, the tray shook ever so gently.

"Can I help you with that?" I asked, standing.

"No, I'm fine. Just forgot to eat lunch is all," she said, and focused back on the tray.

I observed Mr. and Mrs Ayres for a moment and picked up the tea from the coffee table.

"Thank you very much," I said, with a smile, after sipping the tea. "When you last saw Jacob, did he seem off, to you?"

"Off? Well...I didn't think so at the time."

"But now?"

"Well, he was a bit more...affectionate. Told me 'You know how much I love you, brother, don't you?' At the time I thought it was just the wine we'd been drinking talking, but maybe it was something more. He's always been...sensitive, but looking back I think his tone was different. I'm babbling, forgive me."

"Not at all. You're being very helpful," I assured him and smiled. "One last question. Have you visited the hotel since you've been back?"

"No. I met my brother here and drank at home. If you don't mind, I need to start packing."

"Packing? You're not staying for the funeral?"

He glanced at his wife and then back at me.

"I'm afraid something important has come up at work, and I need to head back." He scratched the back of his head.

"More important than a funeral?"

"Yes, you little shit!" he yelled and then put his hand over his mouth, realising what he'd done. "I'm sorry detective. My emotions are still close to the surface. I'm not happy about leaving, but life does move on, and I can't lose my job as well as my brother."

"I see," I said, standing. "I have some things to do, so I will let you get on with your packing."

"Thank you," he said with a wide smile. Light bounced off a gold tooth in his mouth, forcing me to look away.

"Oh! Before I go. I know it's a longshot, but did you happen to take a photo of Jacob before the incident? The one they sent me isn't very recent."

"Actually, we took a selfie together. My phone is charging, but I'll send it to you later."

"I appreciate it. Thanks for your time," and with that, I headed for the door and out of the house.

After standing in the icy wind for half an hour and starting to lose the feeling in my face, a taxi finally picked me up. On the way back to the hotel, my thoughts went back to Mr. Singleton, my prime suspect. Love is a potent potion, once drunk, it can make you capable of almost anything. Mix it with being tossed to the curb, well…that spells trouble.

At the hotel, I got out of the taxi, tipped the driver, and walked to the entrance. There was no sign of the front of house manager as I stepped inside, but I did spot the bellhop.

"Please tell Mr. Singleton I'm back and want to speak with him immediately in the chef's office."

"Yes, sir. Right away," he said, and scurried off, while I headed to the office.

Inside the office, I paced the floor, anticipating another long wait for Mr. Singleton. Five minutes had passed when he finally walked through the door.

"Is something the matter, detective? I heard you needed me urgently," he said, tapping his fingers against his leg.

"I'm afraid so. It's about your relationship with Mr. Ayres, that you neglected to mention."

Mr. Singleton blushed and glanced at the floor while tugging at his collar.

"Care to explain, Mr. Single—"

My phone vibrated in my pocket. "Excuse me."

I pulled out my phone and it vibrated again, causing it to go hurtling towards the floor. I swung both hands towards it but to no avail. It bounced on the floor from left to right while I cursed the heavens. After calming myself down, a vibration noise started again. I crouched down and picked up the phone. It wasn't vibrating, yet I could still hear a vibration noise.

I started opening cupboards one by one, nothing. I opened several fridges, nothing. *Where could it be?* I needed to be fast before the phone stopped. *Think, think!* Closing my eyes, I listened for any sound to give me a clue… *That doesn't sound like it's vibrating against wood… The floor!*

I got down onto my stomach and checked underneath the cupboards on the floor, and there it was. A phone right by the wall. I reached my arm out for the phone… "Got it." I pulled out the phone, turned it on and there on the home screen was a file titled **'For you, my brother'**. I checked who had called before playing the video, but it said *unknown*… With that lead dead, I clicked on the video. Mr. Singleton leaned in close as we watched it together.

The video showed Jacob Ayres, standing in the kitchen. He spoke into the camera with tears cascading down his cheeks.

"Brother…" he said. "I know I should be happy, on top of the world, now I have this job in such a prestigious restaurant, but I'm not… This is not the life I wanted. I thought it was, and I even slept with the owner to help me get it. However, now that I have it, I realise that I was just trying to win the approval from a father that never cared. In the process, I have hurt an innocent man's heart. I-I don't know who I am. I don't feel like I belong, I…" He stared at a cup. "I'm sorry brother." With his hands shaking, he raised the cup and drank from it. Foam flowed out of his mouth, he gasped for air and walked around the room banging into cupboards until he fell into the chef's office.

"Oh my god. He killed himself?" Mr. Singleton exclaimed.

"It certainly looks that way," I said, tapping my finger against my lips and peeling my eyes away from the phone.

"How dreadful…"

"I'll see you around Mr. Singleton," I told him, as I placed a hand on his shoulder and then walked out of the kitchen.

So, there you have it. No crime of vengeance from an eager worker, no love crime from a former lover. No. In the end, it was a

man who was lost in the woods and saw no way out. Or was it…?
Something in my gut didn't feel right.

I walked into my room and shut the door. It had been a long
day, and so I headed straight to the bed. I took the photo of Mr.
Ayres which had been sent with the case letter and stared at it as I
laid on the bed. *What am I not seeing? Think, think.*

I awoke the next morning and peeled off the photo that was
stuck to my cheek. Looking at my phone, I saw I had a message.
It was the selfie of the Ayres brothers outside the little house. A
large drum banged inside my head which meant only one thing,
I needed coffee and a cigar. After making a cup and grabbing a
cigar from a box, I headed out of my room.

In the lift, I watched the video of Mr. Ayres again. People kill
themselves for all kinds of reasons. Mr. Ayres' reason was perfectly
valid, and yet it was something I wasn't able to accept. *What is it,
John? What is your gut te—* The lift dinged, and the doors opened
at the ground floor, breaking my trail of thought.

After exiting the lift, I sent over the video, selfie, and a digital
copy of the original photo to my contact. I asked for him to carefully inspect them, telling him something didn't feel right.

As I exited the front door of the hotel, the cold wind slithered
around my body and down my back. In the distance, I spotted a
bench and headed for it. After wiping away the snow, I sat down
and placed the cup and saucer next to me.

"You know," a voice said from behind me, "the front of house
manager would go crazy if he saw that cup out here."

As smoke flowed over my shoulder, I knew exactly who it was. "Hello
Ms. Constantin, care to join me?" I asked without looking around.

"Da," she replied and came around. Her hair danced in the wind, and as she sat, a smile escaped from the corner of her mouth. "I thought you would be gone. You solved the case, da?"

"Sort of."

"Sort of? What you mean by dis?" she asked and inhaled her cigar.

"The evidence is there. A video explaining why Mr. Ayres died, how others in the hotel are innocent but…"

"But what?" she said, her head titled.

"My gut tells me something doesn't add up."

"And this 'gut'. Is normally correct?"

"Yes. It is."

"Then go with it," she said as she placed a hand on top of mine.

I caressed her hand, and she gazed into my eyes, before leaning in and imprinting a kiss on my lips. I pulled her in close and kissed her again, my hand caressing the back of her head. When she eventually pulled away, she bit my upper lip.

"I like you. You need some…" she pursed her lips, "…release, detective. It will help you think more clearly." She stood and walked away. As she did, I spotted something drop into the snow. When I walked over and bent down, I discovered it was a hotel room key. With the key in hand, I stood, straightened my tie, and headed for Ms Constantin's room.

I knocked on the door, which then opened as if by itself. *Where is sh—?* She pinned me against the wall and kissed me vigorously. I spun her around, pushed her back against the wall and locked my lips onto hers. Her body was warm as I caressed it. After a while she placed her hand on my chest and pulled away. "Let me slip into something more comfortable," she said and walked to the bathroom.

I sat on the bed and took off my jacket and shoes. When she came out of the bathroom, I realised she was most comfortable in her own skin, and nothing else.

I pulled her in close. She smiled, then ripped my shirt open sending buttons flying across the room. She bit into my shoulder, and my adrenaline hit the ceiling. I threw her to the bed, took off my clothes and had the most passionate, rough sex I'd ever had. Afterwards, while we both sat in bed, smoking cigars, I realised she was right. It was exactly what I needed.

As much as I would have enjoyed staying in bed all day, I had work to do. After finding my trousers, I got dressed and so did she.

"So, what now, Mr. Detective?" she asked as she pulled her skirt up her body.

"Speak to the brother, tell him the bad news and see what he thinks about the video," I said, pulling my jacket over my now buttonless shirt.

Ms Constantin buttoned up her blouse, slipped on her high heel shoes and walked towards me. "Good luck," she said and dug her nails into my ass as she squeezed it.

"It was—" She put her finger on my lips.

"Don't talk," she said and left the room.

Once I got downstairs, I asked for a taxi to be sent to the hotel. Hopefully, a trip to the brother's house would bring what my gut was telling me to the light.

As the taxi approached the house, Mr. Ayres and his wife, were outside, closing the front door.

"Mr. Ayres!" I shouted over. The two of them glanced at each other and then gave a half-wave towards me.

"We're on our way to the airport..." Mr. Ayres said, tapping his case.

"This is important. It won't take long."

"We really must go," the wife insisted.

Mr. Ayres looked at her and gave a gentle shake of his head. "Of course, detective, let's go inside."

I walked past Mr. Ayres and his wife. Mr. Ayres then put his hand on her shoulder, looking her in the eyes.

"There's nothing to worry about Mr. Ayres. I just have some light to shine on your brother's cause of death."

"Okay detective. Mary, would you make some tea for the detective?" After a few seconds of hearing no reply, he looked to his wife and spoke a little louder, "Mary?"

Mrs Ayres snapped out of her daydream. "Oh! Of course. I'll be right back."

"Thank you," I said and turned to Mr. Ayres. "It would appear that your brother wasn't murdered, Mr. Ayres. I found a video on his phone which was meant for you. He had tried to send it, but the message failed." I pulled out the phone, pressed play and showed him.

I studied Mr. Ayres' face while he watched the video. He didn't cry, but not everyone cries. His fist rested against his lips, and his eyes widened. When the video was almost over, he moved his fist, and I saw a… *was that a smi—?*

"Oww! Mother fu…" Hot tea flooded my crotch.

"Oh, I'm so sorry detective! I'm so clumsy!" Mrs Ayres said, attempting to dab my trousers, but I moved away.

"It's fine, don't…" I took a deep breath. "Don't worry."

Mrs Ayres handed me a tea towel, with which I soaked up as much tea as I could before heading to the bathroom.

After a few minutes of cold-water therapy, I came out of the bathroom, to the living room and sat back down. "So, Mr. Ayres, back to the matter at hand."

"Yes. It is sad to see that he was that depressed. He never told me things were so bad."

"Forgive me Mr. Ayres, but you don't seem very upset."

"Not everyone wears their emotions on their sleeves detective," he said, with a stern look in his eyes.

"I see. He mentioned your father. I take it they didn't get along?"

"That's putting it politely. My father never gave him the time of day, and when he did, the bastard made him do menial tasks and then criticised all of the work. He didn't give a shit—!"

"Calm down, Mr. Ayres."

His chest puffed in and out, but he eventually calmed. "I'm sorry."

"I find it interesting that you called your own father a bastard. I thought you would be in high praise of him. I did some research and saw he helped you out with a house, a car and so on."

Mr. Ayres opened his mouth, but nothing came out.

"Are you okay?"

"Yes, sorry. My mind just…drifted away, that's all. You're right. My father was a…" he swallowed hard. "He is a great man. I shouldn't have said that about him. He gave…me, everything I needed."

"I'm sure you're just upset how he treated Jacob, right?"

"What? Oh, you mean. I mean. My brother."

"Are you sure you're okay, Mr. Ayres?"

"Yes. Of course. Just the shock of it all, I think. I guess my emotions have finally reached the surface. My brother committed suicide detective. Your case is over, and I have a plane to catch," he said and stood up.

I had visited Mr. Ayres hoping he would spot something on the video I hadn't. I wanted him to shed light on my gut' thoughts that lay hidden in my mind, but alas. "Well, I'll be on my—" My phone rang. "I'm sorry I have to take this." Mr. Ayres nodded.

"Banks."

"John. I have news on the photos and video you sent me."

"That was fast."

"I must've watched the video hundreds of times until a few things started to stick out."

"Such as?" I said, adjusting myself in the chair.

"I noticed that Mr. Ayres looked to the side of the camera several times during the video."

"Meaning?"

"Meaning that he was probably looking at someone else. I looked into this further, and there's no way he could have been holding that camera himself. Even using a selfie stick, you would've seen it in the video."

"Could he not have just placed it somewhere?"

"That's what I thought, but looking closer, you can see movement in the camera. Someone was definitely behind it. At the end of the video, something spooked the cameraman. I thought the camera falling was because of the death of Mr. Ayres, but I think the cameraman dropped it as he ran."

"I see. Anything else?"

"Yes. It's about Jacob and his brother. I looked at the photos and the video back and forth until I spotted something unusual."

I attempted to lower the volume on my phone.

"Jacob Ayres has a gold tooth. You can see this in the original photo, but in the video, the gold tooth is go—"

I fell to the ground and passed out. After what must have been a while, I shook my head and opened my eyes to see broken glass and blood all around me. The back of my head throbbed.

"What are you doing?" Mr. Ayres whispered to his wife.

"He knows!" she said.

"You don't know that! Now what do we do?" He paced the floor.

My phone rang again, and all of our heads turned. I scrambled towards it as Mr. Ayres' eyes darted around the room. It was within my reach. I reached out my arm and grabbed it, but as I went to pull it towards me, Mr. Ayres stood on my hand. I winced but then managed to knock his leg away with my other hand. As he rebalanced himself, I answered the phone call. I had a second or two at best.

"HEL—" Darkness…

"You could've killed him. What were you thinking?"

I pried my eyes open. Mr. and Mrs Ayres were talking in the corner of the room and I was tied to the chair.

"This was not in the plan, Mary."

"What did you want me to do? Let him ruin this for us? I thought you loved me, would do anything to be with me."

"Have I not proved that to you alre—" Mr. Ayres unclenched his fist. "He's awake." They both turned to me.

"Sorry to spoil your lover's quarrel," I said and spat blood onto the floor.

Mr. Ayres walked towards me and put on a false smile, "I'm sorry about my wife dete—"

"Wife? No, I don't think so."

Mr. Ayres took a step back. "I'm not sure what you mean."

"Well, allow me to explain," I said. "In the beginning, I put a lot of things down to emotions over the death. Mrs Ayres seemed very on edge in my presence, she couldn't even carry over a tray without shaking. And Mr. Ayres, you also went to say 'Matthew' when referring to your brother."

"That's ridiculous. Like you said, we have simply been emotional."

"That's true, Mr. Ayres, you have been emotional. But not in the way most would expect. You got angry at times, but no signs of tears or sadness. Even when I showed you the video, nothing. Nothing...but a smile. I've seen that kind of smile before. Many criminals have done it when talking about or looking over their work. And that's what you were doing. You were happy with *your work.*"

"Don't be absurd!" He said, getting closer to me, his chest puffing in and out.

"My gut told me something was wrong when I saw that video and then I got a call from my contact. Something was missing in that video."

"What?"

I smiled.

"What?!" he said and backhanded my face.

As I turned my head back towards him, I smiled again. "A gold tooth." I spat blood at the floor and then looked up. "Hello... Jacob."

"I told you he knew!" Mrs Ayres shouted.

"Shut up!"

"That's no way to speak to a lady," I said, smiling.

"And you can shut the fuck up too."

"Now, now Jacob, play nice," I replied. "So, tell me, why'd you do it? Why'd you kill your brother?"

"You're mistaken, detective. I am *Matthew*. Those blows to the head must have affected your judgement."

"Maybe you're right. You are Matthew. You're not that loser Jacob. What a fuck-up he is, right?" Mr. Ayres' vein in his head throbbed. "No wonder his daddy wasn't proud of him. He couldn't get a beautiful wife. He was a weak little man who had to fuck another man just to get a good job."

107

"Shut up!" Ayres said and broke my nose. "Is that weak? Am I weak now?!"

As blood cascaded over my lips, I knew I had him. "Well, well Jacob, the mask has finally come off. Now, I told you a story, but I think you would tell it so much better. Enlighten me. Tell me the truth about your life and what happened in the end."

"You wanna know? You fucking want to know, huh?!"

"Yes, I fucking want to know."

"Fine! Like I said before, my father is a bastard. Nothing I do is ever good enough for him, NOTHING." He clenched his fists. "I worked my ass off, trying to win his appraisal while my brother just breezed through life and got everything that should have been mine. My brother knew it and mocked me, his 'poor little brother'. Even after Matthew left the country, I still couldn't get out of his shadow. Matthew was 'Mr. Success', working abroad for a big company." He picked a photo of Matthew off the wall. "Well, I decided I would take everything from my perfect brother. Starting with his wife," he said and smirked. "You see detective, my father is a bastard, but I still want his praise. You may think I'm craz—"

"Yep," I said, which got me a punch to my broken nose.

"As, I, was saying. I still want my father's praise and the only way to get it is to *become* my brother. I will fuck his wife, do his job, and my father will love me for it."

"Careful Mr. Ayres. I don't think you'll be married for much longer if you continue talking like this."

"She will do as I say. Unless she wants to join my brother," he said, glancing at her.

Mrs Ayres looked shocked but stayed silent. Shaking, she walked out and into the kitchen.

"A quick question. Was it you who I saw in the hotel on that stairwell?"

"What? The big bad detective doesn't know?" he scoffed. "Need me to do your job for you?"

I gave him a steely glare. "Well you do seem to enjoy the sound of your own voice," I said and spat blood onto his shoes. He swung his leg towards my face, but I caught it, "Playtime," I said with a wink and swung him into a glass cabinet. He crashed to the floor and I headed towards him.

"Stop right there!!" he yelled with a large piece of glass in his hand. "Get the fuck back! On the floor, hands behind your back."

"Okay Mr. Ayres, I can do that," I told him and sat down.

"Now," he said, chest puffing in and out, "Where was I? Oh yes, doing your job for you," he smirked. "Yes, it was me on that stairwell. After killing my brother, I heard a noise and dropped the stupid phone. I went back later to put it somewhere more obvious, but after you chased me, I realised it wasn't safe for me to be there."

"But a woman told me nobody had come out that door."

"Recognise these?" Mr. Ayres said, pointing to some sunglasses attached to Mrs Ayres' case. "She was there to keep a lookout for me."

"So, she was willing to get her hands dirty, I see," I said, wiping blood away from under my nose.

"Like I said, she does what I say. I click my fingers, and the doggy comes running. I'm going to get my father's approval, and when I do, she will be sitting on a leash right bes—" Mr. Ayres fell to the ground. Mrs Ayres was stood behind him, blood dripping from a knife in her hands. Her eyes were wide open, and her body was still. After a few seconds, she stared at her bloody hands and turned to me.

"I really thought that he loved me…" A tear rolled down her cheek.

"I don't think he knew how to love."

Mrs Ayres nodded. "Oh. Let me get that rope off you." She came over and untied me just as the door crashed open. She looked petrified.

"Get down! Get down! Hands behind your head!" An officer in uniform yelled.

"Relax!" I shouted at him. "I've got her," I said and held out my hand, which she took. I walked her to the police car and put her inside. As it pulled away, I caught a glimpse of the sunset. Such a beautiful place had been stained with blood and tears. I closed my eyes and took in a deep breath. "This is going to sting," I told myself, grabbed my broken nose and popped it back into place, "Mother fu…"

With one last look at the little house, I took out my phone and booked a flight back to London. Romania had been intense, for both good and bad reasons. But for me, it was just another day on the job and another case…solved.

THE CLOCK STRUCK DEATH

Case #225

The sun shone through the office window as I sat, examining a parcel. Something was off about it. When I ripped the brown paper off, it all became clear. Some schmuck had messed up the order. They'd sent thin cigars; the kind a female villain might have in a film noir movie. Not a great start to the day.

Over the next hour, the cigar company received a piece of my mind. They apologised profusely. Not seeing much use for the cigars, I threw them into the bottom drawer of my desk. With a quick push, the drawer slammed shut and I reached for my next case file.

What have you got for me today, God?

I struck a match, the flame danced from side to side as it ignited my *non-imported* cigar, and I opened the envelope in front of me.

Dear Detective Banks,

You might not remember me; we met only once when you were a child, but I'm afraid I have some bad news. My brother Daniel Choen died late last night while sitting at his piano in his store. I know you two were close, and when I found out, your name was the

*first that popped into my head. You see, something
doesn't feel right about his death. I always knew him
as a healthy man, eating right, going for long walks,
so to die so suddenly doesn't make sense. I am no detective, but I can think of a few people with motives
to get rid of him. Could you please look into this case
as a personal favour? Once solved, my heart will be
able to rest, and I can grieve.*

Yours faithfully,

Mr. J Choen

I couldn't remember pouring any whiskey. But before I'd finished reading the letter, a glass had almost been drunk. Once I'd
finished the letter, I downed the last of it and poured another.

The logs crackled, and the heat from the fire caressed my face,
as I stared endlessly at the grandfather clock. Mr. Choen had
given it to me as a gift when I moved into the private detective
business. He told me the clock was strong and that the heart of it
would never weaken, like mine. With one last big sip of whiskey,
the bottle was empty.

The next morning my head felt like a coke can that was about to
burst. The logs on the fire had turned to ash, and as I stood, the
clock chimed, loudly...I sat back at the desk, my hand caressing
my sore head and looked at the case again. After re-reading it for
the fifth time, I put emotions into my back pocket and called Mr.
Choen's brother. The talk was brief, and when it was over, I put
out my cigar and headed to the scene of the crime.

After a thirty-minute walk, I arrived at the store. It hadn't changed a bit. Dark green paint licked the walls, a cream sign with fancy writing stood above the door, bearing Mr. Choen's name. A smoke was needed however, before going down memory lane. And so, I reached into my pocket and pulled out a cigar.

With a last flick of the thumb, an avalanche of ash fell off the cigar's edge and smoke pirouetted around my lungs. I sent the finished cigar spiralling to the ground and watched as it met its fate, crushed by the heel of my boot. I pushed open the door, and when the bell jingled, I was transported back to when I was nine years old. My father died when I was four, and as a result, I'd always felt a part of my life was missing. When my mother sent me to Mr. Choen's store to have her watch fixed, little did I know it would have such an impact on my life.

Aged nine, walking into that store, I fell in love right away. My senses were in heaven. Smells of pine, oak and maple wood floated in the air. Soft ticks and tocks trickled down my ear and a pleasant tune played by Mr. Choen danced around me. There was so much beauty to see. The grandfather clocks always received the most of my attention — such fantastic craftsmanship.

A voice came from behind, "Can I help you?"

I snapped out of my dream, turned and saw a short, red-haired lady in a suit, "Yes. I'm Detective Banks. I'm here about Mr. Choen's death."

"Ah yes, his brother mentioned you. Here's a key for the shop, should you need it. Feel free to look around and just ask if you need anything."

I took a deep breath, and allowed myself to forget the case, that Mr. Choen was gone, and to enjoy the store one last time. My fingers ran over the carved clocks. Smooth polished surfaces allowed my fingers to glide like a skater on ice. I closed my eyes and listened to the ticks and the tocks. My fingers came to a crashing halt when I reached the piano, where Mr. Choen had taken his last breath. The piano had captured so many happy moments in my life. But now, I had to see if it had captured any evidence that would tell me a tale of murder.

I dusted the piano for prints only to find Mr. Choen's fingerprints and nobody else's. He had a strict policy of nobody playing the piano but himself. There was, however, one exception to that rule...me. On my tenth birthday I watched in amazement as Mr. Choen fixed an old pocket watch. When he finished, he turned and said to me, "I think it's about time you learned to play the piano."

I wiped the powder off the piano, held that old tune inside my head and began to play.

"You're getting rather good at that tune," Mr. Choen said, his ghost standing next to me. "That E chord don't sound quite right though."

I played the chord again, and he was right; it sounded off. After playing it a couple more times and inspecting the keys, the problem became clear. Something was stuck between two of them. I grabbed a piece of paper, folded it in half and placed it between the keys... "Voila! Got it!" *What could it be...?* I thought, scratching my head. The truth is, it could've been anything, a mint, sweetener for coffee, pills... *hmm, pills.* I placed the broken pieces into a container, ready for later analysis.

Walking around the store, I knew there was a slim chance the killer had made an appointment with Mr. Cohen, over a broken item perhaps. It would create a good excuse to see the victim. If so, their details would be in a record book.

Mr. Choen's desk was neat, as always, and had a ring stain that was there the last time I visited, all those years ago. That man loved his coffee...*Now where did he used to keep his record book...? Bottom drawer!* It turned out Mr. Choen had been busy yesterday, plenty of repairs both coming in and going out. What caught my eye, however, was a repair coming in at 9pm. The store always closed at 6pm on the dot — a *new lead*.

I strolled around the office searching for evidence showing this death suspicious an—

"Who the fuck are you?!" A man shouted.

"I'm De—"

"On second thoughts, I don't give a fuck who you are. Get out!"

"Jack Cohen hired me. I'll leave my card right here," I said, looking the man in his eyes. "Give him a call, and I'll be in touch," I told him as I walked past.

On that note, I left the building. The door hit the bell as it closed behind me while the case rang in my head. There were a couple of leads to go on, for the time being, what I didn't have was cigars.

On my way to buy a case of cigars from Arlo's, I wondered if Mr. Choen's son's anger was out of grief or fear. Was there something incriminating to find?

After I entered Arlo's store, I saw something I wasn't expecting. A tall, beautiful woman browsing the cigars. She wore black high heeled shoes and had legs that went up to heaven. Her eyes were so enchanti—

"The usual?"

"W-what?" I said, turning and seeing Arlo standing in front of me.

Arlo smiled. "I said, 'what'll it be today, the usual?' Are you with me? Hellooo."

"Erm…" I said, eyes focused on the woman.

"I don't normally see your head turned quite so hard."

The woman smiled from across the room and after catching her eyes in mine, I turned to Arlo.

"Yeah, the usual, please Arlo. Online company messed up, but I can always count on you." I then whispered in his ear, "Who's the lady?"

"Never seen her before. Think I stand a chance?" he chuckled.

"Maybe if I wasn't here." I smiled, patted him on the shoulder, and headed over to the woman.

"Need some help?" I asked with a smile.

"Do you work here?"

"No, but I like to help a woman should she need it. That, and I happen to be a bit of a cigar connoisseur."

"Is that so? Well, if I need you, I'll be sure to let you know," she said and turned back to the cigars.

A challenge. I liked that. With a nod and smile, I turned and pretended to look around the store. When Arlo caught my attention, I gave him a wink, grabbed another case of cigars, and walked over to his desk.

"Here's your usual," he said, placing a box of cigars on the table. "You want me to put that one on your tab too?" he asked, pointing to the box in my hand.

"Yeah…thanks." Keeping one eye on the woman, I wrote a note and put it with the cigars. "Until next time Arlo," I said and headed towards the door. As I got close to the enchanting lady, I strategically dropped my box of cigars near her feet.

"Clumsy aren't we Mr…?" she said, bending over and picking up the cigars. She looked deep into my eyes, and I knew I had her.

"Banks, but you can call me John when we have dinner tonight." I handed her a box of thin cigars with a note that read:

I'll pick you up at 8pm, text me your address,
07564587765, John

Meeting in the evening gave me time to go home, get ready and think over what I'd found at Mr. Choen's store.

I pressed a cigar against my lips and lit a match. As the smoke filled my lungs, I breathed my kind of oxygen and relaxed. Sitting in a room of smoke, I studied the white substance I'd found earlier. Holding it close to my eye, I gave the container a little shake. *What are you little one?*

A while later, with the cigar nearing its end and the smoke dancing in the air, I placed the container back in my pocket. The grandfather clock chimed, which was my cue to move if I wanted to drop the evidence off before my date. I liked the fact that I didn't know her name yet; it was a small mystery for me to solve.

I arrived at my date's apartment building at 7:59pm. The icy wind whistled through the trees and down my back. I went to knock on the door, but it opened before my hand could reach it. She was more beautiful than I remembered. She was wearing nothing but a short silk robe. With a smile she told me, "I do like a man who comes on time. Please forgive me for not being as punctual. I was just finishing up a drawing. My passion for art sometimes takes over me, allowing me to lose track of all time. Please come in. I won't take long." She walked into her apartment.

"No bother at all." A tiger lay on the back of her robe, and I could tell she was going to be a handful. I'd have to keep my eyes wide open with this one.

I took the liberty of pouring myself a drink while waiting in the living room. As the whiskey trickled down my throat, a soft hand caressed my shoulder. I turned around to find her dressed, not in an evening outfit, but in lingerie.

"Normally I like to make a man wait, but you're in luck, John. I want you and I want you now," she said, leaning in. I pulled her close and kissed her hard. "I like a man who takes control," she said, running her fingers down my back, "but now it's my turn." We headed into the bedroom and closed the door behind us. The temperature rose, bodies entwined, and the intensity was high. After the final breath of passion, we sat up and lit a cigar.

"You have good taste, John."

"I told you I know cigars."

"I wasn't talking about the cigars," she said and kissed me softly on my neck.

When I awoke early the next morning the enchantress was still sleeping. With a case to solve and not wanting to disturb her, I left a note on her pillow.

On my way out of the bedroom, my jacket got caught on a handle and pulled open a sliding wardrobe door. As I looked inside, I discovered a collection of wigs, all excellent quality. I've seen it all over the years, fake nails, tattooed eyebrows, implants, so the wigs didn't bother me at all.

As I stepped out into the fresh air, the wind shut the door behind me. Having not heard from my contact, I headed over to Mr. Choen's last customer's home.

Finally. After so many months of visiting suspects in the ghetto, I found myself in a rich neighbourhood. This time there were only six steps to climb instead of six floors, and there was no stench of sick or urine. The stunning three-story house in front of me belonged to a Mr. Johnson. After knocking on the door, a Hispanic housemaid greeted me.

"Good morning. I'm Detective Banks. Is Mr. Johnson home?"

"No. Señor Johnson is out running, but you're welcome to wait.

"Gracias," I said, as I entered the home.

"De nada. Would you like a drink?"

Too early for whiskey, I thought.

"Maybe a glass of lemonade, detective?"

"That would be great, thank you."

As the lemonade quenched my thirst, I looked around the living room. The first thing that caught my eye was a one-pound coin in a frame. I'd never seen that before. The rest of the room consisted of things such as fine art, a big TV, golf clubs in the corner and oh, a grandfather clock. The front door opened and closed. Mr. Johnson was home.

Criminals come in all shapes and sizes, from poor families to rich families. Mr. Johnson entered the room, all six feet eight inches of him, built like a brick house. He took off an expensive watch and put on a cheap looking one from the coffee table. *How peculiar...*

"I hear you've been waiting for me. I hope I haven't kept you waiting too long."

"Not at all. I'm Detective Banks. I was wondering if you could answer a few questions."

Mr. Johnson looked over to his maid and then back to me. "Umm, sure."

"My records show you visited Mr. Choen's store late on the 8th, a bit unusual don't you think? The store closed several hours before."

"I suppose you could say that."

"May I see the repaired item?"

"I'm afraid not."

"I see," I said, rubbing my hands together. "Are you sure that's what you went there for that night, Mr. Johnson?"

He looked over at his maid again.

"Does your maid have the answers?"

"What? No of course not. I...erm..." He looked at her again. "Did your maid, Ms...?"

"Gonzales," he replied.

"Thank you. Did Ms Gonzales ever accompany you to Mr. Choen's store?"

"N-no, of course not, why would she?" his voice losing its confidence.

I scratched my chin and observed his body language, "Have you always been happy with the results of Mr. Choen's work, Mr. Johnson?"

"Yes."

"Are you sure?"

"Of course," he said, scratching his arm.

"You seem on edge, is everything okay Mr. Johnson?"

"W-why wouldn't it be? Look, I've just realised I've got to be somewhere."

"That's fine. I have enough to go on for now. But I'll be in touch again, Mr. Johnson."

Mr. Johnson took one final glance at Miss Gonzales and left.

After Ms Gonzales showed me out of the house, I headed into a nearby park. I lit a cigar and pondered over my brief encounter with dear Mr. Johnson. I had the feeling he might be hiding something, only time would tell.

The light blinked on my mobile phone. A missed call from Mr. Choen's brother and a text message. In a voicemail, Mr. Choen's brother informed me he had spoken with his nephew. He also said I shouldn't have a problem visiting the store anymore. An angry relative bouncing round the store was never good, so I was grateful for the good news.

On my way over to the store I checked the text:

Hey there Mr. Detective. I had a great time last night. Since we missed a chance to have breakfast together, I thought we could have lunch and this time maybe try leaving our clothes on...at least for a little while.

Aurora xo.

The offer was more than tempting, but my job always comes first.

When I walked into Mr. Choen's store, the doorbell dinged, and I checked to see if anybody was around. After finding nobody there, my body gravitated to the piano. I started to play the tune Mr. Choen had taught me again, this time it sounded just right. Allowing myself to get lost in the music, my mind floated with the melody, and my body began to rela— Mr. Choen's son approached and watched from behind.

"Your father taught it to me when I was a child,"

"Wait! Are you...John?"

"Not a lot of people call me that these days but yes, how did you know?"

"He talked about you all the time when I was young. You had a special place in his heart. I sometimes think he loved you even more than me." He paused. "Anyway, how are you? Can I interest you in a liquid lunch?"

I looked him up and down. "Sure." And with that we headed out the store and to a nearby bar.

As we walked through the door into the dimly lit bar, he patted me on the back.

"What'll it be, John?"

"Whiskey, no ice, thanks," I said and headed for a table while he headed to the bar.

We drank together for a couple of hours. He didn't like to talk much about my time with his father. Instead, he spoke about things he had done for Mr. Choen, while drinking, *a lot*. He also told me they had lost touch for a while when he went to college. He was about to change all that before the sudden death took away the chance. I asked him about any possible suspects to his father's murder. He told me, however, he firmly believed it wasn't a suspicious death. Everyone loved his father, all except perhaps some store competitors.

"So, what will happen to the store now?" I asked.

"My father told me he was about to put that into his will. He told us how we had no passion for the business and so was leaving it to someone who did...you," he said and looked me right in the eye.

"Me? You must be mistaken."

"Are you k-kidding?! You are John, the Golden Boy. The one who was always so fascinated by my father's work." He downed the last of his drink. Judging by his face, that last drink had hit him hard. While heading for the bar, he swayed back and forth. He almost missed the stool while trying to sit down to order a drink, but made it in the end.

I needed to clear my head and so headed outside for a smoke. *The store was going to be mine?* I knew his son had grown apart from him, but still. I always thought he'd keep the store in the family. Was he afraid it would get sold? He knew I could never do that, even if it meant someone looking after the store for me. In the time I'd now come to know Mr. Choen's son, I realised I hadn't even learned his name. Perhaps that was the reason he'd been eyeballing me so much. Another reason could be the apparent lack of love he'd received in comparison to myself.

The last of the ash fell off my cigar, and I headed back inside.

"I took the liberty of getting you a drink, whiskey, lots of ice, right?" He was starting to slur his words.

"Sure kid." I smiled. "You said '*us*' when talking about who wasn't interested in the repair business. Did you mean you and your uncle?"

"Nno course nnott. I meant my sister and me," he just about managed to say.

"Sister? I was never aware Mr. Choen had a daughter."

"That's c-ccos she was a bit of a bad apple that one. Sshee left when…"

"When?" I urged him on.

"Oh yeah. S-s-hhee l-left when she was yo- young."

I asked if he knew where she lived, but from what I could understand from his drunken mumbling, he didn't. He did, however, give me her name, age, and the last place he'd seen her.

He stumbled towards the bar, and I put my arm around his shoulder. "I'll call you a taxi."

"Get the fuck offa me!" he yelled and took a swing at me. I dodged it, and he fell to the floor. Jealousy can do a lot to a person...

The sunlight outside was blinding. My phone vibrated, but the message was hard to read with all the floating spots bouncing in front of my face. Once my vision became clear, a light blinking from my phone caught my eye. With my fingerprint, I opened the phone and found a message from Aurora.

Hey there Dragon. I'm cold and thirsty. Come have a drink with me and help warm me up Xo

With a slight grin I replied,

Make it dinner. It will give us energy for…later on Xo

★ ★ ★

124

The wind caressed my cheeks as I left the tube station. Pulling the pocket watch from inside my jacket, I realised I was going to be late for dinner with Aurora. *Shit.* Nancy made fun of me for still using this watch. "You have a clock on your phone, old timer," she'd say with a smile. Her smile could calm any storm in my mind. "This is a classic, Piglet." I'd reply. The truth is this is the first watch I ever fixed with Mr. Choen. Even after our falling out, I always believed as long as it kept ticking, my relationship with him would be okay. Time is tricky. It can heal, but also pass you by in the blink of an eye and now I will never be able to reconnect with him. *Maybe if I solve this case, it could be my final gift to a great man.*

"Where've you been?" Aurora asked as I reached the restaurant. She looked incredible, standing there in a red dress which clung to her body, a cigar in her right hand.

"It's that damn tube. You look amazing."

"What? This lil ol' thing?" she said, but she knew how good she looked. "You look alright, I suppose," she said with a cheeky grin.

Once inside, I gave my name and the waiter took us to a table near the fireplace, as I'd asked for.

"Thankin' you kindly, young man," Aurora said in a strong Texan accent.

"I didn't know you could do an American accent, it's very good."

"What are you talking about?"

"That accent you just did when you thanked the waiter."

"I didn't thank the waiter…"

"Yeah you…" I stopped myself. *Maybe she's tired,* though I didn't care. I was just glad to see her.

The sweet smell of food flew from the kitchen and up my nose. The door opened and a juicy seitan steak, with herbs and spices massaged into it, headed my way. It smelled amazing. Once placed onto our table, steam rose from it, while I savoured the moment. Having not eaten for a while this was going to be heaven. Aurora started to speak but I remained enthralled with my food.

"...John?"

I sliced a piece of the steak off and placed it into my mouth.

"John?"

My teeth sunk in...

"John!"

I turned to Aurora who looked less than pleased.

"Shit. I mean, I'm sorry," I said, breaking free from the food spell.

"Hungry aren't we...dragon?" she said and gave me a wink.

"Yeah, sometimes I don't register I need food when working on a case."

"A case? What are you working on?" she said, leaning forwards, red wine in hand.

"I don't discuss my cases, Aurora."

"Not even for me?" she said, moving her foot up the inside of my leg.

"It's...personal," I said and looked towards the window. Rain had started to fall.

"John. John look at me," she said, and I turned to her. "I know we haven't known each other long, but you can trust me."

"I trust you it's just—"

"Argh..."

"What? What's wrong?"

"Oh nothing. Just another headache," she said, popping a painkiller from a packet. "It's been happening for a while now but I'm fine. Tell me about the case."

This girl was persistent, but I still wanted to be brief at least.

"It's a possible murder case. A man died in a store and his brother hired me to solve the case."

"What store? What was the victim's name?"

"Why are you so curious?"

"I'm not, I'm just…taking an interest in your life that's all. But if that's so bad then—"

"No, no it's not. like I said, it's personal, that's all. Maybe we can talk a little more about it over wine, at your place?"

"I'd like that."

We talked throughout the rest of dinner about our interests, love of cigars, places we'd travelled. Afterwards, it was back to her place for another memorable night.

The next morning something pleasant climbed up my nose. "Something smells good," I murmured, eyes still closed. I moved the quilt cover off and sat up. Breaking the seal on my eyelids, I found a tray on the side table. Next to scrambled eggs, toast and orange juice was a note,

I thought my dragon might be hungry. See you soon, Aurora Xo

The food hit the spot. Great lover and a great cook, I was a lucky man. Suit on, the hunt for my tie began. "Oh, that's where I left you," I said and untangled it from a bedpost. The next suspect on my list was Mr. Choen's store's competitor.

As I reached the competitor's store, a stone's throw away from Mr. Choen's, the sign read, *Tanaka Clocks, est. 1978.* This store was here before Mr. Choen's store but now the outside of the shop looked rundown. The paint had faded, and parts of wood had chipped off. It wasn't a store that was thriving.

I turned the handle and as the door opened, the bell dinged. Through a sea of old clocks, half labelled SALE, there was an old Japanese man sitting at a desk.

"Kon'nichiwa, Mr. Tanaka," I said bowing my head.

"Hello," he replied, looking me up and down. "That suit is old, I know person who make good one, you call him."

"Thanks for the offer but I'm here about Mr. Choen. He lives, lived near—"

"I know who Mr. Choen is," he said and went back to writing in a book.

"Right. I was wondering if you saw anything on the night of the 8th?"

"Saw what? Mr. Choen? I have no see that man in long time and good riddance."

"You two didn't get along?" My ears pricked.

"You could say dat."

"And the reason being…?"

"Take a look around here. You think all this SALE if I do well? He has store same as mine. He does better, so I do worse," he said and banged a cheap coffee machine until black liquid came out.

"Can you tell me where you were on the night of the 8th?"

"I fix car all night. Engine broken. My wife, she tell you," he said, as he slurped his coffee. A bell dinged and he looked over my shoulder, "Oh, hey son."

"What's up dad? Who's this suit?" the young man asked.

"This is, erm…"

"Detective Banks. I'm here asking about Mr. Choen."

"That dick, what's the problem?"

"Manners boy!" the man shouted at his son.

"The problem is," I said, then covered my mouth. I took in a deep breath. "The problem is, he's been killed. You seem pretty upset. You don't like him?"

"You could say that," he said, itching his fist.

"And where were you on the night of the 8th?"

"Huh? Erm…at the…gym. Yeah that's right, I was working out."

"You don't sound so sure."

"You calling me a liar?!"

"Son, God sake! Calm yourself. Go eat."

"I don't ne—"

"I said go eat!"

The son left the room, while giving me a stare. The old man didn't like Mr. Choen's store doing better but the son appeared enraged with it all.

"Sorry 'bout him. He crazy sometime, but he good boy."

"How could I reach your wife. I'll need to verify your story. You understand?"

"I understand; you speak to her when she come down."

"Can you think of anyone else who would want to harm Mr. Choen?"

"I try not look at his store or care 'bout it, but I did see man who look angry go in store, I think 9pm. I had smoke with wife, break from fix car."

"Thank you for your co-operation."

His wife later verified his story. It was always hard to tell whether to believe information when a spouse gives an alibi. That day, however, my gut told me he didn't have a killer *feel* about him. His son on the other hand…

I left the store and headed for an early lunch. There was a noodle bar not too far away which had space outside for eating. Perfect, as I needed a smoke.

Sitting down with overpriced noodles in front of me, I checked my phone but there was nothing. *Why haven't I heard back about that white substance...?* I thought, while bringing a prawn to my mouth with chop sticks. Ten minutes went by and I'd checked my phone twenty times. I needed some good news, and guilty evidence is great for that. *What the fuck is he doing?*

I struck a matchstick against its box once, twice, *come on...* three times, it snapped in half. "Jesus H!"

"Is everything okay sir?" an employee asked.

"I'm fine," I said, and the person left.

A match finally struck a flame, "Don't you dare blow out, you son of a bitch." I brought it to the cigar, took a deep, impatient breath, and *relax...* The smoke caressed my tongue and sneaked out of my mouth. I wanted to solve the case so bad that it was getting the better of my emotions. After taking another deep breath I called Charlie. Straight to voice mail. That wasn't like Charlie. He's usually on top of things, lightning fast too.

With no luck finding information on the white substance, I decided to head to Mr. Choen's store. Maybe there was something I'd missed. I grabbed the key and headed out. Upon arrival, a chill ran down my spine. A ghost, or just the English weather? With the key turned and with the softest of touches, the creaky door flew open. Mr. Choen had never been one for modern day things, and that included new doors apparently. He liked old fashioned things, just like me. The clocks played their beautiful ticking tune and smelled as sweet as ever. Some were easier to move than others as I checked around them looking for clues. Nothing, but then...a grandfather clock the same as mine sounded a little off. *Why hadn't I noticed this before?* I opened it slowly. Something dropped onto the floor.

I bent down and picked up a photograph that had fallen. As I turned it over a tear came to my eye. It was Mr. Choen and myself when I was about eleven years old. *I was so happy.* He'd managed to convince me bow ties where cool that year. Friends didn't agree, but their opinion didn't matter as much as his did to me. Mother used to joke I'd jump off a cliff if he asked me to. He knew a lot about everything, and I always thought he had the wisest eyes of all, what stories he could tell.

Placing the photograph into my pocket, I continued to look around. Nothing stuck out to me, nothing except something covered in dust on top of a bookcase. The wheels of a chair screeched as I dragged it over. Two feet steady on the chair I reached up and grabbed the item. I sat at Mr. Choen's desk, grabbed a cloth and dusted the cobwebs off. An expensive bottle of whiskey with an attached label on a piece of string revealed itself. The label read,

For when John and I reconcile.

A tear rolled down my cheek, something which hadn't happened in a long time.

Picking up the glass now filled with whiskey I made a toast, "To you Mr. Choen, may we be together in spirit at least." The whiskey hit the back of my throat, again, and again, and again. I must have stared at that photo for hours… My phone vibrated and I almost hit the ceiling, "Wha-what?" I said, reaching for it but knocking the bottle off the table instead. "Shit!" I dove down to rescue it. "Wait a minute. What's this?" The whiskey on the floor rolled towards one place, where it slowly disappeared. *Some sort of under floor safe?* I tried to lift the floorboards, but only managed to break a small piece off which in return put a splinter in my finger. It did however reveal that it was indeed a safe. As I dragged the splinter out of my finger, I realised it wasn't a good idea to try breaking into this while drunk. I sat back in the chair, poured myself another drink and fell asleep.

The next morning, my head was pounding as if the Gods had been banging it against the wall, over and over. Then, something strange happened. The Gods spoke to me. "John? John? You there?" My head cracked like a mountain in a storm as I opened my eyes and discovered I was still in Mr. Choen's store. *Who would know I was here?* Realising the voice came from the door, I walked towards it. I placed my ear close to the door. *Bang bang bang,* a thunderous fist hit the door, my head almost exploded. "John?"

"What the hell do—" I yelled, opening the door, but I stopped when I saw Charlie's face. "Sorry Charlie. My head's cracking open. How'd you know I'd be here?"

"I have my contacts t-too," he said with a wink. "Still a fan of the whiskey I see. Still no ice?"

"Still no ice," I said, inviting him in. "Where the hell have you been?" I shut the door. "I need work done and you drop off the planet. No calls, no texts. Nothing."

"I'm sorry, John, it's just, my…" he looked to the ground, his shoulders slumped. "my..."

"Jesus Charlie, spit it out."

"My dog died…" He turned away, bringing a hand to his face. "I know it's not a reasonable excuse. I should be professional and g-g-get work done. I should—"

"Charlie, it's okay. I understand."

"You do?" He turned towards me.

"Yeah. I'm not *completely* cold you know. I had a dog. Died a few years back. I used to think he was a better detective then I was," I said, attempting a smile. "What happened?"

"Poisoned. Reckon it was that b-b-bastard next door. There's something about him. I swear, whenever he looks at my, at my dog, there is the *devil in his eyes.*"

"Woah, Charlie. Comin' off a bit strong there. Do you have any other reasons to believe it's this neighbour? Besides the devil in his eyes?"

"Yes. I was playing in my garden with my new diabolo set, when the diabolo flew over into my neighbour's g-garden. It smashed one of his precious gnomes."

"And he flipped out?"

"No. He just s-s-…smiled and told me not to worry."

"Right…"

"Look John, I know he did it, he did it!" Charlie's chest puffed in and out while he searched through his pockets and pulled out an inhaler.

"Alright, alright. Calm down, Charlie. You're gonna give yourself a heart attack."

Charlie shook his inhaler and took in a breath. "Can you look into it for me, John? *P-Please.*"

"A pet detective, huh?" I raised my eyebrow. "Only for you, Charlie. Only for you," I said, placing my hand on his shoulder.

"Oh my gosh, thanks, John! Again, I'm sorry about the lab stuff. I'll g-get too it asap and call you the second the results are in."

I showed him out of the store, and across the street, I was surprised to see Aurora heading for a taxi. *What the hell is she wearing? Looks like an old librarian…*

"Aurora. Aurora!" I shouted across the street. I stepped onto the road and shouted her name again. When she finally turned and looked at me, it was as if she was looking at a stranger. A car ran by in front of me, making me jump back. By the time it passed, she had gone. *That was weird…* A thunderstorm still crackled inside my head. I needed coffee and a cigar. Luckily, I had both in my office.

It didn't take long to get there. The steps creaked as I climbed them and with each one it felt like a cat was clawing my head. At the top of the stairs I flung the door open, went inside and clicked the espresso machine on. I'd had enough hangovers to know it made sense to have my own coffee machine. As the coffee poured into a cup and the aroma filled the air, I searched the cupboards for tools. There was something else that needed to feel like it was cracking open today, Mr. Choen's hidden safe.

Ash snowed from my cigar onto the ground as I left my office building. Tools in hand, I was ready. While walking down the street the sound of shoes hitting the floor echoed around me. A chill blew over my shoulder, a feeling I get when someone is following me. Walking a little further to test my instinct, it soon became obvious I was right. Whenever my steps stopped, so did the others and when I moved again, so did they. I bent down pretending to tie my laces and quickly turned my head. The man dove into a doorway. It was Mr. Choen's son.

"What are you doing?" No reply. "Look, I can see you." No movement, and so I walked up to him and dragged him out of the doorway. "I asked what you are doing?"

"Me? Umm…I came to say…sorry for the incident in the bar."

"Really?" I said, not believing a word.

"Umm…yeah of course. Why else would I be here?"

"And hiding in the doorway? I suppose *that* was part of speaking to me?"

"No, I saw something I liked, is all."

"In a…" I looked inside. "A wheelchair store?"

"Yeah, I know people," he said, speaking in a sharp tone.

"Tell me something else you should know. Where were you at the time of your father's death?"

"You calling me a suspect? You saying I killed my old man?"

"No, I'm jus—"

"Who the fuck do you think you are?! I oughta!" Red mist was descending over his face.

"Listen lets—"

"Fuck you!" he said and pushed me in front of a bus. *Darkness.*

✷ ✷ ✷

Beep...beep...beep.

"I'm up, I'm up," I said, reaching for an alarm clock that wasn't there. I was in hospital.

Shit, I almost died, I thought while lying in the bed. Two faces flashed before my eyes as that bus was coming, Nancy...and my dead wife. Makes you think. What's important, what's not? *What am I doing with my life...?* I fell back asleep.

"Sir. I'm sorry, sir."

"Wh-wha?"

"Sir, there's a call for you. I said you were resting but she insisted," a nurse told me while tapping her foot.

"She?" I managed to pry my eyes open. My right arm felt heavier than usual.

"Yes, said her name's Nancy."

"Unc! PICK...UP...THE...PHONE!" Nancy's voice shouted down the phone still held in the nurse's hand. She rolled her eyes and handed it to me before leaving.

I raised my right arm towards the phone and saw a cast covering it. With a little bit of difficulty, I took the phone with my left hand. "Hey Piglet."

"Oh my God, Unc. The hospital called me. Are you okay? Tell me you're okay. You're not okay. Okay I'm flying over. I'll start pack—"

"Breathe, Piglet, breathe. I'm fine."

"Really? You're not just saying that. I know you are this big tough guy, but it's okay to say you're in pain. You're in pain. Right I'm coming over."

"Hey! Are you on drugs or something?"

"What? Oh! No, of course not. It's early in the morning here. I've been having shots of espresso while trying to get hold of you."

"It's good to hear your voice, Piglet."

"You too, Unc. I don't know what I'd do if you died. You're the only superhero I know," she laughed, then sniffled. I imagined her wiping a tear from her face and my heart ached.

"I'm not going anywhere. Just a few bruised ribs, and a sore shoulder, I'll be fine, I'm sure. Luckily, nobody has found my kryptonite yet." I didn't tell her about the broken arm. She would worry too much. We talked for hours. She told me of her life, friends, work, girlfriend.

"Wait! Girlfriend?"

"What? The great Detective Banks didn't know I was gay?"

"Well, erm…you know I don't like to think of you *with* someone. And I don't care if it's not a guy. I'll still kick her ass if she hurts you."

"I don't doubt that for a second. I love you Unc. "

"You too, Piglet."

"So, how's your work?"

"Well…you know. There's a lot to do. Bad guys need taking down and I'm good at it. This accident has had me questioning whether it's all worth it though. I could've died. Should this be what I'm doing with my life?"

"Unc, you were born to do this stuff. I'm sure a lot of people will sleep better at night knowing you're there to help, I know I do. I think you just need some good ol' R & R. Recharge the batteries and come back to work fresh. When was the last time you went on a holiday?"

"Almost forgot what one of those are."

"Well think about taking one, okay? For me."

"I will."

"Promise?"

"Pinkie promise, Piglet. I hate to say it, but I've got to go. I need rest and have a case to solve."

"Get that rest. We'll speak soon."

I hung up the phone and messaged Aurora. I told her what had happened, not to worry and we'd speak tomorrow. Right now, I needed rest. Tomorrow I had that son of a bitch to visit.

★ ★ ★

I knotted my tie and brought it towards my neck as the nurse walked in.

"What are you doing Mr. Banks?"

"I'm leaving."

"I'm afraid you can't. Doctor O'Hara said you're not allowed to leave until this afternoon."

"Well you can tell the doc I had a difference of opinion." I stood and walked towards the door. She stuck her hand onto my chest to stop me and was surprisingly strong. Pressure on the broken ribs caused me to lose my breath.

"*That* would be your painkillers wearing off. Best lay down and I will get your medicine," she said, pushing me towards the bed.

"Yes, ma'am," I replied with a salute. "I guess that bastard will have to wait," I mumbled to myself. *At least it gives me a chance to go over the case.*

Mr. Johnson was a man with secrets. It was clear his maid and himself were up to something, but what, and were there any other secrets in his dark chest? What was that white substance? Why was it not all ingested? Forcefully put into Mr. Choen's mouth?

Toast crumbled as I bit hard into it while thinking about Mr. Choen's son, "Bastard." He was unhappy about the attention Mr. Choen gave me over the years. Also, his father saying I'd get the store could have tipped him over the edge. He didn't much enjoy being accused of his father's murder either. Guilty response or just insulted? I slugged some tea into my mouth, "Argh!" My tongue felt like lava. "Damn tea!" I yelled and slammed the cup down. "Just great." A pool of tea formed around the cup.

"Everything alright?" A new, young blonde nurse asked.

"Yes, fine," I said and smiled. "I'll be better once I can get out of here though."

"Don't you worry," she said, dabbing the pool of tea close to my— "We'll have you out of here in no time. Shame..." She smiled, and wrote something onto the cast on my arm.

I can help with all your...needs.
07873421562

This was a tempting offer, but I wasn't looking for someone new. As she left the room, I scribbled the writing out and laid back.

✳ ✳ ✳

Once discharged from the hospital I hit the ground hard and fast. "I'm coming for you, you son of a bitch," vengeance pumped through my veins.

Outside, the sun shone bright, but a strong wind whipped fast in the air. "If I were a rat where would I crawl to? He wouldn't hang out at his home, he's not that stupid. Nowhere near his father's store either. Maybe the bar we drank in?"

I approached the run-down bar, the sign faded and just about hanging to the wall. *Don't kill him John, you need answers, don't kill him, KILL HIM.* I shook my head, took a breath, and headed inside.

It might have been midday but inside the bar was dark, dimly lit, and full of creepy characters. This scumbag would fit right in. I did a quick scan and headed to the bar.

"What'll it be?" the bartender asked.

"A guy's location. Is *that* on the menu?"

"Depends."

"Have you seen this guy, Danny Choen?" I pulled up a Facebook image on my phone.

"Oh him. Yeah, that won't cost you. He's in the toilet."

I looked left and right.

"Over in that far corner." And as I turned, there he was coming out. I walked towards him but not directly. If I could go undetected it would make my job a lot easie— *Shit.* He saw me and ran towards the exit by the bar.

"Stop him and I'll give you fifty pounds!" I yelled to the barman. He stuck his large arm across the doorway, which got him a kick to the balls. Door open, I grabbed Danny's shoulder and yanked him back into the bar and to the floor. "One hundred pounds if you close the bar and let me deal with this loser," I said. The barman, recovering from the kick happily obliged.

"Well well well. What am I going to do with you Danny?" I said, towering over him. He tried to kick my crotch and I stomped on his kneecap, the sound of breaking bone echoed around the bar. "Now now Danny. You don't want to piss me off more than you already have." *Don't kill him.*

Danny winced as I dragged him to his feet and he put weight on his damaged leg.

"So, tell me punk, you often push people into traffic?"

"Fuck—"

"Wrong answer." I kicked his kneecap and he fell like a sack of spuds. "Let's try this again." I dragged him to his feet. "Why were you following me that day?"

"I don't have to say shit to you." I smashed my cast across his face and broke his nose.

As blood cascaded down his face, he looked as if he was coming around to the idea of talking.

"Like I was saying, why were you following me?"

"I wasn't following you. I mean, I was but I hadn't intended to."

"You're not making a lot of sense Danny. I don't like that," I said, inching towards him. He flinched.

"I mean I saw you in the street and decided to see what you were up to, that's all."

"Sounds like an awful coincidence to me."

"Fuck coincidence," he said but then staggered backwards. I smiled.

"You don't like me, do you, Danny? Well I'll let you into a little secret." I leaned in close and whispered, "I don't like *you* either."

What's that? Something had fallen out of his pocket. *Pills.*

"And what do we have here?" I said, picking them up. *Motherfucker.* "What are you doing with the same pills I found by your father's dead body?"

"They're umm, ummm…"

"Umm? I haven't heard of *Umm* pills before."

"They're just my meds. Can I not have fucki—" I smacked him to the ground. I'd heard enough. This guy had incriminating evidence against him and had followed me. He almost killed me and had a shitty attitude. The police could have him for now. *That way I can't kill his arse.*

I threw him into a nearby police station. "This guy tried to kill me. Here's the witnesses' names and numbers, Jones. See he gets a few nights in a prison cell."

"Nice to see you too, John."

"I haven't got time for this, Jones. I have a case to solve." I put my mouth next to Danny's ear, "I'll be back for you. You're gonna die in a cell."

Matches shook in my hand. The adrenaline was coursing through my veins hard.

"Need a light?"

"Oh...hey, Angel," I said, to an old flame.

She flicked her lighter towards me. "No matches?"

"You're welcome. It's been a long time, John, almost five years."

"That long huh?"

"Yeah, *that* long. You *said* you'd call when you left that morning. I'm still waiting," she said, curling some hair between her fingers.

"About that..." My phone rang. "Thank Christ."

"What was that?"

"Sorry. It's a call I've been waiting for." I hoped she bought it and turned around to take the call.

"Hey Dragon," Aurora said. I looked over my shoulder, to see if Angel heard anything. Luckily, she hadn't. *That* would've been a fun conversation.

"Listen Angel, this is an important call. I gotta go."

She looked into my eyes and said, "Don't make me wait another five years, John," and headed back inside the station.

"Who's Angel?" Aurora asked.

"That's a story for another day. What's up?"

"I was just lying here naked in the tub and I thought of you."

"That's erm, good to hear. Is there any…evidence of that?"

"I'll send you some…*evidence* later. But play your cards right and you might open this…*case* wide open." Water splashed in the background. "Anyway, I know this secret bar and was wondering if you fancied a drink tonight?"

"Sounds great. I'll pick you up at eight," I said and hung up the phone.

Charlie lived about a ninety-minute drive from the city centre. Because of this he was able to afford a decent enough two-bedroom house with a lush green garden. Pulling into his driveway, I looked out the window. Dog toys lay on his front lawn and a leash was hung near the door. As I turned off the engine a dog toy went flying past my windscreen.

"What the f…" I said turning to my right. An upset postman walked past my car, so I rolled down the window, "Excuse me, sir," I said but got no reply. Opening the car door, I said again, "Excuse me, sir." Son of a bitch was ignoring me. The door almost fell off as I slammed it shut, walked up to the man, and grabbed his shoulder, "Hey I'm talki—" It was then that the man pointed to his ears. He was deaf. "Oh, sorry, I didn't reali—" I stopped myself, realising he couldn't hear a word I said. The man stood there, staring blankly at me. I patted down my pockets, searching for pen and paper, but it was to no avail. The man turned and walked away. "Wait! I mean…" I walked ahead and turned to face him. *How can I get my message across?* I pointed at the house, to the dog toys and pretended to slit my throat. I observed his face. *Okay he either knows what I said or thinks I'm a nut. Hmm...* The man had a smile in the corner of his mouth. I think he got the message and judging by the smile and flung dog toy, I believed I had suspect number one. Unfortunately, my sign language skills were awful, and he was in a rush. *How do I ask him if he'll be here tomorrow...?* I pointed at him, then to the ground and did a forward circle motion with my hands. He gave a nod and walked away.

After watching the postman leave, I turned to check if anybody was home either side of Charlie's house. There were no cars, just a couple of cats hovering round the door of the house on my right. I inspected Charlie's front garden but found nothing of interest. With this, I headed around the side of the house.

Charlie didn't have a lock on his side gate. Bad move. This meant anyone could easily walk in and out. Closing the gate behind me, I headed for the back garden. I moved a few wheelie bins out of my way which revealed a garden in need of a little T.L.C. A rusted lawn mower had been put out for pasture in the corner of the garden. No other tools were in site. There was soil running up either side of his garden. The only thing that was living in it, however, was an old apple tree in the top corner. But as I walked up the garden towards the tree, something caught my eye. There was a disturbance in part of the soil. As I got closer, I realised it was a shoe print. Judging by the size of it compared to mine, I'd say it was a size 12 or 13. *Could it be Charlie's?*

After inspecting the rest of the garden, and finding nothing more than a few old chewed up toys, I headed inside the house. I shut the back door and began looking for shoes. I found a pair of Charlie's shoes near the bottom of the stairs. *Size four? Wow your feet are small Charlie.* This pointed towards an intruder in the garden. I'd call Charlie later to confirm, but it was a good lead to go on.

I checked my watch and realised I needed to head out if I wanted food before meeting Aurora that night. I headed out the house, locked the door and left.

Later, after placing the dinner dishes in my sink, I headed over to Aurora's place. When I arrived and walked up the few steps to the door, I wondered what the secret bar would be like. This girl was wild at times. I'm open to most things, but how far would she go?

The door opened; she was dressed to impress. A sleek black dress cascaded down her body leaving her long smooth legs on show. Her lips were a bold red and eyeliner was the finishing touch. She didn't need a lot of makeup as she was a woman of natural beauty. She always looked amazing in the mornings.

"Ready to go?"

"Sure."

I hailed a taxi and opened the door for Aurora to get in. "So how did you hear about this place?"

"You know what…? I don't recall. It's meant to be amazing though. I've been waiting to go for a while now."

"Why wait so long?"

"Oh, you know, just didn't have the right person to go with…" she said, brushing a hand through her hair.

She slipped out a thin cigar and I rolled down the window.

"Mam there is no smoking in here," said the driver.

"Take it easy," I said and gave him some money.

"Please make sure it goes out the window mam."

She looked at me and smiled. I still don't understand why people smoke those thin things, but dam she looked good doing it.

The taxi stopped at the end of a dark alley and I looked at Aurora with a raised eyebrow.

"Perfect," she said. "Thanks…Rajesh."

After closing the door behind us, wheels screeched, and the taxi sped off.

"This way," she said as she flicked her cigar to the floor and crushed it with her high heel.

The alley got darker the further we went in, with the slightest noise echoing against the walls.

"Right, now we can't see. Time to break out your matches," I said, wondering what we were gonna do next.

"No need, silly." She held my hand. "RELEASE THE BEAST."

"What the hell are you doing?"

A bright light shone, and a door shape appeared in the distance.

"Let's go," she said, and I walked curiously behind her.

Inside, the walls were painted red and the floor was black. Old fashioned chandeliers hung from the ceiling and a cloud of smoke circled them. *Finally, a bar I can smoke in.*

We sat at a table with an old-fashioned oil lamp as the centre piece and a waiter approached.

"Welcome back," the man said to Aurora.

"I thought you hadn't been here before."

"I haven't."

"Sure you have. I saw you the other day. Although you looked a little...different," said the employee.

"That wasn't me," Aurora insisted to me.

"Pardon?" said the man.

"She told you you're mistaken. Now bring us a whiskey no ice and a white wine."

The waiter took the hint and walked away.

"You know, John, this is a cocktail place. They make the best ones in town," said Aurora.

"And you'd know, right? From being here before."

"I don't appreciate your tone. Like I said, I've never been here."

"He mentioned you in a different style of clothes…" I said as I rubbed my chin, "…and I saw you the other day dressed like a librarian."

"What are you talking about? I didn't see you the other day. I would've said hello. And librarian clothing? I'd rather be dead than caught in old stuff like that." She rubbed the side of her head and took out a packet of painkillers.

"You sure they'll be okay to have with alcohol?"

"Yes, I'm sure, John! First you call me a liar and now you treat me like a child! You know what? I thought this would be a fun night, but I guess I was wrong." She stood up and headed for the door.

"Aurora come back."

"Don't bother following me," she said and slammed the door behind her. She had a lot of passion, but at times it meant a short fuse too.

"Your whiskey and wine sir." I gave the waiter a glare, downed the whiskey and left money on the table.

Instead of doing the sensible thing and going home, I told the driver to head over to O'Rourke's.

I impatiently pushed the door open and headed to sit at the bar.

"Hey John, how've you been?"

"Been better, Jimmy."

"Problems? What's on your mind?"

"I'll tell you what's on my mind when I have a whiskey in my mouth."

Pouring a whiskey, he left out the ice. "I've taught you well," I said, bringing the glass to my lips.

"Yeah, years of training led me to this point," he replied with a slight chuckle and turned to clean some glasses. "I've seen that look before."

"Really? And what's that?"

"What's her name?"

"Hey, I'm supposed to be the detective around here."

"I guess you coming here so much has rubbed off on me."

"It's nothing Jimmy. Don't worry about it."

"Wow, that bad, huh? She's really got a hold on you."

"Don't be ridiculous. You know I don't go heavy into things like this. Not since…"

"I'm just saying, I haven't seen you look like this in a long time."

"Would you give it a rest, Jimmy?! And pour me another drink. On second thought, leave the bottle."

"Never drink when thinking about a woman, man."

"I asked for the bottle. Not your opinion."

"Fine." He slammed the bottle onto the bar. "Take it to a table," he said and turned his back to me.

Halfway to the table I turned to apologise but he was serving another customer.

The bottle of whiskey went down quicker than I'd planned, and Jimmy's shift looked as if it was coming to an end. I walked over to apologise, but he headed into the back before I could reach him. *Fuck.*

I left the bar more irritated than when I entered and needed something positive to pick me back up. Time to see what was in that safe.

After stumbling up the stairs, I grabbed the tools from my office and headed to Mr. Choen's store. The keys didn't fit into the front door. In fact, they were so big they kept falling to the floor. After debating whether to use the crowbar to get inside, I came to my senses, wrong key. I shook my head, concentrated with the correct key, and went inside. I slurped the coffee I'd brought with me from the office and headed to the floor safe. *Time to be nice and precise.* Flashes of Danny, and Aurora leaving flashed in my mind, I smashed a hammer into the floor over and over. Breathing heavily, I pulled myself back and looked at the obliterated wood.

Piece by piece I placed the broken floorboards into the trash can. With a safe laying in front of me, I put my stethoscope on, placing the end piece onto the safe. I turned it left until...click, then right...*click*, left...*click* and finally right...*CLICK. Open sesame.*

The heavy old safe door creaked open and I dug my hands inside. I pulled out a photo and needles. There was also something buried deep, almost camouflaged in the bottom corner. A camera hard drive. *I didn't notice a camera in here. Where is it?* I looked around the office, along the bookcase, at the paintings on the wall, "Aha!" There it was. Disguised as a horse's eye, was a small camera lens. Question was, what was on it? With no laptop to plug this into, it would have to wait.

I turned over the photograph. *Mr. Choen's ex-wife? Why was he keeping a photo of that witch?* Onto the needle which I'd made sure not to put fingerprints on. Inside the glass there was a dot or two of fluid. *What was in there? Did you do something to yourself Mr. Choen?* There was only one way to find out more, and that was to send it off to a professional. Luckily enough I was his pet detective.

My head was still pounding from the whiskey as I drunk dialled Aurora, luckily, she didn't pick up.

In a taxi I fell asleep but woke when it came to a sudden stop outside my place. Time for some much-needed rest. As soon as I hit the pillow on my bed I was out for the count.

The next morning, I headed over to Mr. Johnson's house in Chelsea. The video footage found on the hard drive from Mr. Choen's store revealed his visit to the store wasn't a pleasant one. After three tubes and a twelve-minute walk I was there. I walked to the door and used the knocker. Ms Gonzales answered the door.

"Señor Banks. How may I help you?"

"I'm here to see Mr. Johnson. I have some more questions."

"I'm sorry, Señor, but Mr. Johnson told me to tell you he's in meetings all day."

"How convenient. How did he know I was coming?"

"Erm, he just told me to tell you when I saw you next, is all."

"Let him know I was here. Have a good day Ms. Gonzales."

I don't like having to wait, so I headed over to Mr. Johnson's work.

Pulling up at the tall glass building there was the man himself coming out the doors. I rushed over, "Mr. Johnson. Mr. Johnson." But he didn't appear to hear me. He got into his car driven by a chauffeur and left. *Where's a taxi when you need it?* I paced up and down. I wanted to chase this guy; the video put him high on the suspect list. *There!* "Taxi!"

I jumped in the taxi, "Follow that black car."

"Who do you think you are, 007?"

I threw money at him. "I said follow that car."

"Yes sir." And we pulled out onto the road.

Mr. Johnson's car was pulling further away, and our traffic light was on amber.

"We're going to lose them! Who taught you to drive, your grandmother?" The tires screeched and we sped through a red light, drifting around the corner.

"That better for you?! Better? You want it like this huh?!"

The guy was going crazy, but at least we were fast. We were gaining on them. I was getting close to Mr. Johnson's window and a red light was about to light up. The taxi driver hit the gas and we went through the lights, leaving Mr. Johnson behind.

"What are you doing?!"

"You said go fast."

"You went right past the other car!"

"What? No. There is the car there!" He pointed at another black car.

"You idiot. Do a U-turn."

"I can't do that, sir, it's illegal here."

"Do it!"

"Well…maybe I could. Oh shit. We're in a left turn only lane. We have to turn off."

"You're kidding me." But he wasn't. "Pull over, I'm getting out."

Mr. Johnson's car flashed by and there was no sign of another taxi. I would have to wait. In the meantime, there was another person I wanted to talk to again, Danny Choen.

As I headed down into the tube station my footsteps echoed against the wall and the case echoed in my mind.

As I reached my front door and put the key into the door, my phone vibrated. I pulled it out of my pocket, and the screen lit up. Charlie had sent me a dog emoji and a question mark. *Don't people use words anymore?* Tapping the screen, I wrote, *I'm on it,* pulled my key out of the door and headed to my car. I turned the keys and revved the engine. It was time to pay Charlie's neighbours a visit.

By the time I arrived at Charlie's, I needed a cigar, but not as bad as I needed a piss. I slammed his front door shut and headed up the stairs. As I was about to reach the bathroom, I spotted something out the corner of my eye. I turned and looked out of the window. Charlie's neighbour coming out of his shed. *Wait. What was that in the shed?* I thought, but before I could squint my eyes to look closer, he shut the door. *Hmm…* I scratched my head and then realised I still needed the toilet.

After I left the bathroom, I headed back to the window and looked for the neighbour, but to no avail. *I guess I know whose door I'm knocking on first,* I thought to myself and headed down the stairs.

Standing at the front door of Charlie's number one suspect, I looked around for anything of interest. There were rose bushes and an acer tree in the front garden, and a pristine lawn. There was nothing left out from days gone by, no mess, nothing. I turned back to the door, reached up to the chrome door knocker and tapped the door with it three times.

As the door began to open, I didn't know what to expect. Charlie felt so strongly about this man, but was it all in his head.

"Can I help you?" A woman with long straight black hair asked me.

"I certainly hope so," I said with a smile and she smiled back. The sound of footsteps echoed behind her rapidly, her husband I guessed. A man in his early fifties gave her a look, to which she lowered her head and walked away.

"May I help you?" he asked me with a smile. There were no scars or wrinkles on this man. He was clean shaved, smooth skinned, and had jet black hair. *What's this guy's secret?* I thought, running my thumb over my cheek. "Hello?"

"Sorry, yes. Name's John," I said, not wanting to reveal my detective status yet. "And you are?"

"Mr. Gunderson, Paul."

"Well, Paul. I don't know if you've heard about Mr. Dalston's dog."

"Oh no, nothing bad I hope," he said with a tilted head.

"Unfortunately, it is. His dog died and I'm looking into the matter."

"That's awful news. I'll have to send him a sympathy card."

This guy looked genuinely concerned, and had a pleasant aura about him. *What was Charlie seeing in him?*

"Have you seen anything strange lately?"

"Like what?" he said, leaning towards me.

"Someone going into Mr. Dalston's garden unannounced. Anybody treating the dog poorly. Anything like that."

"Hmm, let me think. Well I know the postman doesn't care too much for the dog. Who can blame him, it chases him every chance it gets? I once saw him walking off with shorts ripped to shreds," he said, and chuckled.

"I see. Anything else?"

"Not that I can think of, I'm afraid. When I'm outside, my garden gets all my attention. My wife thinks I love it more than her." He laughed and patted me on my shoulder. *He's strong.* "I could just stand here talking all day, but unfortunately I have things to take care of in the house. You understand."

"I do. Thank you for your help sir."

"If you ever need anything don't hesitate to knock."

I gave him a nod, turned away and walked down the pathway. I walked towards the house on the opposite side of Charlie's. There, three cats hovered outside the front door. They were loud too; so loud in fact they sounded like they were right next to m— "Achoo!" I looked down and discovered a ginger cat rubbing against my leg. As I nudged the cat away with my boot, a woman came out of the house.

"Excu—achoo. Excuse—achoo me," I shouted over at her. She turned towards me, but looked at her watch right after. Hurrying over, I tried to hold in the sneezes.

"Can I help you?" The short brunette-haired woman asked.

"I'm here ab—Achoo, about—Achoo!"

"You're here about...?" she said, tapping her foot.

"Ab—ab—about—ACHOO!" Mucus flew everywhere.

"Look I'm in a hurry," she said, patting her coat, "Take my card and call me when you manage to stop sneezing."

I nodded, "Achoo!"

She got into her car and drove off. After getting away from the cats as quickly as possible, I headed for Charlie's bathroom. While scrubbing my hand, face, arms and then blowing my nose, I cursed myself for how I was in front of the woman. "Damn allergies."

Once I was back to normal, I checked out the card the neighbour had given me. Grace Bishop, manager at a cattery. *Does she do the same at home, or simply a crazy cat lady, I wonder...* I chuckled to myself. I called the number on the card, but it went straight to voicemail... I tried a few more times but got the same result. *I have more important things to take care of, screw this, I'm going to her house,* I thought in frustration. On an average day, I would have more patience. Right now, however, finding my father figure's killer outweighed everything.

Going through Miss Bishop's front door would be too public. With Mr. Gunderson busy in his house, I reckoned I'd be safe jumping over her back fence, and so that's where I headed.

Charlie's backdoor squealed like a cat hung from its tale. "At least I'll know if Mr. Gunderson is paying attention to outside or not," I said, shaking my head. I edged towards Miss Bishop's fence and looked over my shoulder for any signs of Mr. Gunderson. The coast was clear. All I had to think about was how to get over the fence which was surprisingly tall. No ladder or a box in sight. I rubbed my chin trying to think and then remembered

Charlie had some wheelie bins round the side. I rolled one over to the fence and raised my foot up on top. As I put my other foot up, the bin slipped, and I crashed to the floor. The back of my head was wet, but I saw no puddles, no water... I reached back and touched the wet spot on my head. When I drew my hand back, blood covered my fingertips. I took a photo of the back of my head with my phone. No stitches required. I rinsed the back of my head with the hose and headed back to the bin.

With the bin upright and with more caution, I got on top of the bin. Miss Bishop's garden had mice corpses everywhere. Some toys, many not... I climbed onto the fence and lowered myself down, trying to avoid the dead. Once on the ground, I headed for the shed. There was no lock on the door and after looking over my shoulder towards Mr. Gunderson's house I went inside. I just about fit inside and then discovered it was filled to the roof with cat food and cat litter. "Jesus, how many cats does this woman have?" I left the shed and walked towards the back door, dodging cat mess along the way. Standing outside the door, I dug out my lock picking tools and within seconds the door was open. A sudden rush of bad smells smacked me in the face and crawled up my nostrils. "Jesus..." I exclaimed, holding back my body's urge to vomit. *Maybe she's got other dead dogs in here...* As I braved the stench and headed inside it became clear what was wrong inside.

Newspaper skyscrapers, empty food packets, clothes and more filled the room. She was a hoarder. Cat litter boxes were everywhere where there was a space to put one, but there wasn't an air freshener in sight. "Achoo." As I walked through the kitchen, loud scratching noises echoed around. "Where the hell is that coming from?" My senses where overloaded with the stench and sight of this hoarding city. *What was that?* I turned left and right.

With no sign of anything around me, I continued on, squeezing between stacks of newspapers. *No dead dogs...yet. "Achoo."* After a while of walking around, I couldn't recognise which room I was in. A living room? Dining room? I could've been anywhere. A deep growling noise echoed around the paper towers, *where are you cat?* There were no clues, no evidence, only a pissed off cat hunting me down. I was on his turf and didn't know the lay of the land. I closed my eyes and took deep breaths. "Where are you cat?" I focused my hearing. The cat growled again; it was coming from the corner of the house. I eased my way around a corner of newspapers, "JESUS FUCK C..." I yelled as a cat ran past my ankle. I turned around as it ran between paper stacks and out of site. *Hopefully, that's the last I'll be seeing of—wait. What was that?* I turned and lifted my head to discover a cat on top of a paper tower which was crumbling down towards me. The cat jumped off and before I could move the tower smacked my head and the rest of me to the floor.

"Where am I?!" I said as I woke up, disorientated. I took a deep breath through my nose and threw up. I remembered where I was, Hoarder Hell, where an evil cat was the mayor. *How long was I knocked out for? Has she come home? I need to get these papers off me and get the hell out of here.* The papers were heavier than I thought and as I tried to move them again, someone put keys into the front door. "Shit". I looked for something to grab, anything. By some miracle I found the leg of a piece of furniture and grabbed onto it. The door creaked open, "Fuck, come on..." Lying on my stomach, I pulled myself forward. *Gotta be quick, be quick.*

"Hello, my babies," Miss Bishop said in the distance.

My upper body was out from under the pile of newspapers and with a couple final tugs I was free. *Time to get the hell outta here.*

I crept towards the back door. As I shut the door Miss Bishop said, "Mr. Huffington, have you been knocking over the papers again?" *Yeah that psycho cat tried to kill me, lady,* I thought to myself and headed to the fence. It was dark outside and as I went to climb, God's sense of humour kicked in. I put a foot forward and stood in cat shit. I clenched my fist, stood on a chair, and grabbed the top of the fence. I hurdled myself over and landed in Charlie's garden. I washed the bottom of my boot with the hose, *I'm never getting a cat, EVER.*

Someone shouted in the distance, "Is that coming from Mr. Gunderson's house?" As I peered over the fence and looked through a window, Mr. Gunderson was there, standing in front of his wife. He looked right at me and quickly closed the curtains. Mr. Gunderson spoke loudly, but it was hard to make out. "I'm sorry!" Mrs Gunderson shouted. *Couples argue, could be a normal fight, or is it something worse.* I took in a deep breath and realised how bad I smelled. I needed to get home and take a much-needed shower. With a last look over at Mr. Gunderson's house, I headed for my car and went home.

The following morning, I rolled over and hit the alarm clock, but it wasn't making a sound. When I looked at it, I realised why. I'd slept in and it was now three pm. I jumped up and got dressed in a hurry. I walked to a nearby café that served an all-day breakfast and authentic Italian coffee.

As the afternoon turned into evening and with my stomach satisfied, I knew where I needed to go next.

I try to avoid the police station as much as possible these days. Too many enemies inside and bad memories. A place that once felt like my home, was now a place I never wanted to be. But I wanted to see Danny Choen and that's where I'd left him.

It didn't take too long to get in front of Danny. I'd worked hard as a policeman and made friends with a few decent people there. As a result, they were happy to help an old friend.

"So, Danny, have you enjoyed your new home? It's not the Ritz I'll give you that, but home is where you lay your hat right?" He didn't reply. "I've got the best people helping me on this case and you gave me all the evidence I needed last time I saw you. You might as well confess and who knows someone might throw you a bone, for your honesty."

"I ain't done nothin'," he mumbled.

"I'm sorry, I couldn't hear that. Did you say, you're guilty?"

"I said I ain't done NOTHING!"

"There he is. There's the real Danny." I gave him a grin. "Those tests of the pills are going to come back any second and—" My phone rang. "Just the call I've been waiting for."

"Banks, I've got the results back on those white pills." I smiled at Danny as my contact continued to talk. "Turns out they're to treat heart disease. I ch-checked the records and both Mr. Choen and Danny have it. It's hereditary."

"You're shitting me?" I said, brushing a hand through my hair, "Could they have been used to kill Mr. Choen?"

"It would be highly unlikely. I don't think this is your g-guy."

"Thanks Charlie," I said, rubbing a hand over my forehead.

"Bad news John?" Danny grinned. Bastard looked like he'd slept with a coat hanger in his mouth.

"You're still in here for attempting to murder me punk. How do you like them apples?" I stood and left the room, slamming the door on the way out. There was no evidence of Danny killing his father, nothing placing him at the scene of the crime. He was more pissed at me than his father. His name just went to the bottom of the list. *Fuck.*

The lights of a bar beckoned me to go inside and I was happy to oblige. As I slammed the door open, the hinges almost flew off. I thought I was going to walk out of that station knowing I'd caught the killer. Instead, I felt like someone had kicked me in the balls.

"Whiskey, no ice." I told the bartender.

The bar had white walls, white floors, and black furniture. It was like being at a funeral, but with a lot of booze. *Someone should call the decorator and have him shot.*

Sipping on the whiskey, I thought about what Jimmy said. Was he right about Aurora? Was I falling for her? After a stressful day, all I could think about was calling her. Not for her body, but just to spend time with her, be around her. I had to speak to her and later apologise to Jimmy.

On the way over to Aurora's I made a couple of stops. It's the extra touches that count. As I leaned forward to knock on her door, the wind blew the red rose out of my hand. I caught it and pulled it tight against the box of premium thin cigars. I ignored the pain from the rose thorn I'd inserted into my skin and knocked on the door.

"What do you want?" was Aurora's greeting.

"I've come to apologise," I said, and she shut the door. I rubbed my forehead and then leaned it against the door which to my surprise slowly opened.

By the time I went inside and closed the door, Aurora was already in her kitchen pouring a drink.

"Can I have one of those?"

"Help yourself John," she said, avoiding eye contact.

Sitting on the couch, she looked stunning. Her hair flowed like a river down over her shoulders. Her skin was as white as snow and as I sat, her eyes hypnotised me. *Keep it together John*, I told myself. "Aurora listen—"

"No, you listen, John. I want to apologise."

"You? But—"

"Please, let me finish. I…overreacted when we last spoke. It just grinds my gears when someone calls me a liar or tries to tell me what to do. And also…I think it's because it came from you. You mean…a lot to me. And I don't want you to run a mile when I say—"

I placed my hands on her shoulders and looked her in the eyes. "I feel the same way." I pulled her close and kissed her lips tenderly. Afterwards, I held her in my arms and stroked her hair. She sat up, "Where are you going?" I asked.

"It's time to open the good stuff," she said, picking up the glasses from the table.

As she left for the kitchen, I discovered something poking out from the side of a cushion. I pulled it out of the sofa. It was a receipt for Botox. *The things people do to look young.* At the bottom of the page the signature belonged to a Mia Jones. *Aurora doesn't have any housemates… Why would she sign Mia? It's probably nothing, and I don't want to mess this night up.*

"What you got there?" Aurora asked. I shoved the paper back into the couch, while knocking over a bottle of pills.

"I'm sorry, I—"

"John relax. They're just pills for my headaches."

"Still getting them?"

"Unfortunately, oui," she answered in a French accent.

What is with these accents? Too many hours of international TV? She leaned forward and gave me a deep kiss. The glasses in her hands fell, splashing whiskey everywhere, and our bodies entangled. That night we didn't have sex, we made love.

In bed I tossed and turned. I couldn't shake the thought that Mr. Gunderson might be abusing his wife. Unable to sleep, I got dressed and went outside to have a smoke. The crisp air grabbed hold of me as I inhaled smoke from the cigar. As the smoke swayed in the air, I thought about how I would rather it be Aurora who was grabbing hold of me. I knew however, there was only once place I was going, to Mr. Gunderson's house. I left Aurora a note and headed home to get my car.

Driving at that time of night was peaceful. There were no people in a rush, nobody beeping their horns, in fact there were few cars on the road at all. After a short drive I pulled into Charlie's driveway. Charlie's car was parked in front of his house as well as his neighbours parked in front of theirs. It was a full house tonight.

I didn't want to wake Charlie with regards to Mr. Gunderson. This was more of a hunch than anything solid to report. The gate at the side of Charlie's house was still unlocked and as the rain poured down my face, I walked to the garden. I didn't know what I expected to find. Mr. and Mrs Gunderson were most likely sleeping, but I wanted to investigate, and I wanted to do it there and then. I grabbed hold of Charlie's not so trusty wheelie bin and dragged it over to Mr. Gunderson's fence. Having already fallen victim to the bin's unsteadiness, the rain poured down, adding to the fun. I decided I needed to find something extra to help with a secure jump over the fence. Looking round the garden, I found huge dog toys and balls. I wedged some balls and chew toys underneath each side of the bin. I shook the bin to test its stability, I was good to go. With one leg over the fence, my cast resting on the edge, I looked at Mr. Gunderson's windows but there was nobody there. I swung my other leg over and jumped down, right on top of a gnome, which sent me flying onto my back. It was dark around me with the only light coming from the window. I winced as I stood up and put weight on my foot.

But that wasn't my main problem. The motion lights came on in full beam. Mr. Gunderson's bedroom light came on as I scrambled towards the shed. As I approached it, the hall light came on. I threw myself into the shed and pulled the door shut, as noises from the backdoor got louder. I peered through a crack in the shed. Mrs Gunderson being edged out of the kitchen by her husband, *Classy...* As she stepped into the light and looked around, a dark bruise could be seen circling her eye.

"Oh no," she mumbled.

"What? What is it?"

"Well, um…"

"Spit it out."

"Well, um…"

"Don't make me come out there Elaine."

"One of your gnomes is broken…"

"What?! That fucking bastard. Hasn't he learned his lesson already?"

Mrs Gunderson shrugged her little shoulders and walked to him. As she reached the kitchen door she said, "Sorry about your gnome." But something was wrong. Mr. Gunderson got angry and shoved her down onto the kitchen floor and slammed the door. Then it hit me, she smiled after saying that. It must've slipped out. Next things to slip out were gonna be my fists, right out of my jacket and into that wife beater's face. As I went to stand, there was a crunch. Looking down, I feared it was my ankle after my leap into the shed, but I smiled when I saw it was a broken dog bone treat. *Why would he have dog treats? He doesn't have a dog and Charlie said he hated his one.* I looked around, close to the bones, for anything suspicious and discovered a sack of rat poison. Looking back at the bones, I could see some were hollow, others…were filled in with the rat poison. *I guess Charlie was right about him. This wife beater is going to taste my fist and then smell the inside of a jail cell.* "I'm coming for you Mr. Gunderson," I said and kicked the shed door open.

The floodlights shone through the rain and onto me. As I paced towards the house, the kitchen door opened and Mrs Gunderson was flung outside. She was startled when she saw me, but I just moved her to the side and picked up the pace.

"What the f—" Mr. Gunderson said, then received my fist to his jaw sending a loud crunching sound echoing around the garden.

"So, you like to beat women, do you?" I said as he fell to the ground. I grabbed him by his clothes and dragged him to his feet. "People like you make me sick," I exclaimed and crashed my head into his, sending him spiralling to the ground. My chest puffed in and out as I stood over him. I raised my boot above his head when—

"No! Please don't." Mrs Gunderson pleaded from behind. "He's a good man."

I blinked rapidly, "This man beats you and is treating you like shit."

"I know but...the man I married is still inside there." She kneeled next to him and stroked his hair.

"No woman should ever have to put up with this Mrs Gunderson."

"I know..." she said, looking to the ground.

I put my hands under each of his arms and dragged him up onto a chair. "I still have questions for you, arsehole. She might love you, but I don't."

Mr. Gunderson wiped blood from under his nose and attempted to talk. "What, Ow. What, Ow!"

"That's what happens when someone busts your jaw. Hurts doesn't it?" I said with a grin. "We can get back to your cowardly wife beating later, but I have something else I want to talk to you about." Mr. Gunderson raised an eyebrow. "Earlier on I asked you about Mr. Dalston's dog and you seemed genuinely upset. I found this a little odd as Mr. Dalston pointed you out as the lead suspect for the killing. Maybe he'd got it wrong, a bit paranoid. A few things like this crossed my mind. I came here tonight to find out how far you were going with your wife, but stumbled upon something rather interesting in your shed."

Mr. Gunderson turned away. "No no no no, over here Mr. Gunderson." I grabbed his chin and as he winced, I brought it forward to face me. "I saw how you reacted tonight after finding a broken gnome. When Mr. Dalston broke one however, he told me you appeared perfectly fine. Kinda odd, don't you think?" Mr. Gunderson didn't say a word, but just glared at me. "Don't worry," I said, staring into his eyes. "The feeling's mutual. So, Mr. Dalston breaks one of your little gnomes, which to be honest I don't see the fascination with. They look like children would play with them. Actually, scratch that, even children wouldn't want those awful things. I guess if you're okay with Charlie breaking one, you won't mind me br—"

"Do and I'll kill you too!" he yelled then held his jaw as he winced in pain.

"Welcome to the room, killer. You love those freaky gnomes, so you killed something Mr. Dalston loved, didn't you?" Mr. Gunderson leapt forward right into my face, but didn't say a word. I looked him up and down.

"Well, if you won't talk after receiving a broken jaw, I'll just ask one of your gnomes. Now which one looks the most expensive...Gotcha!" I walked towards a gnome by an acer tree—

"I killed that fuckin' dog! Now get the fuck away from my gnome," he yelled, then screamed with the pain in his jaw.

I grabbed his wrists and handcuffed him to the pipe on the outside of his house. Taking my phone out I called Frank at the police station. "I've got a wife beater here, who's confessed to killing his neighbour's dog. Can you send someone out?" As Frank confirmed he could and the call ended, I raised my boot and crushed the gnome into a hundred pieces.

"NO!" Mr. Gunderson screamed.

I smiled and under the shelter of a tree, I pulled out a cigar and lit it up. Cigars always taste sweeter when catching a bad guy and the look on his face made it even better.

It didn't take long for the police to come and take Mr. Gunderson away. Once he was gone, I drove back to Aurora's, put the note I'd laid out into the trash and held her in the bed. When I awoke in the morning, the aroma of whiskey washed over my face. The bottle stood on the bedside table, the lid nowhere to be seen. Aurora laid there sleeping. I brushed her hair behind her ear and kissed her softly on her cheek. She smiled and went back to sleep.

I had learned from Ms. Gonzales that Mr. Johnson usually goes for a run at 7am and leaves for work at 8:15am. I looked at the clock, 7:45am. This gave me just enough time to get over there before he left.

Fine rain sprayed onto my face as I approached his home. I wiped water from my eyes as Mr. Johnson was closing his front door.

"Mr. Johnson," I shouted over.

He glanced at me and hurried down the stairs.

"We need to talk Mr. Johnson."

"And I need to go to work so if you don't mind."

"I'm afraid I do," I said, standing in front of him. "This won't take long." I placed my hand on his shoulder and turned him towards the front door.

Inside, I brushed the hair away from my eyes and hung my coat. Mr. Johnson paced in the living room/office with a lit cigarette in his hand.

"I don't know why I should talk to you. You can't keep me in my own home," he said as he walked to the bay widow.

"Nice place you got here," I said, trying to make him feel more at ease. "Elephant tusks. Are they real?"

"Yes. They were a gift. Do you like to hunt Detective? I do." He turned towards me.

"Actually, I'm plant based."

"One of *those* people..."

I gritted my teeth, "We're getting off topic Mr. Johnson. I'm here because I saw a very interesting video from Mr. Choen's store's security camera."

He stared at his hands and fiddled with his fingers.

"Did you hear me Mr. Johnson?"

"Yes. I fail to see what that has to do with me," he replied, scratching the back of his head.

"It has to do with *you* assho—" I took a breath. "It has to do with you because from this footage it would appear you weren't too happy with Mr. Choen. This is despite you telling me earlier that all was good between you two. It has to do with you because Mr. Choen happens to be someone very important to me. I don't take kindly to people who threaten people I care about."

"I never threatened Mr. Choen!"

"Sure, you did. And it looks to me that you were so angry you could *kill*. In fact, before the footage cut out, it looked as if Mr. Choen was going for the phone. To call the police maybe?" I said and stepped in close to him.

Mr. Johnson clenched his fists, which revealed bruises and broken skin on his knuckles.

"Been fighting Mr. Johnson? After say, a disagreement?"

"What? No."

"Then what's with the knuckles?"

He tucked them away and then looked at me, "I do martial arts. Keeps me focused."

"And you can prove that can you?"

"Call my shifu anytime," he said as I strolled around his office.

"You smoke cigars too?" I said, noticing a box on his desk.

"Actuall—"

"What the...?" I said as I opened the box and revealed needles. The same kind of needles that were in Mr. Choen's safe. "What are these for? If you don't mind me asking."

"What? Oh, they're for, my, my—"

"Spit it out."

"My speech slows when I'm, I'm stressed okay?!" He rubbed his left arm up and down. "They're for my diabetes. H-had it all my life."

"Hmm...likely story." I placed one of the needles into a clear bag and then into my pocket. "So, Mr. Johnson. If you're so innocent, can you tell me why you were shouting at Mr. Choen."

"No."

"Tell me, *now*."

"No."

"Fucking tell me!" I shoved my forearm into his throat.

"I can't. I can't."

"You can and will!"

"I mean...I...can't...bre...breathe."

I let him go. "I can do a lot worse." I moved towards him.

"Please no!"

"Then talk."

"I can't!" He stumbled backwards and fell to the floor. "It would ruin me."

"And what do you think I'll do to you?"

He looked left and right, there was no escape route.

"How much?"

"Excuse me?"

"How much will it take to make this all go away?"

I grabbed him by his suit jacket and shoved him up high against the wall. "I'm not some whore you can just pay so you can do what you want. Time to say goodnight prince." I raised my cast.

"NO! I'll talk! I'll talk! I was arguing with him because, because…"

"Why?!" I yelled, bringing his face inches from mine.

"Because I'm having an affair! Alright?! Perfect Mr. Choen caught me kissing Ms González in the store and told me about it during a late-night watch repair he'd arranged. Said I needed to confess. Told me he wouldn't lie to my wife, who enjoys visiting his store. I wrote him a cheque, but he tore it up and threw it in the trash," his chest puffed in and out. "I can't lose everything and him tearing that cheque got me…it got me mad. I threw my pen against the wall, clenched my fists but as I got closer to him, I pulled myself back. I may be a cheat Mr. Banks, but I'm not a killer. Do any test you want; I'll even go to the police station to make statements."

I released him from my grip and glared deep into his eyes. He blinked several times and with his shaking hands, adjusted his tie.

"I'm going to have this needle tested Mr. Johnson, and I want you to go down to the station. Ask for Frank O'Donovan, tell him I sent you. If I find out you haven't made the journey, I will come after you. I will find you, and I will make today look like a stroll through the park. Are we clear?"

"C-clear," he said, adjusting his clothes.

Affairs can make people desperate. Desperate enough to kill? Sometimes. This guy might be a slimeball, but his aura didn't scream killer. *Hmm...*I decided to leave without Mr. Johnson in cuffs. I would, however, be checking those needle results and would talk to Frank later on.

Flickers of rain bounced around my eyes as the wind blew in every direction. I pulled up the collar on my coat and started to walk. It had been a hectic morning and my body itched all over. It had been a while since I'd had a cigar and patting my pockets, I found nothing. Fortunately, a fresh box lay in my office and so I'd found my next destination.

On my way to the office the heavens opened for business and the rain crashed down hard. The wind had too, resulting in the death of my umbrella. As I opened my office door, I shook my head, flicking water onto the floor. I hung my coat over the back of a chair and placed it near the fireplace. I struck a match and allowed myself to get lost in the smoke from the cigar. I needed to empty my thoughts and just...*be.* I closed my eyes.

"I am at peace. Everything is going the way it's supposed to." *And breathe...1, 2, 3.* After a while my body started to shiver. It was reminding me that I was still cold and wet. I threw logs on the fire and soon there was a nice warmth coming towards me. I lit another cigar and blew smoke rings into the air. The final ring landed on the grandfather clock next to the fire. I caught a glimpse of myself. "I'm going to catch the killer Mr. Choen," I said, imagining it was him who was sitting in the chair looking at me in the clock.

There was one person I hadn't paid a visit to yet. I was dreading it. Last time our paths crossed things didn't end too well. The person I'm talking about...Mr. Choen's ex-wife.

Five years after his wife's death, Mr. Choen met a woman. She was ten years younger than him and was keen on him from the start. Her name was Rebecca Crawler. She worked at a convenience store stacking shelves. Mr. Choen, one day while in her store, knocked a tin of beans onto the floor. She picked it up for him and things developed from there. I believe she preyed on his kindness and was after his money. He wasn't rich but was a lot better off than she was, stacking shelves for a living. He wasn't a fool, but she was good at acting, *real* good. When I brought all this up with Mr. Choen, well...he didn't want to hear it. I even photographed her kissing another man once. When I tried to present the photos to Mr. Choen, he threw me out of the store and told me to never come back. I was in a dark place for a while after that. And after weeks of trying to get back in touch with him and failing, those weeks soon turned into months, and months into years. Now divorced and back to her old lifestyle, did Rebecca have motive for killing him? You're damn right she did.

After getting through the traffic jam from hell, I arrived outside of Rebecca's bungalow. I parked on the opposite side of the road, took the key out of the ignition, and searched for matches. *Not today God, not to-fuckin' day.* "Where are you, you little bastards?"

After what felt like the longest two minutes of my life, I finally found the matches. *I need to have an official place for these.*

"Finally..." I said as smoke flowed over my tongue and out of my mouth. The windows remained closed. I wanted all the smoke I could get right now. As the fog massaged my body and cleared my mind, I said a mantra in my head. *Good things come to those who tackle their emotions. Good things come to those who tackle their emotions.*

The car door handle clicked as I opened it, then pushed it against the strong wind. The clouds had darkened, and the trees swayed side to side, like an unsettled child. As I crossed the road a drop of rain hit my cheek and dove to the ground.

I stood outside Rebecca's door.

Knock, knock, knock…

Knock, knock, knock… no answer.

"Doesn't anybody stay home anymore?" I said and glanced over at the window. The curtains were open.

With hands cupped against the window, I looked inside. No sign of Rebecca, which I was almost grateful for. A wine glass left on the table, *is she in or too lazy to put it away? What else? What else? Wait. Is that? What is that doing the—*

"Wanna tell me what the fuck you're doing?" a voice said.

I turned, putting a smile on, "Rebecca. It's nice to see you too." This received a glare. "I was checking if you were in. Can we have a word?" I asked as the rain started to come down hard.

"No. I'm busy."

"Doing what?"

"That's none of your fucking business, John." She hadn't lost her charm.

"What, no, how are you?" No reply, she just put her key into the door. "Come on Rebecca, you're not gonna leave me out in the rain are ya?"

"That's the plan, asshole," she turned the key and opened the door. "Have fun in hell." She started to shut the door, but when it didn't close, she looked back confused and then discovered my foot was wedged in the way.

"I'm not here to fight. We need to talk about Mr. Choen. You know he's dead, right?"

She nodded, left the door, and headed inside.

I stepped inside; my body gave a shiver down my spine. I slipped off my jacket and hung it near the front door. Above the coats was a photo of Rebecca, with a new, older man and a calendar to the side of it. *July 12th Trip to Bahamas,* it read.

"I thought you said you wanted to talk," Rebecca said from the living room.

The smell of cat darted up my nose as I went to sit on the sofa, then when I turned around there it was. A black cat lay on top of a bookshelf staring at me. *Like owner, Like...cat.*

My nose itched just looking back at that cat. "Thanks for letting me in, Rebecca. Achoo!"

"I need a drink. You in?"

"Sure," I said, taking in a deep breath.

Handing me a glass of red wine, Rebecca stared at me as if to say, 'let's get this over with'.

"So, you're aware Mr. Choen died recently?"

"Yep. Dick got what he deserved."

I broke the stem of the glass, digging it into my thumb.

Managing to keep the glass from falling I replied, "You fu—"

"What was that John? I couldn't hear you. Too much bullshit in that mouth of yours?" She grinned and took a sip of her wine.

"Let's get straight to it. Where were you on the night of June 8th?"

"You're kidding me? You're accusing me of killing that prick?"

"Well you're obviously not a fan," I said, blood dripping onto her white carpet. A small justice.

"Doesn't mean I'd waste my time killing that old fool."

"I thought you "loved" old fools. Seems you've got a new one, if that photo is anything to go by." It was my turn to grin, and she was a little lost for words. "Allow me to continue. A little bird told me you didn't get too much from the divorce except for this place. You wanted more, much more. Can't go on fancy holidays to let's say…the Bahamas with the lack of money Mr. Choen left you. Maybe you knew exactly where he left sums of money. A safe in the floor perhaps? Or did you just kill him for revenge and take a souvenir?" I pointed towards one of Mr. Choen's favourite clocks that was now on her mantelpiece."

"That clock, was a gift. We'd talked on the phone and it didn't end well. That was his apology."

"You two don't speak for a year, have one conversation and he gives you his favourite clock? Sounds a bit odd, don't ya think?"

"I don't have to *think* anything. He gave me this clock and that's that. When that loser died, I was buying wine round the corner and drank it here."

"With your new, I mean *old* lover?"

"No. I've answered your questions, now fuck off outta my house before I call the *real* police."

I stood and then collected my coat in the hall. Before leaving, I turned and said, "Don't go leaving town anytime soon Rebecca." To which I received the middle finger.

The front door slammed behind me and the heaven's opened in front of me. I ran across the road and jumped into my car, but still managed to get soaking wet. I threw my phone onto the passenger seat, it lit up. After unlocking the phone with difficulty due to my wet hands, I discovered it was a video message from Aurora. After pressing play, I looked over my shoulder to make sure no one else was looking. The video showed Aurora from behind taking her bra off. She held it to the side of her, dropped it to the floor and then, "Shit! Mother fucking piece of shit!" My phone died. I turned the key in the ignition and sped off down the road, creating a tidal wave to the side of the car. *Where can I get a car phone charger?*

I pulled my pocket watch out and checked the time. 7:54pm. After driving for what felt like an age, I slammed the breaks after spotting a store. I got to the front door just as a man turned over the sign to CLOSED.

"Come on!" I said, banging on the door. "I'll make it worth your while." But as he turned, light bounced off wireless headphones in his ears. "Fuck." I paced in front of the door for a while and then took out a cigar.

With every attempt, the cigar failed to light and when I tried in the car, the cigar was too wet. After cursing all the names under the sun, I turned the key in the ignition and headed for a nearby bar.

Inside and soaked, I walked up to the bar and sat on a stool. "Whiskey, no ice and do you have a Samsung phone charger?"

"Yeah, somewhere... Let me get you that drink first."

The barman placed the drink in front of me and took my phone. The only thing distracting my mind from Aurora's video was thoughts of that bitch Rebecca. Mr. Choen was a great man and she spoke of him like he was shit on the bottom of her shoe. I knew I was right about her all those years ago, but at the time I'd wished I was wrong.

Like any "son" I wanted my "father" to be happy. However, he ended up with the wicked witch of the west and lost me in the process.

After finishing the whiskey, I headed for the toilets. Turned out they hadn't cleaned in there for a while. It smelled like someone was dead on the toilet or giving birth to a giant turd baby. I finished as quick as I could while hoping there was enough charge in my phone.

"Can I check my phone?" I said before I'd even sat on a stool.

"It's still only like, 3%. Maybe finish your drink first?"

I puffed out a long breath, "Fine."

I focused on my breathing and sipped some whiskey. After allowing my mind to wander, drifting into the air, I started to think of my memories with Mr. Choen...I hummed a tune and thought about the time Mr. Choen took me to the fayre. He took me on every ride, let me eat everything I wanted until I almost vomited...

"Sir?"

"What?" I said, and came down from my daydream.

"Your phone. It's at 50%."

50%? Wait, how long has it been?"

"Sorry sir, it's been about an hour. It got busy in here all of a sudden," he said and passed me my phone.

I gave him a nod and smile to say thanks.

"Messages, messages." I whispered to myself. "Gotcha." I clicked on the message, pressed play and... *unable to play file.* "What?"

"Oh man, I hate it when that happens. Was it anything good?" the barman asked and received a glare from me as to say, 'what the fuck do you think you're doing?' He understood and pretended to dry some glasses on the other side of the bar. Another message came through. Just a text.

I guess you didn't like my offer and it's getting late...

I hammered a reply, almost cracking the screen.

Phone been a pain in the... I can come over now.

I waited for what felt like an hour but was probably only a minute.

Sure John, but I'm still tired and have a busy day tomorrow... Wine on the sofa and then bed sound good?

It was, although I wished I had been able to take up that offer in the video.

Sounds great. I'll be there in 10.

As the engine came to a halt outside Aurora's place, I searched in the car for cologne. This was usually used when I was meeting higher up clientele. Aurora, well, she was in a class of her own.

Heading up the steps the wind blew my hair all out of place. While I attempted to fix it, Aurora looked at me through the bay window. I smiled, covering my embarrassment at being caught.

"Looks like a tornado ran right through you," she said, opening the door.

"Umm, ye—"

"I think it's cute. Get in here," she said, pulling me in by my jacket.

As we walked towards the couch, a glass of whiskey was already waiting for me on the glass coffee table. *She knows me already.*

"I know I said wine, but I know how much my dragon likes his whiskey," she said, sitting down and tucking her legs to one side.

"Allow me to pour you a wine, madam," I winked.

"Mr. Banks, you are spoiling me," she said with a cute giggle.

As I sat down, she snook underneath my arm, resting it behind her neck. "Tell me something about you, John. Something more… I know! Tell me about your childhood."

"Well, for as long as I can remember, I loved the police. My grandfather was the chief of police and sometimes allowed me to ride around in his police car. He was a great man." I paused.

"You okay?"

"Yeah. Just…haven't talked about him in a long time. You would've liked him," I said and managed a smile.

"If he's anything like you, I'm sure I would. I'll have to thank him in my prayers for inspiring you to be you." She put down the wine and wrapped an arm around me.

"What about y—" she'd already fallen asleep. *Rest easy my sweet*, I thought and carried her into the bedroom.

★ ★ ★

The next morning, I was awoken by thin branches banging against the bedroom window. Pulling out the pocket watch from my jacket on the chair, I cursed the Gods, *five am*. Eyes still closed, Aurora rolled over towards me, "I'll keep you warm. Come here," she whispered, to which I gladly obliged.

"John? John?" an angel said. "John! It's eight o'clock. I've gotta get going in a minute."

I opened my eyes to a lovely smile from Aurora.

"There you are. I've got something for you."

"For me?" I sat up.

"Close your eyes," she said, and I did. She placed something soft into my hands. "Okay, open them!"

It was a black scarf, thick and crisscrossed. "This looks great," I said and gave her a kiss.

"I didn't want my dragon getting cold in the stormy weather," she smiled.

"When did you learn to knit?"

"Umm last night I guess."

"You guess?"

"Yeah, I was watching TV and next thing I knew I was finishing a scarf. My first ever."

"Don't you think that's a bit strange?"

"Nah, I'm super talented. Didn't I tell you? I pick up things, just like that," she said, snapping her fingers.

"Hmm, I'll take your word for it," I said and gave her another kiss. Out the corner of my eye I spotted gothic clothing in her wardrobe. "I didn't know you liked those sorts of clothes."

"Huh?" she said and turned to the wardrobe. "Oh…I have so many clothes, I don't even remember buying half of the stuff. I should throw those ones out. I've never worn them. Anyway Mr. Dragon, you are too much of a pleasurable distraction and I have to go. See you for lunch?"

"It's a date," I said and watched her leave the room.

After making myself a piece of toast, I headed out of Aurora's place. This case had been a frustrating one so far and one I wanted solved soon so I could grieve. I decided to head to Charlie's workplace.

After I entered the ten-story building and began to walk, my movements echoed along a silent white hallway. I knew Charlie's office like the back of my hand, and it wasn't long before I walked through his office door.

"Tell me you've got something," I said, tapping my foot, "God, tell me you have."

"Well I'm no G-God, although the ladies tell me I am," he said and snorted.

"Charlie…"

"Actually, my new assistant seemed to have missed something earlier. He's just found a couple of long hairs on Mr. Choen's clothes. Fake hair, g-great quality."

"Didn't Aurora have…? No. Must be a coincidence."

"What was that?"

"Nothing, nothing. Thanks for the info. Any news on those needles I sent in?"

"Not yet. I'll call you when results come in though."

"Any idea what they could be used for?"

"Possibly for diabetes, but I'm not s-sure. There was a strange substance inside the needle which is being t-tested."

"Okay thanks," I said, turning away.

"John?"

"Yeah."

"My dog…"

"Jesus Charlie I can't believe I haven't told you yet."

"Told me what?"

"I caught your dog's killer."

"When? Who?"

"In the early hours of yesterday morning."

"And you're only t-telling me now?!" Charlie's eyes widened.

"Yeah, sorry Charlie. I know it must have been wrecking your brain lately."

"And the killer? Was it that b-b-bastard?" His chest puffed in and out.

"Yeah, sick son of a bitch."

"I kn-kn-knew it!"

"Turns out it wasn't just dogs that he was hurting. He was also beating his wife."

"I'm going to r-run over th-there and g-g-give him what he deserves," he said, grabbing a scalpel.

"Woah Charlie, calm down," I said with my hands against his chest. "We've got him; he'll get what he deserves."

"No, he w-won't. Jail's too g-good for that b-bastard. I'm gonna f-finish the job." A vein throbbed in Charlie's head. This was so out of character for him. I couldn't imagine Charlie hurting a fly, let alone killing a man.

"Charlie, look at me. Look at me!"

Charlie's eyes turned to mine. "He was like a s- a son to me, John. Like a son…" he said and fell into my chest.

"I know buddy, I know," I said, patting Charlie on the back while debating whether to have Mr. Gunderson beaten up. I had *acquaintances* on the inside, it would be easy, hmm...

After making Charlie a tea and sitting with him for a while, I told him I had to go. After thanking him again for his hard work, I headed out and towards my office.

Walking through the door of my office, I caressed my chin while thinking about that fake hair. After placing my jacket on the coat rack, I searched for any spare clothes. I was in luck. There was a navy-blue suit and shirt in the wardrobe. The shirt could have done with a little ironing, but with the jacket buttoned up, it would work fine.

Suited and booted, I went and sat at my desk. A couple of unopened cases lay with a letter opener on top, the scent of perfume coming from them. *Interesting.* I pulled a cigar from my inside pocket and struck a match against my nail. I thought about Aurora and the time we'd spent together so far. Before I even realised, smoke clouds filled my office, and the cigar was almost finished. Sitting upright, I checked the time. *Time for lunch with the lady herself.*

As I arrived at Barrafina for lunch, there was Aurora, dressed in black but shining brightly.

"Hey there stranger," I said, as I leaned in to kiss her on her cheek.

"Yeah it's been forever," she smiled. "I thought we'd eat outside in case you wanted to smoke."

"I don't usually smoke when I eat but thanks for thinking of me."

"How's your case going?"

"Developing ok. Little slower than I'd like but I've got a lead or two to go on."

"Oh really?"

"Yeah. Anyway, tell me about your day so far."

"Long. Lot of phone calls, a couple of interviews. Nothing fun to talk ab—"

"What are you doing here?!" A guy shouted. I turned and saw Danny Choen.

"None of your—"

"I'm not talking to you, asshole. I'm talking to Jenny, my sister."

"Sister?" I turned to Aurora. "You're Jenny?"

"I don't want to talk to you Danny," she said, looking down as she stirred her coffee.

"Ohhh you don't wanna talk to me? Is that so?"

"Yes, it is," I said, standing up, coming face to face with him.

"I see you've got a bodyguard. How quick did you fuck this g—?"

His jaw popped as my fist smashed into it and he collapsed onto someone's table. The manager came running out.

"Apologies," I said, grabbing Aurora's hand and walking away from the restaurant.

"I can ex—" she said, but I yanked her arm forward. "I can ex—" I did it again. She looked at me, but I kept my eyes forward. Wind and rain bounced off my face, and my knuckles turned white. I didn't know where I was going, I needed to think. *Mr. Choen's daughter? Why? How? She kept this from—*

"John! talk to me." She turned me around.

My blood was boiling, my mind working overtime. "No." I said and turned away.

She turned my shoulder again, "Talk to me."

"Don't push me."

"John! Can you please just talk to me, let me ex—"

"No!" I yelled and kicked a bin over. "I told myself not to let anyone in, *no one!* But like an idiot I let you slither your way in and sink your poison into me."

"John, I—"

"Don't! *Just* don't. It all makes sense now. A woman like you paying me so much attention, being almost *perfect*. You were just trying to get information out of me about the case, weren't you?"

"No! John, you've got to believe me I—"

"Believe you. *Believe* you? Until a few minutes ago, I didn't even know your real name. God knows what else you've lied about. I'm such an idiot."

"If you'd just let me explain."

"I don't want you to explain, I want you to leave." I paced back and forth.

"But John."

"Leave!" I shouted inches from her face.

"No."

"Fine. Then *I* will. Goodbye Aurora."

"John."

"I said goodbye!" I yelled and hailed a taxi. As I stepped into the car and closed the door, she stood outside begging for me not to leave. "Get me outta here."

"Yes sir," said the driver.

As the car pulled away, my heart sank, like a rock thrown into the ocean.

As I walked through my front door thoughts and emotions flew around my head like a hurricane. I yanked open a drawer and pulled out tape to strap up my wrists and hand.

With the tape applied I took a deep breath, clenched my fists, and started beating the shit out of my punching bag.

Beads of sweat ran and then leaped off my face as I moved side to side, killing the punching bag. *Why did she lie? What does she want from me? Am I just a source to her?* I crashed my knee into the bag. *I bet she tells all the guys she fucks a new name. No, that's not her…is it? No.* My other knee smashed the bag. *How do you know anything, John? She lied and her name could just be the start of it.* My fists were tight like welded iron and I let out all my emotions through them as I hammered the bag once more.

I hit that bag until my arms and legs became numb and I couldn't stand anymore. I sat on the floor panting, sweat stinging in my eyes and reached for a bottle of whiskey which lay on a side table. Before I finished my first drink, I was out for the count.

I was in a deep alcohol induced sleep, that was until a bird tapped on my window, again and again. "Stupid bird," I said and threw my shoe towards it. *Tap tap tap.* "What the f—" I looked over to the window again but there was nothing there. *What's going on?* I walked towards it. "Shit!" I yelled as a rock smashed through the glass. "What the fuck?" I carefully got closer and lifted up the window frame. I poked my head out and received a rock to the forehead. "Mother f—…!"

With a hand in front of my head for protection, I put my head out the window again and looked down. It was Aurora. I mean, Jenny…

"What do you want?"

"I want to…"

"What?" I said, cupping a hand around my ear.

"I want…"

"I can't hear you," *damn busy streets.*

I didn't want to see Aurora, let alone speak to her, but I found my heart taking control and dragging me down the stairs.

As I walked down the last step and towards the building's front door, I tried to keep calm. As I approached the door and saw Aurora's… Jenny's silhouette, my feet turned to stone, I couldn't move.

"John? Is that you?" Aurora asked and pressed her face against the glass.

I closed my eyes, took a deep breath and another. My heart rate began to lower. I opened my eyes and walked to the door. As I pulled it open and saw Aurora, my heart rate smacked into the ceiling.

"John," she said with a little smile.

"What do you want?"

"Oh my god. You're bleeding."

"What?" I said, taken aback by her comment.

"Here. Let me help you," she reached forward but I moved back.

I rubbed my forehead with my fingers and when I brought them back, they carried a small amount of blood.

"What happened?"

"Someone thought it would be a good idea to throw rocks at my window," I said, pulling a handkerchief out of my sleeve and wiping away the blood.

"Oh...yeah, sorry about that." She looked to the ground, and twisted her tiptoed foot side to side. "I must have pressed the buzzer for your apartment a thousand times, but you didn't reply so..."

"That thing hasn't worked for months."

"Oh, I see."

"I only came down to ask you to try to avoid breaking any more of my windows and I've done it, so goodbye." I said and turned to walk away.

"No! Wait. Please..." I'd missed her voice. It had only been hours, but it felt like I hadn't seen her in a week.

With my back still facing her I told her, "I can't, I just..."

"I understand. And you have every right to hate me right now, I deserve it but—"

"I don't, hate you..."

"Thank you. I love you, John, and…and…and I could never forgive myself if I didn't at least try to fix this, us."

"I…can't."

She placed her hand gently onto my shoulder, "Please, let me at least explain everything. Then, if at the end you still can't see a way past this, we can go our separate ways. John?"

I looked over my shoulder and into her eyes. "I'll get my coat," I said and walked away. I wanted to be mad at her still, I wanted to push her away, but I couldn't.

Inside my apartment I grabbed a coat and held it, almost hugging it. My heart wanted Aurora enclosed in my arms, my mind wanted her out of the city. I opened up the coat, slid it on and headed out.

As I reached the main door of the building, I took a deep breath, preparing my mind and heart for a war of emotions.

"I like that coat on you," Jenny said, with a nervous smile.

"Let's walk," I told her, not meeting her eyes.

We must've walked for ten minutes and not a word was spoken. My heart raced. I was so focused on controlling my breathing that I hadn't even thought about talking. Jenny on the other hand, well, she was nervous I'd guess. She had to convince me to trust her, understand her reasons and even come back into her arms.

A drop of rain landed on my face, then another. I looked to the sky, and then the heavens opened. Heavy rain bounced off my face and as I turned to Jenny, I realised her coat was wafer thin.

As we continued to walk, and the rain poured down, I took in a deep breath and placed my coat over Jenny's shoulders.

"Oh no, you don't have t—"

"You'll catch a cold, take it."

"But."

"Take it. You won't be able to…explain things to me if you're sneezing all over the place."

She smiled, "Thank you." I smiled back. *What are you doing? You're supposed to be mad at her.* I got rid of my smile and paced forward.

"Are we going somewhere in particular?" Jenny asked. "Or is it a mystery for me to solve?" She hugged my arm.

"This isn't a game Auro— Jenny," I said and shrugged her off my arm.

"No, of course not, I didn't mean, umm, I meant," she looked to the ground.

The streets were empty, and all was silent except for the pitter patter of rain on the parked cars. Every now and then I caught a glimpse of myself in a puddle, and I didn't like what I saw. I felt weak, yet the demon of anger lay waiting in the shadows. I could see it in my eyes.

"John? Are we going to talk?" Jenny said and stopped in her tracks.

I looked over my shoulder at her, "It's not far now."

"Trés bien."

"Did you say…? Never mind."

Why's my hand hurting? When I looked down, I realised why. I must've been scratching the top of it the whole time. A layer of skin had been etched off. I dabbed it with my thumb and as I breathed through my nose, familiar smells came back to me. Pine trees, wet leaves, we were at the park.

"There's a shelter over there," I told Aurora pointing to the spot.

The shelter lay at the top of a hill, overlooking a long, beautiful park. Even in the rain it brought a sense of peace. The tall trees acted like a border. In the middle of the park was a small lake, with an old wooden bridge across the middle. Further on you could see the rest of London.

"It's beautiful. I can't believe I've never been up here." Jenny said, looking out onto the park.

"This place is very important to me," I said and stood next to her, "When I was about twelve years old, Mr. Cohen brought me to this same spot. Some kids had been making fun of me at school. We didn't have a lot of money back then. It was just my mother and I, so times where tough. Kids don't think about that though, they just think of ways to make you feel even more like shit."

"Oh John, that's awful."

"Anyway, on that particular day, those kids came at me, making fun of me and then, they mentioned my mother…"

"What happened?"

"I broke one guy's nose, the other's jaw before a few others jumped on top of me. The headmaster suspended me an hour later. With my mum pulling double shifts, she couldn't get out of work to get me, so Mr. Cohen came. As we drove away in his car, anger still coursed through my veins. I was ready to kill those kids."

"But you didn't, right?"

"No. We soon arrived here and stood right where you're standing now. He looked at me, pointed out at the city and said: 'You see out there? Well that world is a messed-up place, full of assholes who want to beat you down and make the world a miserable place too. There are people, however, who can make it a better place to be and I truly believe that you could be one of them. Those kids probably deserved what they got, but if you want to make a real difference, you should ignore those idiots, focus on working hard and then kicking bad guys asses when you're older.'

"And that's what I did. I knuckled down, worked hard, trained harder and after becoming a police office, rained hell on all the sons of bitches in London."

"Wow, that's—"

"I'm telling you this because that was a pivotal point in my life, and I feel this might be too. A part of me wants to scream at you for lying and then leave."

"And the other part?"

"The other part...the other part feels like Mr. Choen is on my shoulder whispering, telling me to hear you out."

"Well I'm glad there's that part," she said with a nervous smile.

"Don't be too happy. He's small up there on my shoulder and I can easily flick him away. You've got five minutes Auro—start talking."

"Well, you've told me some of your history. I think it's only fair that I share some of mine."

I leaned back against the wall, the cold concrete against my skin, and listened.

"When I was fifteen, I was young and naïve. One weekend I went to a carnival with friends and it was there I met David. We hit it off right away and started dating."

"What does this have to do w—"

"Please. Let me talk. Anyway, I started growing feelings for David and I *thought* he was feeling the same way. He told me he loved me one day, but it turned out he just said that to get me into bed. He dumped me the next day and I was crushed. But what was even worse...I fell pregnant. Then, my father who was never around, who loved spending time at his job more than his home, made me...made me...he made me kill my baby, John." Her eyes welled up with tears. "After that, I rebelled, got in with the wrong crowd, drank too much, smoked weed. One day after drinking heavily, me and my friends decided to break into my father's store. We continued to drink and then a friend handed me a baseball bat. He made me kill something dear to me and so I destroyed something dear to him. His piano. In my drunken state, standing over his busted-up love, I'd forgotten my father's shop had a silent alarm. The police came and got me from the shop moments later."

She paused for a moment and lit a thin cigar. Puffing the smoke out into a great cloud, she continued, "My father didn't press charges, but he didn't let me back into his house either. Mum protested but he wouldn't listen. I looked him in the eye, told him he was dead to me and left."

"I'm sorry to hear that happened, but it doesn't explain why you lied to me, or prove you're not up to something. Why did you lie? Why?" I yelled, banging my fist against the wall.

Jenny flinched. "I was scared," she mumbled.

"You'll have to speak up."

"I said I was scared ok?" Tears rolled down her face. She turned away from me, the moon reflected in her eyes. "Look, I came out of the shadows to see that man get put into the ground. I didn't expect... I didn't expect to find you and fall for..."

"Out of the shadows? Don't be so dramatic. Plenty of people go to a funeral of an estranged father without giving a fake name, come on Jenny!" I shouted and kicked a coke can. "You know what I think? I think it makes more sense that you wanted information about this case. So, you followed me, even knew where I bought my cigars. Then all you needed to do was put on the charm and slither your way into my life."

"No! It wasn't like that at all. If I wanted to know about the case, I'd just say it to your face in the first place. My father has been dead to me for a long time, but yes, I admit, you being on the case did intrigue me."

"I knew it," I said, standing up straight and getting closer to Jenny.

"But John, I didn't know you were on the case until after we met, I swear."

"Even if I believed that, you still haven't explained why you lied about who you are. If you didn't know I was on the case, then why call yourself something else?"

Jenny exhaled long and hard. "I'm going to tell you something I haven't told anyone before and something I prayed I wouldn't have to tell you... When I was young, Danny, he, he...he abused me. At first, he would try it when he was drunk, but...it got progressively worse—"

"Son of a bitch," I said, under my breath.

"I've never been able to trust men since or let them get close. Knowing Danny would be around, I was scared someone might mention my name in conversation and he'd come after me. I've even bought a dark veil so he can't see my face at the funeral," she said and rubbed her fingers across her eyes. "When I met you," she said, making eye contact, "I didn't think things would get serious, so continued using the fake name. After my feelings for you got stronger, the urge to tell you my real name got stronger. I nearly told you several times too, but after finding you were on the case...I thought you would leave me, say it was a conflict of interest. I even thought you might associate me with the bad feelings you're having with my father's death. John...I don't wanna lose you. I l..." She turned away, trying to hide her face as she wiped away a tear. "Maybe you're better off without me. I wasn't good enough for my father and I'm clearly not good enough for you. I'm gonna go..." She stood up, looked at me and turned away. "Goodbye J—"

189

"Wait," I said, as I stood up and put my hand on her shoulder. I felt her trembling as she turned around. I looked deep into her eyes, "I want you to know that it's not easy for me to trust people or let them in. So, when I let you in and heard what you had done, it felt like a betrayal, that I was right not to let anyone in. If it had been anybody else, I wouldn't even be having a conversation with the person. But it's not just anybody, it's you... I'm not saying what you did is right, but, I understand, and...I don't want to lose you either."

"John, I—"

"Don't talk," I said, then pulled her in close and kissed her intensely. My heart raced as her soft lips fired the furnace inside of me and I got lost in the heat of the moment.

Later, we walked back to my place and finished what we'd started outside, in the bedroom. Passion fired all over the room until our bodies gave out and we collapsed into each other's arms.

Jenny was gone when I awoke the next morning. Another note lay on my pillow, which I read with a morning coffee, and then planned my day.

Mr. Choen's ex-wife mentioned she had bought wine at the time of his death. Time to check that shop out and find out if the bitch was telling the truth or not.

As I walked up to the store, a broken letter on its neon sign flickered on and off, the broken lights causing me to close my eyes.

"Watch it!"

I opened my eyes to see an angry woman pointing a finger at me.

"Asshole," she said and walked away.

As I opened the door, the rain stopped. "Just my luck."

The small off-license had the usual zombies roaming the aisles. They were putting things on shelves and almost drooling while serving at the counter. I followed a worker down an aisle who ignored me the whole time. At least that's what I thought. Turned out he was deaf... *Better luck at the counter maybe.* My feet skimmed round the wet floor signs on the way like a pro skater.

"Can I help you?" said zombie number two.

"I certainly hope so. Have you seen this woman?" I showed him a photo from Rebecca's Facebook.

He shrugged his shoulders.

"Did you see her on June 8th?"

"Urr..."

I shook my head and rolled my eyes, "I have a better idea. Can I see your security footage from June 8th between 8pm and midnight?"

"Ummm, Mike's not here yet."

"Who's Mike?"

"The manager, duh."

I had the right mind to knock him silly, but held back. "And he's the only one with access to the footage I'm guessing."

Zombie two nodded.

"I'll wait. Don't work too hard zombie."

"What?" He looked at me confused.

"I said I'll see you when Mike gets back." I turned and headed for the door. With a cigar in hand, I stepped outside and lit a match, which went out. *Damn rain.* I didn't let it stop me, however. I found a tiny area sheltered from the rain and sparked up the cigar.

After twenty minutes, a man in his forties came running through the car park. A glimpse of his name badge as he passed revealed he was the man I was looking for. I followed him through the door, "I need to talk to you."

"Jesus! I'm through the door two seconds. This better be important," he said, turning.

"Actually, it's about a murder case."

"A what?! Oh, I'm so sorry..."

"Banks. Detective Banks," I said as I put out my hand to shake his.

"I didn't hear about a murder here...I'm the manager, so I should be the first to know..." he said, scratching his head.

"It didn't happen here, don't worry. I just need to see some security footage."

"Sure, right away, sir," he jittered and walked me to the office.

After rewinding a lot of tape, there she was. Nine-thirty pm buying some wine and stumbling all the way to the counter. *She could've still made it to Mr. Choen within the time of death time frame, but she would've had to do some skilful, fast driving. In the state she appears in, it doesn't seem likely. 'Doesn't seem likely', doesn't get people off with a murder charge though, hmm...*

I left the store to dry weather but as my car door slammed shut, the pitter patter of rain fell onto the roof. The engine roared as I turned the key, the window wipers came on.

Traffic was building up and just as I was about to yell at another driver, my phone rang.

"Hey Charlie."

"Hey John, I got the results back from those needles."

"Oh yeah?"

"Yeah. T-turns out they weren't used for diabetes, like I thought."

"Well don't keep me hanging here, Charlie. What was in it?"

"Botox."

"Botox? Why the hell would Mr. Choen have Botox?"

"A fresh look," he giggled.

"I'm serious. He wasn't that kind of guy."

"Right, right, I'm sorry. Yeah, I thought it seemed strange too. Another th-thing was there were no prints at all on the needles though they've clearly been used."

Didn't I see a receipt for Botox at Jenny's? No, no, it's a coincidence. Lots of people use it nowadays.

"Banks? You there?"

"Yeah, of course. Any other info?"

"This Botox isn't usually found in England. Must have been shipped in from Bulgaria."

"Interesting. But people use Botox all the time. Harmless right? Except for people looking like motionless fools."

"Actually, if you used enough at one t-time, it can be lethal. Botulism is a serious illness caused by the botulinum toxin. It causes paralysis which can stop the lungs working, then Bob's your uncle, you're dead."

"Bob's your uncle? Really? That's how you're talking over this death?"

"Sorry, sorry. I t-tend to use humour or old phrases when something is so…serious…so…close to the heart."

"It's okay, it's just a sensitive case. Did you find any puncture marks on the body?"

"It took me a while but yeah. There was some an inch above the hairline. Looked like someone had even used fake hair to cover the marks. Crazy, right?"

"Crazy…Look, I've gotta go. Thanks Charlie."

"Sure."

I hung up the phone and tapped it against my head. *Botox, no prints… Does Rebecca use Botox? Mr. Choen's competitor Mr.*

Tanaka had a young son. Could he get some? Jen—No. I needed to crack this case before it cracked me right open. Time for the next suspect.

Mr. Tanaka's son told me he was at the gym when Mr. Choen died, but I got a negative vibe from him. This guy could prove Aurora was innocent. I headed to the gym to check his alibi.

It was a basic gym. Mainly weights with a couple of treadmills and the stench of sweat. Mr. Universe himself 'Arnold Schwarzenegger' was posted up on the wall, along with some motivational quotes.

"Can I speak to the manager?" I asked the blonde female receptionist.

The receptionist took out her AirPod headphones, stuck her gum onto a post-it and said, "Can I help you?"

"I'd like to speak with your manager please."

"What's wrong with me?" she said, leaning forwards in a playful way.

"Nothing at all. I just need to ask about one of your customers."

"Oh, I know all the guys in here," she said and winked. "Maybe I can help?"

"Maybe. Do you know this guy?" I handed her a picture of Mr. Tanaka's son.

"Ren? Sure, I know him. He has a nice smile."

"Was he here on the 8th?"

"He's not in no trouble, is he?"

"Not at all. I'm just curious."

"I was here that night and he wasn't. I would have known if he'd been here," she said while playing with her hair.

"And do you have cameras that would confirm that?"

"We have one. Would have to wait 'til the manager is in to get access to it though. But trust me. He wasn't here."

"Well, thank you…"

"Candice," she said with a smile.

"Thank you, Candice. I'll see you around."

"I'd like that," she said, then put the gum back in her mouth and the headphones in her ears.

If he wasn't in the gym, was he at Mr. Choen's? It was time to pay a visit to Mr. Tanaka's son and get some answers.

The clouds in the sky started to part as my taxi pulled up at Mr. Tanaka's store. As I placed one leg out of the car, I saw the owner's son getting onto his motorcycle. "Change of plans. Follow that bike."

After twenty minutes the bike pulled up outside a place called, *Ku Bar.* I tipped the driver well and exited as the suspect entered the building. As I walked through the doors, I realised I wasn't in Kansas anymore. The majority of the clientele were male and dressed in leather. Some people had tops on, others didn't. Seeing a man do the splits facing downwards while on a pole was a sight, I would unfortunately not be able to forget. *Mr. Tanaka's son is gay?* I sat at the bar, "Do you know this guy?" I asked the barman, showing him the photo.

"Yeah, he's just come in."

"Does he come here often?"

"Why? You interested?"

"Not in the way you think?" I said, adjusting my tie. "So, does he come here often?"

"Yeah, I've seen him a few times. He was here last on…let me think… When was the Magic Mike stripper night…? Oh! On the 8th. Yeah that's right. Was here all night with that guy over there." He pointed to a booth in the corner, where Mr. Tanaka's son was getting to know a young gentleman up close. That would explain why he lied about where he was. Some families can be strictly against the whole gay scene. Apparently, Mr. Tanaka was one of those type of fathers. Good luck to the kid I say, but it didn't help me get any closer to solving my case.

"Thanks for your help," I told the barman.

"Anytime," he said as I turned to walk away. "You forgot this!"

I turned, a little confused. The barman held out a piece of paper which I took from him.

"Call me," he said.

"I'm honoured. But I'm taken."

"All the good-lookin' ones are," he said with disappointment in his face.

I gave him a closed lip smile and headed for the exit. Outside, I managed to get a light from a man in chapless trousers. I inhaled the cigar and took a walk.

That night I couldn't sit still. Pacing my office floor, cigar smoke filled the room so much that if you walked past you might not even see me. Suspects were being crossed off my list one by one and a woodpecker kept knocking on my head accusing Jenny.

"You're just thinking this because she lied about her name. She explained why, John, we're passed that. Stop looking for a reason to stop someone getting too close to you." I clenched my fists. "Get your act together," I cursed under my breath as the cigar went out for a third time. "Where are those fucking matches?" I said, rummaging through my coat and then my drawers. "I know who'll have matches. That bitch Rebecca. Bet she's got Botox too." I threw the last of my glass of whiskey down my throat and headed out the door.

Pulling up onto Rebecca's drive with a strong screeching noise, I threw the door open and slammed it behind me. Approaching the door, I saw Rebecca looking out the window. "I need to talk to you!" I said. She waited a moment and then closed the curtain. I went to bang on the door, but it opened before I got chance.

"What no—?"

I barged past her. "You got a light?"

"What?!"

"A light. You know, it sparks, lights a cigar."

"You're telling me you've come here just for a fucking light?!"

"Of course not. Where's your Botox?"

"Excuse me?!"

"Don't play dumb with me. You got wine that night but still had time to get to Mr. Choen's shop. And you look good for your age. Now where is it?!"

"I don't have any Botox and I don't have to let you stay in my house either. Leave or I'm calling the police."

"I am the police!"

"Not anymore, asshole."

I ignored her and searched the house. "Where is it Rebecca? Better to tell me now and the police might reduce your sentence."

"Yes, I'd like to report an intruder," she said over the phone.

I didn't have much time. I pulled out drawers, knocked things from off the top of cupboards, searched wardrobes. Sweat started to run down my face as I moved from room to room. Rebecca kept yelling stuff in the background. I blocked most of it out and continued searching the house, anywhere there might be Botox hidden. My heart was racing and the longer it went without finding something the more impatient I became.

After checking my watch for a fifth time, I estimated that I still had another thirty minutes or s—

"Sir? *Sir?*" As I turned, a short, thin policeman stood before me.

"Shit. A murder happens and you people take forever to arrive, but I look around a house and you're here lickety split."

"You need to come with us sir."

"I don't have to do shit."

"Sir? Sir?"

And then I did something I instantly regretted. I shoved the officer to the ground and clenched my fist. Last thing I remember was feeling a pain in the back of my head.

I awoke to a smell of sweat, blood and alcohol. I was in a cell. As I sat up, I looked around at the other men. The smells curled the hairs in my nose and watered my eyes.

A familiar face soon came walking down the corridor.

"Hey Frank, umm…long time." We went way back, Frank and I. We were in police training together, constantly competing for the number one spot. Friends ever since.

"Long time? Really? That's what you're going with?" he asked, moving a squash ball around his hand.

"That's what I got right now. My head is killing me."

"Yeah, I heard you pissed off officer Mendes." Silence. "Look John, I can never repay you for what you did for me in the past, so I'm gonna do you a solid and get you out of here. Just try not to do anything stupid like this again, okay?"

"You got it," I said with a faint salute. He opened the door, and I threw a smile at him. I patted him on his shoulder and said, "Thanks Frank."

It was nearing lunchtime as I left the police station, and I needed a drink. I headed over to O'Rourke's to quench my thirst and to apologise to a friend.

"Hey Jimmy," I said as I sat at the bar, but he just looked at me. "Look Jimmy, I was out of line…I don't like to talk about my feelings and I took it out on you. I'm sorry."

"Okay John," he said and grabbed the whiskey. "Do I dare ask what's on your mind?"

"Don't you dare say... Sorry. Don't say I told you so but..."

"The girl?" he asked with an eyebrow raised.

"You got it in one."

"So, what's up? Trouble in paradise?"

"I'm not sure..."

He raised his other eyebrow. "What do you mean, John?"

"I'm on a case. Closest thing to a father I've ever had has been killed. The woman I...care a lot about...well, there's evidence maybe pointing towards her being the killer."

"Shit John. That deserves a free drink," he said. He poured a shot in front of me but then drank it himself. "I'm kidding," he said and poured me a glass of whiskey.

"Thanks Jimmy," I said, cradling the glass.

"Do you think she's capable of doing something that bad?"

"My heart says no, my head says...well I've been trying to keep it quiet."

"Your mind is afraid it could be yes?"

I gave him a slight nod.

"Look John, you obviously care a lot about her, but things won't be right between you two until you're sure about her."

"Maybe you're right," I said, sipping my drink. "So, I should break into her place, look for evidence and be sure, thanks Jimmy," I said, downing the rest of the drink.

"I didn't quite say th—"

"Thanks again." I stood up and headed for the door.

"John!" he shouted as I opened the door.

"What?"

"I told you so," he grinned, to which I responded with the middle finger and left.

The wind was cold, it whipped around my neck and pushed me from behind. My feet slowly hit the pavement one by one. I was in no rush to break into Aurora's place. My mind, running at 100mph, was debating if I was doing the right thing or if I should just go home. My heart felt nothing but love for her, but my brain knew oh too well how emotions can affect people.

I'd walked slow but it felt like I got to Jenny's in seconds. It didn't happen to me often, but I was anxious. Not because I might get caught breaking in, I knew she was out for the day. No, I was anxious that my brain might be right and my heart might smash on the ground.

With nobody around, I took out my tools and picked the lock on Jenny's door. A drip of sweat rolled down my face as the final click hit—

"Meeeooooww." I spun around and saw a cat stood on the top step staring at me. Relieved, I threw some old nuts from my pocket onto the street which it happily chased after. And I was in.

The mail, on a counter in the hallway, revealed nothing of interest and so I headed towards the living room. I pulled out the drawers of a dresser underneath the window, nothing. In the bathroom, the cabinet contained lots of tablets. Tablets for headaches, a variety of sleeping aids, no needles. In her kitchen I pulled open all of the cupboards. I found some rubber gloves, but that's not unusual to find in a kitchen. Besides poor taste in food, there was nothing else to find there. On to the bedroom.

I remember seeing the wig in her room earlier and headed over to the wardrobe. The door slid open smoothly and revealed a deep red coloured wig. Using some tweezers, I plucked a strand of hair out, to see if it was a match for the one found on Mr. Choen. After inspecting it up close, I placed it in a small bag. Shoes clanged as I shoved them side to side, looking for evidence. "Where's that damn Botox?" The clothes flicked from side to side. "God Dammit!" I shouted and hit the back of the wardrobe wall. *What the...?*

A secret compartment at the back of the wardrobe opened. Inside, there were a few boxes, some dusty, some...fresh. Dust danced around my face as I flipped the lid off a box. *What do we have...?* It wasn't drugs or a gun, but it was still bad. Photos of former lovers with their arms around Aurora. My fist tightened. *Maybe I was right, she's innocent. I bet there's just some diaries in the other boxes.*

I opened another box. It wasn't diaries... It was...a whip, handcuffs, and a gag. *Kinky, but alright.* I moved swiftly onto the next box; it was a little stiffer than the others. *What was that?* I turned and glanced over my shoulder. That damn cat was outside the window. I pried the lid off the box waiting for the diaries and...Botox. *Okay John, you knew she'd bought some, find that they're from the states and let's go.* I searched for an origin. "Aha," I said, then read the address,

192 Vitosha Blvd. Sofia

"Sofia? Sofia..." I said scratching my chin. "Where do I know that city from...? Romania...Ukraine...Bulgaria!" *Shit.* A noise rattled in the house. Damn cat. *Wait! In the house? Shit, she must be home early.* I grabbed one of the Botox needles, shoved the secret door back and bolted for the backdoor.

"Hello?" Jenny asked as I reached the back door. "Is anybody there?"

Little by little I moved the handle downwards. It felt like an eternity. It opened with a small bang and I moved as quick as I could. "I'm calling the police. Get outta my house."

After hopping several fences and releasing my tie from one, I was back in the street. A cold fog ran out of my mouth as I got my breath back. *The expensive wig, Botox from Bulgaria, shit. Why*

God? For fuck's sake why?! I smashed my fist into a wall and watched as blood ran down my hand and dove off it towards the ground. The second time there was more, and the third time? Well…

I crashed into the nearest bar and headed into the toilets. I winced as the cold water brushed over my bloody knuckles while I looked in the mirror. "Everything's fine, John. Get it together," I told myself. Fuck!" The tap had turned to scorching hot. "Everything's fine. I'm sure she has a reason for having Botox there. It might be hidden away but, who doesn't hide things?"

"Are you okay out there, mister?" A voice said from a cubicle.

"Mind your own business," I replied and headed for the bar.

I sat on a stool and placed my hand, now wrapped in paper towels onto the counter.

"Erm…you okay buddy?" the barman asked.

"I will be once people stop asking me that. Give me a whiskey."

"Erm sure."

"What the fuck is this?" I said as he placed the glass in front of me.

"Whiskey, what you asked for."

"No, not what I fucking asked. I said no ice. Do you see ice in here? You Goddam right you do!"

"Sir, you never said 'no ice'."

"Ohhh so you're calling me a liar?"

"No sir, it's just—"

"Just what? Here, take your fucking ice. My gift to you," I said, throwing them at him.

An older man behind the bar looked over to the barman to see if he needed help, but the barman raised a hand to say, 'I've got this'.

The whiskey barely touched the sides of my throat as I slammed it down, "Another one. NO ICE," I said, sliding the glass towards him. He grabbed the glass, gave me a nod, and turned.

Two whiskeys soon turned into four, which turned to eight, which turned into, well…I lost count. After arguing with the barman when he told me the place was closed, I decided to leave. I stood up and stumbled over towards the front door, crashing my leg into several chairs along the way.

Outside, I realised I'd forgotten to piss. "Aha!" I said and dragged myself towards an alleyway. As I began to urinate over some bin bags, my balance started to get worse. "Woooah Betsy," I said, almost falling backwards. "FUCK!" I yelled as I slipped and fell to the ground.

"John? Is that you?"

"Jesus? Is it me you're looking for?" I sang, giggling to myself and still…urinating.

"Oh geez. Come on. I'll help you up," the man said, while he licked my face. Or maybe that was a dog.

"Thanks, erm, man."

"It's me John, Charlie."

"I like your dog."

"It's not mine."

"Then w-whhy iss it with youu?"

"Uck, you smell like gasoline. How many have you had to drink?"

"Ermm, a million!" I said, trying to twirl around.

"Oh geez. Well anyway," he said, lifting my arm back around his shoulders. "The dog is a friend's dog. They th-thought it would help me get over th-the death of my dog."

"Thaat souunds nuts."

"Yep, but here I am, early hours of the morning, cleaning up shit, and dealing with the-the dog too."

"Whaa?"

"Never mind. My place isn't far from here. You can stay with me tonight."

I don't remember going into Charlie's house, but I remember he had a comfortable sofa. "She's ino, ino. What's the word?"

"Innocent?"

"Yes! She's innocent."

"Who is John?" he said with the kind of tone a sober friend says to the drunkard.

"Jo...wait...Jane...Jill...? JENNY!" I said, bolting upright on the couch.

"Lie down John," he said and eased me back down. "I've left a towel, some water and...a bucket by you. Will you be alright by yourself?"

"I'll be..." *hiccup*, "I'll be fine. Thanks Jenny."

"It's..." but he stopped himself finishing the sentence and headed to bed.

The next morning at Charlie's, a woodpecker pounded its beak on my forehead, while a giant pair of hands squeezed my head. *What kind of torture is this? I don't remember having a bird. Wait! Where am...* I sat upright, a little too quick and I dove over to the bucket, paying the consequences. "Where the—"

"You're at my place. Don't you remember coming here?"

"Urr..."

"You tried to flirt with poor Mrs Aldridge next door?"

"The cat lady? Maybe. Did she like it?" I asked, my words echoing around the bucket.

"She's eighty-four. Probably gave her a small heart attack. Anyway...I've got to g-g-go, some of us don't have the luxury of picking our own working hours."

I gave him a thumbs up and pulled my head out of the bucket.

"Okay John, I've put the coffee machine on for you and the shower has plenty of hot water left. Let yourself out."

"Yeah, hey Charlie!"

"Yeah John?"

"I'm sorry about last night. My head's in a bad place."

"I know, John. I hope she's worth it," he said and left.

The water cascaded down my body and the mirror in the bathroom steamed up. I sat in the shower with the hangover from hell pulsing all over my body. *Wake up. Shake it off, John.*

After drying myself off and getting dressed, I made an espresso and took it with me outside.

I shut the front door to Charlie's building and headed towards the tube. *Wait. Is that...?* "Jenny?" I shouted, crossing the street. "Jenny!" I shouted. She looked at me and started to walk away. "Hey! Wait. We need to talk." My stomach made knots as I bent over and tried not to vomit. She was getting further away so I picked myself up and soon caught up to her. "Jenny. Why are you being like this?" I placed a hand on her shoulder to turn her around.

"Get off me, HELP!" she yelled in a French accent.

"What?" I asked, confused, as a man dragged me off her, for which he received a broken nose. I didn't see the other guy coming behind me...

Piss smell, body odour... "Not this place again," I said and opened my eyes. I was in jail. Frank was not going to be happy. "So, what are you in for?" I asked one of the inmates, but the face tattooed man just stared at me.

"Let him out." That was Frank's voice. I looked up, but he wasn't smiling like I was.

"Frank thanks, listen—"

"No, you listen, John," his chest puffed in and out. "I stuck my neck out for you to get you out of jail and here you are again," He said squeezing a small ball in his hand

"I'm—"

"By some God's miracle I've found a way to get you out this time, John, but…" he relaxed his hand and looked at me.

"But?"

"You're not going to like it." He began squeezing the ball again.

"What?" I asked, hoping he was being dramatic.

"You can leave, John, but you've got to go to…a therapist."

"What? You're kidding."

"Afraid not."

"I'll put it in my diary," I told him, pretending to write into a book. I was itching to get out of the cell.

"No John."

"What do you mean, no?"

"You have to go today, right now. A taxi is waiting outside to take you."

"For fu—" I stopped myself and nodded. He was a good guy and probably worked his ass off even to get me this. "Okay Frank, I'll go."

Frank opened the cell door and I headed for the exit. "Oh, and John?"

"Yeah?"

"Come in here again this week and I'll let your latest cell buddy give you a bath."

I shuddered at the thought and headed to the taxi.

The Clock Struck Death

***

The therapist's wall was full of qualifications, awards, and graduation photos. Behind the photos laid a stone-cold white wall. Fingerprints and smudges presented themselves where people had inspected the doctor's credentials.

"Hello Mr. Banks," a voice came from behind me. "Take a seat, please." A man in a green check tweed suit, late fifties I'd guess, sat in front of me while putting on some glasses.

"Sure thing, doc," I said, sitting into a deep leather chair. As he sat behind his desk, he placed a glass of water onto a coaster. Behind him there must have been fifty books on psychology.

"Interested in the books? I could recommend some to you."

"You're alright doc."

"Please, call me Andrew."

"Andrew."

"Can I call you John?"

"Sure."

"So, John, let's talk about—"

"Actually, *Andrew* I've got another idea. What would it take for you to talk about a friend of mine, instead of me? Help me out and I will help you out."

"Now John, I'm a professiona—" £50 on the table, "As I was saying, I'm a—" £100, "I'm a—" £150.

"Final offer doc."

"Well...perhaps just this once..."

"Atta boy."

"What seems to be the problem with your...friend?"

"I'm not sure I would say it was a problem, more that she's acted...strange at times, not herself."

"How so?"

"She has clothes she can't remember buying. I've seen her walking in the streets with the types of clothes that aren't her style at all."

"That doesn't seem too strange, John."

"There's more. There's been occasions where I've waved to her or talked to her in the street and it's like she hasn't recognised me at all. She stands there speaking in a foreign accent, or blanks me and jumps into a car."

"Did you say speaks with foreign accents?"

"Yeah, why?"

"It's interesting that's all. Does she do accents for fun, for a job?"

"That's the thing. When I've asked her about it, she says she can't do accents at all and fails when she tries to."

"Really...?" he asked, resting his chin on his hand.

"I've heard her do a French and Texas accent a couple times. She was actually doing the French accent when screaming for help saying she didn't know me. That's how I ended up here."

"Tell me, John, does she suffer from headaches?"

"Actually, I have seen her taking a lot of painkillers lately. She was taking some when we got into an argument in a bar."

"What was the argument about?"

"This an' that. She claimed to never have been to this secret bar and yet the barman recognised her."

"Very interesting. Has she ever had loss of memory; done things she's never done before?"

"Hmm...let me think. I have had a conversation or two where she's forgotten what I've said almost right away. I put it down to daydreaming."

"Hmm, anything else?" A wind blew in through the open window. "Oh, I'm sorry about that," he said and closed it.

"No problem. Actually, that just reminded me. She made me a scarf, but said she'd never knitted or sewed before. Said one second she was watching TV and the next she had a made a full scarf."

"So, clothes she wouldn't usually wear and accents she could never copy. Minor amnesia, having skills she never knew she had…" He tapped his pencil against a notebook.

"Something coming to mind, doc? Andrew."

"Actually yes. Have you heard of D.I.D.?"

"Can't say that I have."

"D.I.D. stands for Dissociative Identity Disorder. You might have heard its former name, Multiple Personality Disorder. Without seeing your friend in person, I can't be sure but it's ticking all the boxes for this disorder. Multiple accents, dressing differently, not recognising you. Also having new skills without memory of learning them. These symptoms point towards separate personalities, what we call 'alters'."

"What are you saying, she's more than one person?"

"Kind of. During times of 'memory loss' also known as mini amnesia, your friend could be becoming one of the other *alters*. The French person for example. It would be a different person altogether. The person would speak differently, dress differently, have different skills."

"Doc. Could one of these other personalities, commit a crime? One my friend would never know about?"

"It's possible. The alter could look to defend the body, or if it didn't like a person it could even kill them. If there was no evidence, then your friend would have no way of knowing. All she would have was a gap in her memory."

"Innocent and yet guilty at the same time…"

"If there's been a serious crime, I need to let the authorities know."

"No doc, Andrew. Nothing to worry about. Just a theoretical situation. Okay?" I said and slid another £50 towards him. He nodded and took the note. *People are right. Therapists are stupidly expensive.*

"Thanks for your time Andrew. I trust you can take everything from here?"

"Yes John."

And with that, I left with thoughts of Jenny's innocence and guiltiness on my mind. The woman I love killed the father I never had, but it wasn't her, yet it was. *Do I bring her to jail? Do I run away with her?* Questions bounced off every edge of my brain. *The evidence pointed towards her being guilty, but nothing was set in stone.* Was that my head or heart talking?

No matter how many cigars I smoked, I couldn't get my head straight. A leaning tower of cigars piled up and threatened to fall apart at any moment, just like my mind. I needed to speak to a guru, do some meditation and clear my mind. I knew just the man.

✳ ✳ ✳

Ramesh had been a guru for many years. His grey beard expanded down to his waist and his calm aura affected you the second you walked into a room with him.

"Thank you for seeing me on such short notice Ramesh," I said, shaking his hand.

"It is no problem of course," he replied, bowing his head. "What can I do for you?"

"There is a war between my heart and mind. A tornado is blowing around my head and I can't centre myself."

"Sit with me, John, let us meditate." And we did, we both sat, crossed our legs, and began to take deep breaths. "Close your eyes. I want you to imagine yourself walking through the storm, the tornado running around. Look for a house. Can you do that?"

"Yes." I focused hard and looked past the heavy wind. Parts of other houses were flying round, and then there in the corner, was a solid brick house. "Okay, I've found one."

"This house will be safe for you. I want you to focus not on things in this world, but simply about making your way to this house."

"Alright." I continued my deep breathing and focused. I could just about make out a path in the distance, leading towards the house. The wind tried to push me backwards and so I leaned hard against it, edging myself closer to the house.

"You're doing well. Remember, life will push you around if you let it, but you are stronger, you are the creator."

"Yes guru." I grabbed onto a tree's branch. On the trunk there was a heart with Jenny's and my initials carved into it. My breathing became faster.

"Focus. Don't get blown away by negative thoughts."

I left the tree and continued towards the house. After a few paces I fell to the ground as Mr. Choen's grandfather clock came hurtling towards me. The edge clawed along my back.

"Breathe, John, breathe."

I stood up and continued walking. My breathing slowed down, and the path became clearer. "I'm close to the house."

"Good. Head on inside."

As I reached the house I stepped onto the front porch and across to the front door. A clock ticked behind me and thin cigarettes lay in an ashtray on the porch bench swing. I shook my head and went inside. Silence.

"I'm inside."

"You are safe here, John. Free of judgement. Free to just *be*. Take your time. After a while begin to ask the questions, you so dearly need the answers to."

"I will. Thank you, Ramesh." And I did. I took my time, sitting in the stillness, breathing slow and deep. I felt connected to my soul. When I was ready, I began to run through the questions and the case in my mind. After half an hour, I knew what I had to do.

I headed outside of the guru's home; the bright sky blinded me for a moment. I turned and took out my phone. I knew a contact who owed me a favour and it was time for her to pay up. I punched in her number and hit call.

"Yeah," she answered.

"Nice greeting as always Sonia."

"Who's this?"

"Don't act like you don't know."

"John...Bon Jovi? No wait, John Travolta? Loved you in Face Off."

"Ha-ha very funny."

"Oh, hey Banks. When did you come on the line?"

"Remember that favour you owe me?"

"Yes..."

"I need you to track a phone for me, and set it up on my phone so I can follow the...person."

"A girl, huh? What she do, John? Cheat on you? Break your h—"

"Just get it done," I said and hung up the phone.

A flame from a match caressed the cigar in my hand. I inhaled it deeply and closed my eyes. It would all be over soon. Would I feel good at the end of it all? Only time would tell.

The phone rang.

"Bon Jovi, I've done it. I'm sending you an app I created. Open it and you will be able to track your girl."

"Thanks," I said, "Keep out of trouble Sonia."

"I'll do my best," she said and hung up the phone.

Seconds later an app downloaded onto my phone. I opened it and there it was, Jenny's location. She was in St James' Park.

As I headed up the stairs from St. James Park tube station, the signal on my phone kicked back into business. Jenny had left the park. *Damn.* She was heading towards the Westminster bridge. I could catch her if I moved quick enough.

Crowds of tourists filled the streets, taking selfies, listening to tour guides, and wearing ridiculous hats. That slowed me down at first, but I'm used to dealing with these situations and so, soon I was approaching the bridge. There she was.

"Jenny!" I shouted; her head turned as I ran up to her.

"Hey John. Everything okay?"

"Good, it's you."

"Expecting someone else?" she giggled. Such a sweet sound and a beautiful smile…

"Kind of."

A blank expression came over her face.

"We need to talk."

"Oh, here we go," she said, rolling her eyes.

"What?"

"The 'we need to talk' talk. I moved too fast, you like me but it's getting too heavy and—"

"Jenny no. I love you."

"You do?" she said, her cheeks blushed.

"Yes, but we still need to talk."

"Okay… Should I be worried?"

"I know you did it."

"Did what?"

"I know you killed Mr. Choen. Well not you but, the other yo—"

"Killed someone?! This is not funny, John," she said, edging backwards towards the edge of the bridge.

"Which one of you did it? Show yourself!"

"John, you're scaring me…"

"I'm not talking to Jenny now. Come out you chicken shit! Show yourself!"

Jenny stepped back, hands trembling, but then her facial expression changed completely.

"Halo John, looking for me?" A German accent came from Jenny's lips.

"Are you the killer? We haven't met before."

"You haven't noticed me, but I have noticed you," she said and bit her lip.

"You killed Mr. Choen?!"

"That old fool? I took him out, ya. He never loved us, kicked us to the curb like trash. Even in his death he didn't want to leave us anything. He got what he deserved."

"You son of a bitch!"

"But I thought you loved us, John. Those words are hurtful."

"I don't love *you*, you twisted fuck."

"Now now John, we wouldn't want anything to happen to Jenny, would we?" she said, standing up onto the ledge of the bridge.

"Stop!"

"Ohhh, now I have your full attention. Are you going to treat us nice?"

"Yes. But you need to come with me now," I said, reaching a hand out.

The wind started to blow hard, flicking her hair.

"And where would we be going? You know, Germany is lovely this time of year."

"Unfortunately not. I need to take you into custody. It's the best thing for you. I know it doesn't seem like it now but—"

"Doesn't seem like it? Doesn't seem like it?! I'd rather be dead than go to jail, or worse, to the looney bin!" She slipped her heels off and moved backwards. Only the front half of her feet remained on the ledge. A gust of wind blew into her stomach making her sway.

"No! Alright alright, you won't go to jail, you won't! Just let me help you down."

"Okay John," she said and leaned her hands towards me. Her fingertips touched mine, "You're lying, John," she whispered and leaped backwards off the bridge.

"NO!" I ran to the edge.

"John!" The real Jenny screamed.

Time stood still as I watched her fall for what felt like an eternity. I stuck out my arm as though I'd be able to catch her if I tried hard enough. But as the icy wind cut at my skin, a wound opened up in my heart with my brain admitting I couldn't save her.

"FUCCCKKKKK!! JENNY!!!!!"

My eyes wide open, I stared as she crashed hard into the Thames and vanished out of sight. I stumbled backwards as people began to rush to the edge of the bridge, knocking into me along the way. Everything went silent as I continued backwards, blinking and re-running the image of Jenny's frightened face, over and over. My heart pounded so hard it nearly left my chest, which would have been fine with me. I didn't want the pain. "Why didn't I save her? What did you do, John? You did nothing. You let her die! You... you..."

"John. John? John!"

"Huh?"

"John, it's me, Frank. Can you hear me?"

My hands were numb, my face like a block of ice. "Wha... what? Erm..."

"John, I came as soon as I heard on the police scanner."

"You were quick."

"John, you've been standing in the road for hours. I'm surprised nobody tried to get you off here."

I looked down at my hands and saw grazed knuckles. *Maybe someone did try to stop me...*

"Come on, John. You're coming home with me. No arguing."

I didn't say a word. My world was falling around me like ash after a fire, and it covered me like a blanket. I didn't talk much that night or the next week. My mind was like a clock that couldn't tick, and it would take someone strong to help wind me back up.

They dragged the river for days but never found a body. Doctors said nobody could survive that fall. I'd allowed myself to love again only to find it flushed down the Thames. My heart had burned in flames and the ashes spread over London during the weeks that followed. The city, the world, is messed up. I've seen, fought and felt more than an unlucky man should in a lifetime. I needed to get away, I needed to restore peace to my soul, get to the root of it all and start fresh again. I knew just the place.

Another case finished, it almost finished me. But it was another case, SOLVED.

SLICE TO MEAT YOU

Case #226

Welcome to Narita International Airport. We hope you have a pleasant stay in Tokyo."

11 hours and 50 minutes of sitting in a metal tin and I had finally landed. The whole flight I'd thought about nothing but that sweet taste of what would be my one and only cigar in Japan. I needed a clear head and lungs for this journey. I rushed through customs as quick as humanly possible and headed outside. The taste of fresh air hit me, and I immediately pulled out a cigar from my jacket pocket. I moved it slowly under my nose from one end to the other, inhaling the smell, savouring it. I placed it on my lips and struck a match. That first intake felt sweeter than it had in a long time. It tumbled down my body, and the smoke on the outside hugged my face—I felt almost at peace. Almost. That was the reason I came to Japan. To get back to my roots, silence the world I live in and replenish my soul.

I called for a taxi as I inhaled the last of my cigar, which by then was so small my fingertips almost got burnt. I slowly blew the smoke out of my mouth, savouring every sensation... "Are you getting in the taxi?" the driver asked me. I nodded and got into the car. "Yushima Seido Temple," I told him before he had the chance to ask.

Once I arrived, I headed through the Gyohkoh-mon gate and up the stone path. Immediately I started to feel a strong sense of history and former greatness. I spotted a man standing next to a giant bronze statue of Confucius, his back to me. As I approached, he turned around towards me.

"Shifu!" I said, surprised, and immediately bowed.

"Rise," he said and smiled as his eyes met mine. "It has been a long time."

"Too long, shifu. Thank you for letting me stay."

"Nonsense. You will always have a place here, my son. We will never forget what you did for us. Walk with me," he said as he turned and headed towards the Hijiri Bashi-mon gate. "I sense a dark cloud in your mind and a heaviness in your heart, my son."

"You're right, shifu, as always. The path I have walked down of late has been filled with violence, blood, and disbelief in mankind. I am in much need of cleansing my soul and realigning my heart."

Shifu stopped and turned to me. "You know, Confucius once said, 'Life is really simple, but we insist on making it complicated.' Let us go and start your journey."

I forgot how peaceful this place was. Calm, still, and the air filled with positive energy. I closed my eyes and took the deepest breath I had taken in years.

A few moments later Shifu went to take care of some business and a young man approached me, "Your room is ready," he said. He was young, about sixteen years old. Yet, through his eyes, you could see he was wiser than most people on this planet and I bet he'd never used an iPhone.

I slid my bedroom door open to reveal a sheet and pillow laid on the floor. This was to be my bed. A table and candles were in the corner for meditating, and a jug of water was at the side of it. The room was bare and basic, which was what I needed to start my spiritual recovery.

"Arigato," I said and bowed to the young man.

"You're very welcome, Detective Banks. My name is Anzan. If you need anything, don't hesitate to ask."

And with that, he left, and I was alone. I sat down, crossed my legs, and closed my—

"What do you mean you can't deliver the food? We have nothing here." I heard a man saying in the distance.

I stood up and went to see what the problem was. It turned out, some new idiot employee at the delivery company messed up. He'd spilt coffee on the order form and hid the evidence. When the usual delivery guy came into work that day, he discovered the truth and went to the monastery. He was apologetic and informed shifu a new delivery could not arrive for at least two more days.

"I'll hire a car and bring you back the food you need, shifu," I said as I bowed.

"Even though you walk through the darkness, I see you still have a good heart. Thank you, my son."

And with that, I put my meditation, amongst other things on hold, called a taxi and headed into town.

The traffic in the city was hell. I found my fingers twitching on and off. They were missing their faithful companion, the sweet cigar that had always been there. As soon as I rented a car, I headed to the nearest supermarket, not caring if it cost twice as much as the one across town. I parked the car, checked my inside pocket for my cigars, as old habits die hard, and then stepped outside. I breathed in the…semi-fresh air and headed for the store.

"GET OFF ME!" A woman screamed. *But from where?* I thought. I turned a couple of times and then I saw it. A woman being attacked in an alley.

"The lady said, get off!" I said, then I broke the guy's jaw. He hit the ground hard as I turned to the woman. "Are you okay?"

"I think so. I mean, I am now. I...I..." she stuttered.

"Relax. You're in shock. Come with me."

I took her into the nearest bar. "This should help," I said, placing a shot of vodka in front of her.

"Thanks. Actually, I'm more of a whiskey person. No ice though, I hate it when they put ice in it," she said it with a half-smile.

"You heard the lady, whiskey no ice," I told the bartender. "Make it two."

Sipping on her whiskey, she asked, "So do you do this often? Save damsels in distress?" A nervous smile came to her face as she continued to look down into her glass.

"I've saved my fair share," I said. "Comes with the job. I'm Detective Banks, John. And you are?"

"Eleanor," she said, staring into my eyes.

"Well, Eleanor, it's a pleasure to meet you," I said. "You mind telling me what happened in the alleyway?"

"I was searching for answers for..." she looked to the floor.

"For...?"

"I should go. I don't want to get into trouble. Well, I'm already in trouble, but, oh God," she said, trying to keep a strong face, but tears betrayed her.

"It's okay," I said, my hands on each of her shoulders, my eyes looking right into hers. "You're safe. You can trust me. Just start from the beginning, and I promise I will do what I can to help."

Eleanor sipped some whiskey and took a few deep breaths.

"Well, the company I work for has recently opened an office here. It's my responsibility to show the potential investors around the city, make sure they have a good time. I took them for a meal, then some bars and then...well, honestly, I can't remember much after that. When I woke the next day... Oh God. Um..." She scratched the back of her hand.

"Go on, Eleanor, you're doing great," I said, in a reassuring voice.

"I woke up with my head fuzzy, and when I looked down... there was blood all over me, and there was a knife in my hand. Then I realised that I didn't know where I was. I got scared, and ran right out of an exit door and just kept running and running. Eventually, I managed to go into a bathroom to wash the blood off my body, but I still needed some clean clothes. I walked through the streets and noticed a torn open bag of clothes in that alleyway. I know I should have waited to get dressed somewhere else, but I just wanted that blood away from me. Then I guess someone saw me getting changed and he tried to...to..." Eleanor burst out crying, repeatedly trying to continue but failing.

"It's okay, don't talk," I said as she rested her head on my chest. "You need to rest. I'll take you home."

I took Eleanor to her place, made sure she had a drink of water and that she went straight to bed. I told her I'd call her later and headed out.

I arrived at the monastery a lot later than planned with a little more road rage than usual. I found some peace once I walked through the gates again, however. I found shifu, let him know that the food was here, and apologised for the time it took.

"Nonsense, my son," Shifu said. "You arrived here precisely when you were meant to. Now, what is it you *really* wanted to tell me?"

"It looks like the darkness has followed me here. I can't seem to escape the shadows," I told him.

"People bring you the darkness, my son, because you are the light. I see no curse in you, but instead a gift. You know what needs to be done. Rest my son, tomorrow your mission begins."

In my room, I meditated on the day's events, asked for guidance, and then cleared my mind. The road was about to get rough, and sleep would keep me on track.

When I awoke in the morning, I was focused, but something was missing, something I always needed when on a case. Thirty minutes later, I was outside the Davidoff cigar shop, and my old friend had returned to me. I slowly placed the cigar on my lips and struck a match against a wall. The flame caressed the tip of the cigar, *and breathe in*. My eyes remained closed during those first few inhaling breaths and when I opened them...it was time for business.

I called Eleanor and arranged to meet her in *my office* which for now was a bar near her place.

"A little early to be in a bar, isn't it, detective?" she said as she arrived.

"Not for me. You see, I kinda grew up in places like this. My father was a great man, but he drank a lot. You couldn't imagine the things he could still do after a day of booze. Most children had a nanny in their home. Me, I had Rick, the bar owner. So, in a way, these places feel like home. Sorry, I'm letting myself go down memory lane. I'm here for you—"

"No, don't worry! It's actually nice to think of something else for a while. You tell stories well," she said, brushing her hair behind her ears.

I got us both a coffee and went over what Eleanor remembered step by step. She gave me a list of the investors she had taken out; places she had taken them to. She also told me any fragmented bits of memories she could remember, including something about a raven's claw. It was enough to go on for now. With our coffees drunk, I stood up and stuck out my hand to help her up. She looked at my hand for a while, hesitant to hold it. She'd been through a lot.

"Eleanor, you're safe," I said, looking her in the eyes. She took my hand, stood up and then we headed out. It was time to pay a visit to the places she'd been, one by one.

We arrived at the restaurant where she and the investors had eaten. Very friendly place and no discount prices in the window. I guess her company had the money for the finer things.

"Welcome back, Miss Eleanor! So nice to see you!" they said with a big smile and bow. They had received a big tip apparently so who could blame them for their enthusiasm. I asked if they had noticed anything out of the ordinary about the customers, if anyone was following them perhaps, but it was a dead end. We thanked them and left.

Next, we hit the bars they'd visited. Each one gave us a warm welcome. Bartenders nudged each other as if to say, 'she was the big tipper, give her your attention'. But this is not what we had come for, we wanted answers, not smiles. All they could tell us was everyone was lovely. Loud but nothing bad. With not too much to go on, things were looking bleak.

As we left the third bar, a waiter approached Eleanor cautiously and said," Miss, I do remember one thing from when you were here. That sleazy guy seemed to have taken a likin' to you, as well as some of our waitresses. I'd keep an eye on him if I were you." Eleanor thanked him for the information, bowed and then headed for the door.

"Wait," I held her arm and turned to the man. "What did this guy look like?"

"Well he was—"

"Stop talking to those people and get back to work," a man from behind the bar shouted.

"So sorry but I've got to go," he said and ran off.

"Let's take a break," I said and headed for a coffee shop. I had to give my eyes something new to see other than bars, drunks, and dark interiors. "So, that man he was talking about. Do you remember him?"

"Maybe. I've seen my fair share of sleazy men. Comes with the job. Hard to tell who is happy to speak to a woman and who has a rotten kind of mind. I can think of one or two men from last night who it could be. Maybe if I saw his face, I would recognise him. I have some photos at home of the investors somewhere."

I drove her home; told her I'd be in touch and went to investigate a couple more bars.

The staff in the bars weren't quite as friendly now the big tipper wasn't there. They did, however, still smile when they spoke to me.

I asked the usual questions: Did you see this woman with a group of men last night? Anything out of the ordinary happen?

This was met with 'I don't know' or 'it wasn't my shift', except for the last man I spoke to. He was young, early twenties, and when I asked him questions, his eye twitched. I was getting somewhere, so I pushed him harder.

"Listen, this is between you and me," I said as I slid some money towards him. I felt a hand on my shoulder.

"You're finished here," a man said from behind.

"Actually, I was just getting started," I replied.

The man's hand tightened on my shoulder, his fingers digging in hard. He came close to my ear and said, "I will crush you into tiny pieces little man. You are poking your nose where it does not belong."

"That's not what he said," I said and pointed behind the man. He turned, and at that moment, I grabbed his wrist and broke it in two places.

"KUSO!" he screamed in pain.

"Looks like your wrist is what's crushed into tiny pieces. Now tell me—" I blacked out.

***

When I awoke, my head was pounding, and I had what felt like a golf ball on the back of it. Someone had hit me with a club or a giant fist. I looked around; I wasn't in the bar I was in before. They'd moved me quickly. *Did they know I was coming?*

"Mr. Banks," a woman's voice said. "You've been poking your head in matters that do not concern you. I'm afraid I'm going to have to ask you to leave Japan immediately."

I looked the woman up and down. Dressed in a dark green suit, she was no taller than five foot, but looked like she could crush you in a second.

"And if I refuse?" I asked, staring straight into her eyes. I needed to show her no fear and that I meant business.

"Then you will end up on the menu for my dogs," she said, her face emotionless as she tossed meat to her rottweilers, "They're ever so hungry."

As I watched the dogs viciously tore the meat apart a man approached me as she said, "Have a drink, Mr. Banks. Whiskey no ice, right?"

The man placed the drink in front of me, but I didn't pick it up.

"Relax, Mr. Banks. If I wanted you dead, you'd be in the ground by now. Treat this as a farewell drink. It's been in my cellar for years, waiting for the perfect connoisseur like yourself." She smiled just enough for one to notice it.

I picked up the drink, smelt it, and then tasted it. "Aged perfectly. I suppose I could thank you for it, but I would rather get back to the…to the…" My head hit the table, and I fell to the ground. The last thing I saw was that bitch standing over me.

"Banks. Banks." I heard a voice echoing as I pried my eyes open, my vision blurry. "Where is Banks?" I raised my hand slowly as I sat myself up and leaned against the wall. My vision started to clear up, and I saw a policeman coming towards me. I was in a jail cell! Sitting next to me were guys you wouldn't want to meet in a dark alley, who smelt like they'd been lying in one too.

"Banks, you're coming with me," the man said.

He opened the cell door and asked me to follow him. On the back of his neck was a tattoo, a claw of some kind. *A raven's claw!* Eleanor mentioned something about that, I was sure. *Is this guy connected?* He took me into a quiet room and sat me down.

"Mr. Banks, you can consider this a warning. Leave Japan today, right now, and that will be the end of it. If not, well…" he said, caressing his gun. "Am I clear?" He leant towards me.

"Crystal," I replied.

I was thrown out of the police station with everything except the money that was inside my wallet. I hate dirty cops, and I wanted to find out more about this one. I waited for a couple of hours until I spotted the policeman walk out of the station. He looked left and right cautiously before getting into his car. He didn't want to be followed, but this wasn't my first time tailing someone. I allowed him to leave, and after a couple seconds, began to follow him.

After thirty minutes, we arrived at a warehouse. I kept my distance. Through my binoculars, I saw people loading boxes into his car. He must be a delivery guy for the new friends I made earlier. He started to open a box, and I zoomed in. *RING!* "Shit," I said as my phone vibrated, then fell off my lap. When I looked back through the binoculars, the box was closed. My phone was still ringing and when I picked it up, I saw Eleanor's name.

"Hel—"

"HELP!" she screamed down the phone.

"I'm coming!" I threw the binoculars on the back seat, reversed the car, and put the pedal to the metal.

At Eleanor's apartment building, I ran out only to be stopped by the entrance door. I needed to be buzzed through. *Fuck.* I pressed all the buttons on the intercom, waiting impatiently for someone to buzz me in. "Is that the pizza dude?" a stoner said. "Yes, it's the fucking pizza dude. Now let me in before I throw this in the trash!" *BUZZZZZ.*

The elevator was broken, and after punching a dent into it, I charged up the stairs. Finally, I reached Eleanor's apartment and kicked the door down. A man stood behind her, with a plastic bag over her head.

"You gonna die, bitch," he said.

"Not on my watch, asshole," I said. I ran across the room and stamped my foot on his ankle, breaking it instantly.

He screamed in pain, but as I got closer, he swung a knife and sliced my right cheek. I turned, took a deep breath, and then set my eyes on his. He came at me swinging wildly now, shaking his head anytime he put weight on his ankle. He missed me, got the knife stuck in a wall and an elbow in the face from me. "Stay down!" I shouted at him, but some guys don't learn.

He managed to stand, using the table to help him up. His eyes betrayed him; he was scared but didn't know when to give up. "ARRRRR!" he screamed and threw the knife towards my head. I moved to my left, and the blade flickered off the tip of my ear and into the wall. "My turn," I said with a smile, picked the knife out of the wall and threw it into his other leg. He hit the floor hard. Crawling, he headed towards Eleanor. He reached for her but received my boot to his face and said goodbye to his two front teeth.

"Who do you work—" I said, but before I could finish, he'd bitten into something and fell unconscious. *What was that? Not cyanide, I've seen someone take that before, hmm…*

I frisked the man, checking for any clues, nothing in his pockets were of use. I flipped him onto his stomach and there on the back of his neck was a raven claw tattoo.

I turned to Eleanor, who was now sitting up against a wall. I crouched down and checked her over. She had a pretty deep cut on the back of her shoulder. The wound was probably from when the man approached her from behind initially. A mistake, I'm sure, as I think he wanted it to look like a suicide in the end. That's how these kinds of people work.

"Are you okay?" I asked. Eleanor looked at me. Her eyes wide open, she was in shock. I went over to the kitchen and poured her a glass of water and then headed to the freezer for some ice.

"What the hell is that?" I asked, surprised.

I pulled out a bag to see what appeared to be some kind of sushi, but it looked unfinished and made out of…*human flesh? No, it can't be, can it?* I've seen my share of dead bodies. Parts ripped off, pieces all over the place after an explosion, but this looked like some messed up shit. *I'll send it to my contact to analyse it.*

"Eleanor... Eleanor!" I said and lifted her chin up.

"W-wha...?"

"Eleanor, what is this?" I showed her the bag from the freezer. She stared at it, curiously at first. Then her eyes widened, and fear came back inside. "Get it away!" she screamed.

"Okay, okay, it's gone. It's gone, Eleanor. Now, can you tell me why you have this in your freezer?" I asked calmly.

"Th-the man. H-he put it there. I caught him putting it in my freezer, a-and when he turned and saw me, I ran. But he came at me with a knife and-and-and—"

"It's okay. Look at me. It's okay. You're safe now. You're safe," I told her and then she fell into my arms. As this happened, I noticed something on the back of Eleanor's neck. I moved her hair to the side and saw a raven's claw tattoo.

"Eleanor, do you remember getting a tattoo?"

"What? No." she rubbed tears from her eyes, "Why?" she said, confused.

"Well, you've got a raven claw tattoo on the back of your neck. Same as the one I saw in the bar I was drugged in, same as one on a dirty cop and now this guy on the floor. Only yours only has one claw. It seems it's all connected. Do you remember going to a tattoo parlour, bright light sign, anything?"

"Um..." She looked to the ground, tapping her fist against her lips. "A redfish!"

"A fish?" I asked.

"I remember a red neon fish in a window. That's all I remember, though. I'm sorry it's not more." Her eyes looked to the ground as she rubbed her left arm.

"Eleanor, it's great and something to go on. You did well. We'll find that place later, but for now, we need to get you to a hospital and see about getting that shoulder stitched up."

I sent the "sushi" to one of my contacts to get analysed and took Eleanor to the hospital. I also dragged the unconscious man who refused to wake up with us. The doctor told me he was in some sort of coma and didn't know when he would be conscious again.

While Eleanor was getting stitched up, I searched on my laptop for the redfish hoping it would direct me to the tattooist who had marked her. It turned out there were only a few tattoo parlours in the city, unusual for a city this size. They all had neon fish signs on them, all red. As I mapped out the addresses, I discovered one was right in the middle of where Eleanor had taken her clients. As soon as she came out from having her stitches, I told her, and we headed to the parlour.

It didn't take long to get to our destination. I got out the car and opened Eleanor's door for her. We both stared at the building for a while. It was a big place and lit up like a Christmas tree. Eleanor saw the sign and her head twitched. "Are you okay? I can go inside on my own if you need me to," I told her.

"No, it's fine. I think it's just because we're getting closer to it all."

I looked through the window and saw a man counting his money. He had a grin from ear to ear. Then, he glanced up and saw Eleanor. He rushed to the door and tried to slam it shut. "We're closed!" he said as I put my foot in the doorway.

"Not anymore," I said and shoved the door open. The man fell back and then rushed towards me. He stopped just before he reached me when he realised the size difference between the two of us.

"You're gonna sit down nice and slow. We need to talk," I said as I walked towards the man who stumbled backwards. "I can see from your face that you remember my friend here. Question is, why were you so eager to make sure she didn't come inside?"

"I just had to close up is all," he said, avoiding eye contact.

"Bullshit. You took one look at her and panicked." I moved closer and leaned forward on the desk as he sat down. "Now, are you going to start telling me the truth?"

"I am telling the truth—" *BANG*! I slammed my fist hard down onto the table. The man jumped and tried to get away. I grabbed him by the tie and dragged him to my face.

"Start talking!" I demanded. "Tell me how you know this woman and all about the raven claw tattoo I keep seeing."

"Give me money," he said.

I pulled the tie of his knot tight to his throat, causing him to choke. "How about I give you some broken hands instead?! See how well your tattoo business does then."

"Ok, ok, ok! She came in last night with a group of guys and a woman. She was high on drugs or something."

"And you thought it was okay to tattoo someone in that condition?"

"No of course not but, but..."

"But what?!"

"Well, they paid really well," he said, half smiling at the thought of the money.

"Take that smile off your face before I knock it off. Now, I want names."

"I don't know any."

I started to put knuckle-dusters over my fingers.

"I swear! Oh God, I swear I don't know any names!!"

"Tell me what you *do* know, and things here don't have to get...messy." It was my turn to grin now.

"There were a few men, and a woman who looked like there leader. She was built like a brick house that one. I've seen her going into the club up the street, *Dragon Fire*. Here," he said and handed me a flyer. "A charity event is being held there tonight."

232

"Ok, now tell me what you know about this tattoo."

"Word on the street is, if you have that tattoo, you're an exclusive member of a club, a gang. They make the rules around here. All the people who came in here last night have had one done by me or in the other two parlours over the years."

"I see. And why does my friend's tattoo only have one sharp claw on it?"

"That...I heard it means she's only...umm..."

"Spit it out."

"She's only killed once," he said and looked over to Eleanor.

"Wh-what did he s-say?" Eleanor said and fainted.

After making sure Eleanor was alright, I asked the tattooist if he could draw a convincing raven's claw on the back of my neck that looked like a tattoo. He said he would do his best, which would have to be good enough. I sat in the chair while he worked, planning my visit to Dragon Fire.

Once Eleanor was home, I rented a tuxedo from a store and headed to the club. I arrived a little early and so headed into the nearest bar. "Whiskey, no ice." I told the bar man. As he grabbed the bottle, I looked around the bar. Traditional dragon paintings covered the walls, dark mahogany floorboards filled the room. "One whiskey, no ice," said the barman. I tipped the bar man and went over to a booth. I sat down on the red leather cushioned seat and sipped my whiskey. *This is not half bad*, I thought, and took out my fountain pen to wrote down the name of it.

A while later, I pulled out my pocket watch. It was time. I stood up, gave a nod to the barman and left. Outside, there were expensive cars, women wearing diamonds, and plenty of raven claw tattoos. I checked my new tattoo and headed to the door. The doorman was about six foot five and had muscles to spare. He looked like a tank wouldn't be able to knock him over. He slowly checked the back of my neck and then looked me up and down. If he wasn't happy, I was not sure I could take him. But then he smiled. "You've got all your kills. I like it," he said and allowed me to then pass.

Inside the club, I was aware that some people might recognise me from the last encounter which landed me in jail. When possible, I made sure to have my eyes to the ground and to stand behind guests when surveilling the room.

"A drink, sir?" a tall, beautiful woman asked me as she walked up to me with a tray.

"No, thank—" She tripped, and I leapt forward to catch her.

"I'm so sorry! So, so, so sorry!" she said as I lifted her back to her feet.

"It's okay, I'm fine."

"No, no, no, sir, let me help you," she said and began patting me down where the drinks had fallen. Before I could stop her, she'd wiped the water off the back of my neck. Once she'd finished, I prayed the tattoo was still there as I tenderly reached my hand back to touch it.

A large shadow appeared in front of me. I turned around and saw the doorman. His giant fist came towards me and I flew across the room, banging my head on a table. The female leader came towards me with a syringe as I blinked and then passed out.

Time passed, and when I started to gain consciousness, I felt myself being placed onto a table.

"Don't worry. That will keep him knocked out for hours," someone said, my eyes not yet open.

Bits of metal scraped against each other. *Why's that so familiar? Wait. It's someone sharpening a knife!*

"WHAT THE FUCK!" I screamed, opening my eyes to see a woman peeling the skin off my leg!

The woman jumped back. "You're meant to be asleep!" she told me and grabbed a cleaver.

I rolled off the table onto my feet, but my legs buckled, and I hit the ground.

"Come back here!" she shouted and ran towards me. "I told them to kill you first, but they wouldn't listen," she said and swung the cleaver towards my head. I stopped it with both hands on either side of the blade. It was an inch from my face, and this woman was heavy.

"I'm going to enjoy peeling you, and I think I will keep you awake while I do it."

She put more weight onto the cleaver while spreading her legs to get a better stance. Big mistake. I kicked her right between the legs. The cleaver spiralled to the floor as she bent over in pain. I grabbed her head and smashed it against mine. Blood trickled down her face as she fell back but she just shook her head and came toward me again. I grabbed a frying pan and *BANG*! I hit her hard, and she was out for the count. I spotted the back door, limped towards it, and escaped into an alley.

At one end of the alley, I spotted two silhouettes of men. They turned, and when they spotted me, they started to run my way. I went as fast as my injured leg would take me to the other end of the alley, but they were fast. I was close to the street and as I limped towards it, I saw a man getting into a taxi. I barged him out the way and dived in. The men were fifteen feet away.

"Where to?"

"Just drive. DRIVE!" I yelled, and as the men approached, the car tires screeched, and we left. Two seconds later, I passed out.

Waking with a banging headache, I looked out the window. *I must've been out for a while.* "Wh-where are we?"

"We're about to pull into the hospital," he said in an irritated tone.

"I never told you to come here."

"You're bleeding all over my taxi and have passed out twice. Now get out."

The second I was out the door the taxi drove off and I began to limp towards the entrance door. I nearly made it too...

★ ★ ★

I pried my eyes open and a beautiful brunette woman was leaning over me.

"Are you okay, Mr. Banks?" she asked, checking my eyes.

"Feeling better already," I said with a smile.

"Mr. Banks, you have been unconscious for twelve hours. We have taken care of your leg, but it will need a few days to rest to avoid irritating it. Unfortunately, space is low in the hospital. I can only offer you a bed for this afternoon. Do you have somewhere to stay?"

I nodded, as another woman brought me some food. While eating, I couldn't take my eyes off my leg. These guys were some sick, crazy people and I had to put an end to it all. From the look and feel of my leg, I wasn't going to be charging into war anytime soon though. When the afternoon was up, I called Eleanor to explain what had happened and told her to sit tight for now. Then, I headed back to the monastery.

At the monastery, I needed stillness in my heart. Right now, it had a hurricane inside. To beat these sick people, I first needed to be at peace. My spirit had to become like a leaf floating on a calm river.

Over the next couple of days, I emptied my mind. Thoughts of the case were not allowed in. On the third day, after hours of meditation, I opened my eyes. I was ready to begin. My first action would be collecting evidence. When going into the dragon's den, I wanted more than just my fists.

My first stop was the hospital. "I'm here to check on the John Doe I brought in," I told the receptionist.

"John Doe, sir?" she said, looking at her computer screen. "There has been no John Doe's brought in here this week."

"You're mistaken. I brought in a guy who was unconscious the other day. Your doctor said he was in some sort of a coma."

"We have no records of that here sir," she said, still not making any eye contact. People can be like that, I guess.

"Can I speak to Doctor Nakamura?"

"I'm afraid that's not possible, sir. Is there anything else?"

Just then, the doctor who'd treated the scumbag walked by.

"Doctor Nakamura. Doctor!" I shouted to get her attention.

"Can I help you, sir?"

"Yes. I'm looking for the John Doe I brought in, but your receptionist can't seem to find him. I told her about your diagnosis the other day but—"

"I'm sorry, sir, but you say you know me?"

"Yes."

"I'm sorry, sir, but I've never met you before. Listen, I'm swamped. Sorry, I have to go." She rushed off into an elevator.

Something was going on. *Why would the hospital staff be acting this way? What had happened here?* And then I saw it. The same cop who spoke to me at the police station was walking through a door with hospital files in hand. I ran towards him, but some idiot in a wheelchair rolled right in front of me and hit my sore leg. "Dammit!" I yelled as I fell to my knees. *I don't have time for pain.* I got up and ran to the door. When I got to the other side, he was nowhere to be seen. I looked out a window and saw him in his car, staring right at me. He smiled and drove away.

I jumped in my car and decided to head back to the monastery. Something was going on. This was bigger than a club or just a gang. Was it the mafia? Drug lords? Whatever it was, these people had power and people in their pockets. As I got close to the monastery, I saw smoke rising. Something was burning.

I raced to the entrance. Outside were two cop cars, including the guy from the hospital. The front door was wide open, and as I entered, I saw my room on fire and two cops laughing. I crept up behind one of them, wrapped my arm around their neck and said, "You picked the wrong guy to fuck with." I slammed his body to the ground, and as the other man came towards me, I put my fist into his throat. He walked backwards, struggling to breathe, and then tripped, hitting his head on a statue. I sat on top of the other man, lifted his chest up by his shirt and started pounding his face. I couldn't stop. The red mist had descended.

"This is not the way, my son." Shifu said and put his hand on my shoulder. "Violence is never—"

Shifu fell to the ground, the dirty cop stood over him, smiling. I leapt towards him and grabbed him by the throat. I lifted his body into the air and his face quickly started to turn red.

"What are you gonna do? Kill me? Kill a cop?" He managed to say, barely.

"I've done a lot worse. Get ready for hell," I told him. But he started smiling. "What are you so happy about?"

"Him."

I turned and saw the bouncer from the club. Blackness...

Fuck it's hot... Sweat poured down my back. It was still dark, but I was awake. *What...what's going on?* Just then, I saw the slightest bit of daylight. A thin line. I was in a car trunk. As I moved my body a little, I discovered that my hands were cuffed and feet tied. I had a bad taste of plastic or something in my mouth. Duct tape… You never get used to the taste of duct tape, no matter how many times someone has slapped it on you.

I tested how much I could move, to see if I could free myself out of something but to no avail. I hated this part. I put my hands as close together as I could and then…*crack*! I dislocated my thumb. Sliding my hand out of the cuffs, I reached down, untied my feet, and then ripped the duct tape off my mouth. I wiped the sweat out of my eyes and looked for the trunk release cable. It was too dark, so I had to do this by touch. *Got it!* The trunk flew open, and I could see the road. We were moving fast over a bridge.

"This is going to hurt," I said and jumped out of the car. I hit the ground hard and rolled over and over and over. Blood poured down my face and over my hands. The car screeched to a halt. I had to move quickly. I looked over to the car, it started to turn around.

"Here goes nothing," I said and jumped off the bridge. I hit the river and went down deep. Red water floated around me, and my blood clouded my vision. I stayed underwater and held my breath, making sure not to send any bubbles to the surface. While I waited, the current started to move me down the river.

After a while, I washed up onto land. I was going to need a new suit and some supplies. Luckily, I knew a good tailor close by.

Once suited up, I grabbed some supplies and went to stake out the club. It didn't make sense for me to walk into the lion's den, especially when they had that giant ogre at the door. I needed a different tactic. I parked in the street close to the club and waited. The queen bee had to leave sometime, and when she did, I would follow her, get her alone and have a little talk.

A few hours later, she came out of the building with two men and got into a car. I followed them around the city closely. First, she had some tea with a suspicious looking man. He slid her a package underneath the table which she passed behind her to her bodyguard. With a nod, she stood up and left. After driving for half an hour or so, she went to her home, and I continued on a little down the road. The walls around the property were high, and from what I could see through the gate, it would be a long walk up to the house. It wouldn't be long until it was dark, and that is when I would enter.

Once the moon kissed the ground, I began my search for a weak point in the security or the wall. I got out of the car and started to walk.

After fifteen minutes of searching weak parts of the wall or a backdoor entrance, I found my way in. Good thing I'm not scared of heights.

In front of me stood a tree, a very tall tree, with a long branch that leaned over the wall. This was something I'm sure wasn't there when they first bought the property. Their incompetence in regular checks, however, was my gain.

I started my ascent up the tree and was soon in position. This allowed me not only to gain access but also to see the property's layout. Two guards patrolled the grounds. I stayed in position for a while taking note of any routine they had. It turned out that every thirty minutes or so, the men stopped for a cigarette break. That would be my chance.

After a few minutes, it was time for me to cross the branch. It looked thicker from the ground. *Just take it step by step, John.* That's all I needed to do. I was halfway across the branch and going strong. The branch above my head that I was holding, was about to run out. I moved forwards, balancing my— "FUCK!" I yelled as the branch began to break. I leapt forwards and landed stomach first on the top of the wall. The wind was taken out of me, but I didn't have much time. I rolled to the edge of the wall and slid down it onto the grass. I went from tree to tree until I was close to the guards. Slowly, I crept behind them and said, "You know, smoking kills." And as they turned, I smashed their heads together. With the guards now bloody and unconscious, I sat them either side of a tree, tied them together, and gagged their mouths.

Once at the property, I searched for any open windows, but to no avail. It was going to have to be the doors. A side entrance would be best. I wanted to avoid the front door or places like the kitchen. Luckily, I found one on the east side of the building. I took out my lock picks, praying the door wouldn't trip an alarm. If it did, I would have two choices. Run away or run as fast as I could towards the queen bee.

I heard the lock click open and slowly opened the door, prepared to run if needed. "Easy does it…" I was in and no alarm went off, *thank God*. It was time to catch me a killer. I crept in the dark from room to room, searching for the Queen Bee or any evidence that would help me put this psycho behind bars. Then a line of light shone from between two sliding doors at the end of the hall. I slowly approached it and put my eye to the door- *BUZZZZ*. "Shit." It was a text on my phone. *Thank Christ it was on vibrate.*

"Banks. I've got the results. Human flesh. Female. I've seen some messed up stuff in my time, but human sushi? I'll send over the details to you. I just thought you'd want to know."

The doors began to open, and I darted to the left of them. The woman walked through the doorway sweating as if she'd just run a marathon. She walked slowly down the corridor. That was my chance. I wrapped my arm around her neck, but as I did, she grabbed my wrist and moved it with ease. She was freakishly strong. I pushed my arm back towards her throat, but she twisted my wrist, almost snapping it.

"So, Mr. Banks," she said, twisting my wrist a little more. "You think you can just come into my home and attack me?" I swung my other fist at her, but she caught it. "I'll show you what happens to people who disturb me here," she said and crashed her head into mine. I fell to the ground. There was now three of her going around in a circle. I shook it off and scurried backwards on the floor. This was going to be tough.

I went to put my knuckle dusters on, but she kicked them away, and they bounced off the wall, into a fish tank. She grabbed me by my throat and raised me up. I struck her arms with all my might, but to no avail.

"Let me tell you what I'm going to do with you, Mr. Banks. I'm not going to feed you to my people. You're not worthy of that. I'm not even going to feed you to my dogs. No, I'm going to feed you to my pigs and watch them crunch your bones as you scream."

I spat in her face. She didn't like that. She raised me higher and then slammed me into the big fish tank. Water, fish, and blood splattered everywhere. She towered over me and leaned down to pick me up. I smiled and smashed her face with the knuckle dusters. As she staggered backwards, I grabbed a chair and smashed it over her head. *How is she still standing?* I backed up, ran, jumped, and smashed her again in the face with the knuckle dusters. She swayed left, then right and then came crashing down to the ground.

I checked her pulse. Still alive. I tied her hands behind her back and put her in a chair. There was something odd on her bracelet. Some hard-plastic stick. I ripped the bracelet off her wrist. Maybe it was something important. I started to look around the house for clues. I went through her office drawers and cupboards. Nothing. *I guess she doesn't like to take her business home with her.*

Human Sushi. I couldn't get that thought out of my head. Then it hit me. The freezer. That man had put some in Eleanor's earlier on. Maybe there would be something here. I headed for the kitchen. There I found the biggest freezer I had ever seen in a home. *Who owns a walk-in freezer in their house?* I pushed past some cow meat and some lamb. Then there at the back, I saw a freezer box. Locked. "I wonder…" I said and lifted the plastic stick towards it. The lid slowly opened. There it was - human sushi and some body parts neatly piled.

I took out my phone. No signal. I walked outside the freezer and headed back to check on the woman. She was gone. Tie-backs laid broken on the floor. I backed quickly into a room and shut the door. I called the police and waited.

As I looked through the keyhole, there was no sign of the woman. Then came a bang on the front door. *That was quicker than I expected.* Knuckle dusters on my hands, I made a run for the door. When I opened it, I was surprised when I read the man's name tag, 'Commissioner Takahashi.'

A voice came from behind me, "Commissioner, how lovely to see you." It was the queen psycho, now dolled up and smiling.

"Commissioner, you need to come with me quick," I said, turning to head past the woman.

"Is that so?" he asked and looked at Ms. Psycho, who remained calm.

Why is she so calm? Hmm—

"Detective? I thought you had something to show me."

"Yes. Follow me," I said and walked fast to the freezer. Once the commissioner caught up, I opened the freezer chest.

"You see, commissioner. This psycho is killing humans and serving them for dinner!" He moved past me and picked up a package from the same freezer.

"Ah, my package," he said with a smile.

"Wait, what?!"

"You haven't tried it, detective? It's delicious!" he said as he pulled his gun out.

He walked me slowly out of the freezer at gunpoint.

"Detective Banks, I've admired you from afar for a while now. I think it would be a shame to put such talents to waste. So here is what I'm going to do. I'm going to allow you to join us, and in return, I won't serve your flesh at our next event." Turned out this guy was the head of the snake and not the woman. An excellent cover for him though, should things go south.

"And if I say fuck you?"

He pistol-whipped me hard. Blood and teeth fell to the ground.

"Come now, detective. I could kill you right now where you stand," he said, lifting my chin up with his gun. "But I see a better future for you. Join us. Think of what we could accomplish together."

More blood trickled out the side of my mouth. I needed to buy some time.

"And what would you have me do?" I asked.

"We need you to kill someone for us. Don't worry, he's an evil man," he said, moving the gun away from my chin.

"And you can't do this yourself?" I asked and spat some blood on the floor.

"This is the leader of an up and coming Russian gang. He knows all our members. We would never be able to get close to him. But you, on the other hand, I'm sure it wouldn't be a problem. Who knows? You might enjoy it. And then you will have earned your claws."

I went to strike the gun out of his hand but something cold and sharp slipped into my back and blood began to trickle down.

"Now, now. I thought we were past this. I can have you skinned and ready for a meal quicker than you can cry for your mother!" he shouted and then took a deep breath. "Do you want to die, Mr. Banks? Hmm?" He put the gun to my forehead. "Three...two..."

"Okay," I mumbled.

"I'm sorry. What was that?"

"I...want to join you," I said, and the knife slid out of my back.

"Perfect. Now here is what is going to happen. We will give you the weapons and get you in. But, if you have a change of heart Mr. Banks, we will make sure every member of their gang comes flooding down onto you. I'm sure you understand," he said and put out his hand. I shook it and then with a bandage on my back I was escorted out of the house and into a car.

Inside, the car was packed with huge thugs. I fit in the middle, just. The smell was awful. These guys must have missed their yearly bath.

The way I had it figured, this group of people felt they had a win-win situation. Either they would have the Russian gang leader killed and me on board, or me dead and buried along with everything I had witnessed these past few days.

When the car stopped, I saw a familiar sight. A neon redfish. Looks like I was about to get some fresh ink.

"Hello gentle—" The tattoo artist spotted me and turned as white as a ghost.

"This guy needs a tattoo," one of the thugs told him. "Now."

"R-r-right," he stuttered. "The usual?"

"Yes. No claws, for now."

I felt a nudge in my back, and I walked towards the tattoo-ist. "Nice to meet you," I said, reassuring him that I hadn't rat-ted him out. He breathed a sigh of relief. "Is your tattoo room small?" I said, nodding to him. "I can get a little claustrophobic, you see." I mimed my lips, "Say yes".

"I'm afraid the only room I have available now is a small room."

"You two can't be alone," a thug said.

"I'm sure we could squeeze..." he said, and I signalled the num-ber one to him, "...one of you in with us." He smiled nervously.

We went into a small room, and he got to work on my neck tattoo. Some people don't like the feeling of getting a tattoo. Painful, they say. But after what I've experienced in life, it was more like being tickled.

I knocked the tattooist's ink onto the floor. "Oh, I'm sorry," I said. When he bent over next to me, I whispered, "Exit?" He gestured towards a narrow door, behind some supplies. You wouldn't even think it was there unless told.

"And...done," the tattooist told the thug. "Do you want to check it?"

The man leaned in, and I thrust my head back into his. I heard his nose crunch, and then I grabbed the tattoo gun and scratched it across his eyes. He screamed in agony. I didn't have long. I threw the tattooist towards the door and, with a nod of appreciation, I barged the exit door open. Out in the alley, I dragged some heavy garbage cans in front of the exit. They weren't getting out that way. They would expect me to run for the street. Instead, I went up the fire escape to the roof and hid. Crouched down, I tried to control my breathing. Men's feet slammed the ground of the alley. The guys sounded pissed.

It was an hour later when I saw the thugs go out of sight. I assumed they went inside to further question the tattooist. We weren't friends, and the tattooist didn't know where I was. He had nothing to give. I took out my phone and called a contact of mine. I was gonna need a weapon.

Before I could even think of any fighting, I needed to make sure Eleanor was safe. I headed over to her place and explained everything while she packed.

"But where am I going?" she asked.

"As far away from here as possible. You're not safe in Tokyo and possibly not even in Japan."

"But my job. My life here."

"You'll have no life at all if you stay here! Do you want to die?!" I said, looking right into her eyes.

"Okay! You're right…" she said, looking at the floor.

Cars screeched to a halt outside. I looked carefully through a window.

"We've gotta go. Now!" I said and grabbed her by the wrist. She managed to grab her bag as I pulled her out the front door.

We made a run for the fire exit door at the end of the hall. Once on the other side of the fire exit, I peeked through the crack of the door. Six men entered the hallway and kicked her apartment door down. We headed down the stairs and ran out the back of the building. Just then we spotted smoke coming out of the building. They were covering their tracks. Eleanor hadn't agreed to be part of their crew, and that meant she couldn't live.

Once we were far enough away from the building, I took Eleanor into a clothing store. We needed to change clothes, dye

247

Eleanor's hair, and then sneak her out of here. Once we were changed, Eleanor said she needed a stiff drink.

"I'm afraid we can't. We don't know which bars these guys own. We can't take the chance, and I also need your head straight," I said and so instead took her into a little café.

"I-I've started to remember things from that night," she said, looking at the floor, a tear coming to her eye. "I know why there was all that...blood. I didn't drink too much that night, but at one point, the room started spinning. I remembered one of the sleazy guys, and he seemed to be thanking the owner for something. I remember seeing a tattoo on the back of his neck as we entered the tattoo place. Later, some woman told me that I was one of them now. Said I needed to be initiated first though. That's when they put me in front of...of...a body. A man just lay there, barely moving. 'Do this,' the woman said, 'and you will have a new husband and all the members of our group will become your family.' That sleazy man stood smiling in the corner of the room, eating some sort of sushi. Then the woman started to...to peel the legs of the man on the table! When I hesitated to do the same, she made me drink something. Then things went blurry. I can't remember anymore, and I don't think I want to."

Tears ran continuously down her face, but her eyes were blank. When you go through such an experience, it changes you. Sometimes forever. Your soul is buried in a dark pit, and you can spend your life trying to get out of it, trying to feel normal, whatever *normal* is.

I made a few calls and managed to find someone who could smuggle Eleanor out of the country undetected. As for me, this was war. I had my mission, and it was time to execute it. I found a private weapons dealer in Tokyo and bought my own little arsenal. A lot of blood was about to be spilt.

It didn't take long to discover the location of the Russian gang's main headquarters. I kept my distance at first. From a rooftop, I sat patiently gathering intel about the area and the gang. Once I had what I needed, I sat down and crossed my legs. In deep meditation, I spoke affirmations of how everything was in my control and how all would go well. Then I opened my eyes. It was time.

A year spent in Russia has served me well. Being able to speak the language got me out of a lot of sticky situations throughout the years. I went to the main entrance with a case in hand.

"What is this?" the man at the door asked, looking me up and down and staring at the case.

I cleared my throat and started to speak in Russian. "I'm here with a sample of guns to sell Vladimir."

"I have no record of this. Piss off."

"When Vlad sees what's in this case, he will be far politer than you are," I said and opened the case.

Seeing expensive top-of-the-range guns, the man turned and spoke to a man who scurried away. He returned five minutes later, and I was in.

I was patted down by the six-foot seven-inch ogre vigorously. "Why do you have a bible?" he asked as he reached towards it.

Pulling it towards my chest, I replied, "I always like to keep the Lord close to my heart. I can read you my favourite passage if you like."

He looked at the other man and then signalled for me to head inside.

The place was huge. Steel everywhere; steel floor, steel stairs, steel sculptures. Full floor-length windows were at the back of the property with a stretch of land behind it. The front of the place only had a couple of small windows surrounded by black walls making it less easy for a sniper or others to see inside. As I headed up a long set of stairs, I saw something I didn't expect; paintings of ballerinas all over the walls.

"Do you like the ballet?" A voice asked as I reached near the top of the stairs.

A man in an expensive navy-blue suit with a red tie stood behind a large desk.

"I once had the pleasure of watching the Russian Ballet in Saint Petersburg. Quite stunning," I said, never looking away from his eyes.

"I love the ballet. The performers move so gracefully. They work hard at what they want to perfect, and then they execute it beautifully. Like me, in my line of work." He turned to look at a painting of a female ballerina on his office wall. "My man tells me you have something for me."

"I do," I said and opened the case on a table.

He walked over. "These are some nice pieces you have, Mister...?"

"I don't use real names. Code names only. You understand."

"Well, what can I call you?"

"Raven."

"Raven?" he said. "Well, Raven. I like your guns, The FN F200 assault rifle is a glorious piece of craftsmanship. I think we can set something up." He nodded at his guard. "How unusual that you carry a bible," he said, scratching his chin.

"Have you not let the Lord into your heart, Vlad?"

"The Lord doesn't belong in my line of business, Raven."

"Let me read you a passage that might change your mind," I said, opening the book close to my body. "Matthew 24:6, You will hear of wars and rumours of wars, but see to it that you are not alarmed. Such things must happen—" Then I pulled out the gun from inside the book and shot Vlad between the eyes. Shocked, the two guards turned towards me but received the same treatment as their master.

It was only a matter of time before more men came running up those stairs behind me. I picked up the assault rifle from the case in front of me and turned. I opened fire, and the men dropped like flies. Once the last man was down, I went over to Vlad's body and dropped a raven's claw on top of it. One thing I love about Russians is when a leader falls, there is always some-one hungry to replace them. And when that person found the raven claw, there would be a war between the two gangs of the city. All I had to do was wait.

It wasn't a matter of days, but a matter of hours before the fighting began. The city was lit up by gunfire and explosions. And with all gangs busy, with everyone distracted, I had a cou-ple of people I needed to visit.

I could have used a sniper rifle. I could've used a small gun. But these kills needed to feel more...personal. What these peo-ple had put Eleanor and I through deserved a more cut-throat ending. I sharpened a few blades and then rested. The next day was going to be intense.

I spent the day observing both gangs' movements and the queen bee. With the gang war happening, there weren't many guards around her. She retreated to her home, and I got into position.

The night was cold, and my breath danced in front of me. I looked through the lens of the sniper rifle to see if any guards had stayed close to the home. There were two. I didn't know these guys, and they didn't know me, but soon they would be leaving this earth. I held my breath. The guards turned their backs to each other and began a perimeter check. I pulled the trigger, and the bullet flew through the air and then the guard's head. Before he touched the floor, a bullet headed for the other guard. He didn't even have time for a scared expression. When he fell to the floor, I jumped over the wall, dropped the rifle, and headed to the house.

I picked the lock of the side door and pulled out my Gerber Silver Trident blade, a favourite of mine. One by one, I checked the rooms for the queen. Then I heard the crackling of firewood to the west of the building. A long shadow lay on the floor, coming from a tall chair by the fireplace.

"I've been expecting you," the queen bee's voice said from the chair.

"And yet, no guards in the room with you?"

"No, Mr. Banks. Sometimes in life, you have to take the bull by the balls and look it in the eye. Which is precisely what I plan to do with you," she said, standing up and turning to face me. Staring straight into the depths of my soul, she moved towards me.

The veins on her neck pulsated. I swiped my knife towards her face, but she caught my hand and began to squeeze. My knuckles cracked as I dropped the blade. My heart pounded. My breath grew quicker. *What options do I have? What? What?* Her ankle!

I smashed my boot into her ankle, her bone pierced through her skin. She fell to the ground. Breathing heavily, I stood upright and to my surprise, so did she. *What is this woman on?!* The beast hobbled towards me. *Time to put this monster to rest.* I slipped my knuckle duster on and smashed it right into her nose. Blood flowed down. No reaction. She grabbed my head with both hands and began to squeeze. My legs went limp and the room began to spin. As she lifted me back up, I saw three heads coming towards mine. With a smile she slammed me down onto the floor.

"I thought you would be more competition," she said as she turned and looked at the fire. "You disappoint me."

Vision blurred, I told myself, *aim for the one in the middle. The one in the middle...* But when I swung for her, I missed completely. She smirked and put a poker into the fire.

"I'm not going to make this quick for you Mister—" She collapsed to the ground, her body finally giving in. Her ankle bone shone in the light of the fire and I picked up the hot poker and stuck it into the wound.

"RUSO!" she screamed in agony. She tried to reach for the poker but collapsed backwards in pain. She reached into a cupboard and pulled out a syringe. I sunk my blade into her wrist, as a thank you she crushed my balls with her other hand. Blood rushed to my head, I tried to distract my mind. "FUUCCKK!" I yelled and booted her face before collapsing to the ground.

Spitting the cap off the syringe onto the floor, she injected herself in the ankle. She pulled out the poker and pushed the bone back into her leg. Then, she set her eyes on me.

I could see the knife out of the corner of my eye. *Too far away, shit.* I began a brief meditation. My breath came under control, and the pain started to leave my mind. *Round 3.*

I managed to get a few good hits to her face and abdomen. It didn't hurt her much, but it allowed me to reach my knife. I thrust it towards her and sliced into her flesh once or twice. But it was clear that she was not going to be defeated blow for blow, or even knife for knife. Not with that stuff she'd injected anyway. Her one weakness, whether she'd feel it or not, was her ankle. That had to be my focus.

"You know," I said, trying to buy some time. "I admire your physique. Quite an achievement."

"Flattery will get you nowhere," she said, edging closer. "And it won't stop me enjoying killing you slowly."

Her fists felt like iron as they struck my face. Blood painted the walls with each blow. I shook it off and like a mad man went back for more. She guarded her ankle and so I struck her other leg as much as possible, to put her off balance. I had to think outside the box. I held the tip of the blade and sent it coursing through the air and into her wounded ankle. Her eye flinched, and she let her guard down. I ran, jumped, and came crashing down on the knife. She staggered back towards the window. I summoned all my strength, ran, and kicked her chest, sending her crashing through the window.

I cautiously walked towards the window and looked down. There she was, head impaled on a spike. A part of me waited for her to come back to life, come for her final revenge. But she didn't. A river of blood cascaded to the ground like a waterfall, her eyes wide open.

I looked around the room and found her phone near the chair. There was someone else I needed to talk to.

The phone was locked, *shit*. I headed outside and pressed the monster's finger onto the phone. *Bingo*. Time to message the commissioner.

'I have the detective chained up. We need to meet. Come to my place.'

It didn't take long for him to reply.

'I'm about to head to the airport I'm afraid. You should do the same,' he texted back.

"Shit," I said and looked for a vehicle.

As I turned a corner, I saw a thing of beauty. A Honda CBR1000R motorcycle - red, black, and aggressive. This would work perfectly.

Before I could ride, I needed to make a call. I dialled the number of a hacker who owed me a favour and asked him to hack into the commissioner's police car tracker. While I waited, I grabbed some weapons from the arsenal I had seen in the house.

"He's leaving his building now, Banks. Heading north," my friend told me. I put my earpiece in and told him to stay on the line. I would need some guidance.

I revved the engine on the bike, stones flew behind me and then I sped off into the city.

"You're about five minutes away from him so you should be able to cut him off before the airport," my hacker told me.

"The only thing I'll be cutting off is his life supply," I said and moved fast between the cars.

"Okay, you're about a minute away, Banks. He's driving a black Toyota Crown Saloon car. Look for 55-89 on the license plate."

It didn't take me long to find it. I rolled right up to the passenger window and looked in. There he was. I pulled out a shotgun and tapped on the window. "Remember me?" I shouted. He turned, and fear filled his face. The driver speeded up, and I blew the window glass to bits. I couldn't catch up with the shotgun in my hand, so I tossed it. As I came close to a window, I was greeted with a hand sticking out, holding a pistol. Narrowly dodging a few bullets, I pulled out a machine gun and fired towards the hand. The tip of a finger flew through the air, and a scream left the car.

"Time to die, commissioner!"

The car had some serious engine inside it. It sped up again and started to get away.

"Not this time, asshole," I said and shot through the back of the window. The driver's brain painted the window red, and the car swayed. The commissioner stuck his upper body out the window, trying to escape. As his waist came out the window, the car twisted and flipped through the air. The vehicle crashed and bounced off the ground violently. When it came to a halt, only the legs of the commissioner remained… I revved the bike's engine and drove over the blood-ridden road. Hell had just found a fresh soul. Mission accomplished.

The city was up in flames with the gang war, but I knew a place where I could find peace. I rode back to the monastery. Over the next year, I helped rebuild the monastery and shifu helped rebuild me. And the truth was I didn't know if I would ever leave.

What I did know was, in Tokyo another case had been… solved.

AUTHOR BIOGRAPHY

August Lee was born in Liverpool, a city passionate about music and football. Lee wrote his first story when he was 9 years old on his aunt's laptop, which sparked his love of writing.

Lee has previously worked for years as a marketing content writer. A renaissance soul who is constantly learning new things, he taught himself to play the guitar and is currently learning French and Mandarin Chinese. He also holds certificates in film studies, Spanish, and personal training.

A visit to a secret bar in London inspired him to begin writing detective stories and solve fictional cases for clients as an online gig. His stories were intricate and original resulting in 5-star ratings from international clients. This led to him pursuing creative writing full-time and publishing his stories starring Detective Banks which are packed with thrilling actions and gruesome crime.

Lee's biggest dream is to write for the big screen. When not writing he can be found drinking in secret bars until the early hours, traveling the world with his fiancé for story inspirations or teaching his two cats how to do tricks. He enjoys spending time with his family, and is always looking to try new experiences like stand up paddle-boarding, axe-throwing, beer yoga and ultimate frisbee.

Printed in Great Britain
by Amazon